# MURDER IN MINIATURE

## MARGARET GRACE

**WHEELER**
**CHIVERS**

This Large Print edition is published by Wheeler Publishing, Waterville, Maine, USA and by BBC Audiobooks Ltd, Bath, England.
Wheeler Publishing, a part of Gale, Cengage Learning.
A Miniature Mystery.

The text of this Large Print edition is unabridged.
Other aspects of the book may vary from the original edition.
Set in 16 pt. Plantin.
Printed on permanent paper.

**LIBRARY OF CONGRESS CATALOGING-IN-PUBLICATION DATA**

Grace, Margaret, 1937–
    Murder in miniature / by Margaret Grace.
        p. cm. — (A miniature mystery) (Wheeler Publishing large print cozy mystery)
    ISBN-13: 978-1-59722-778-0 (softcover : alk. paper)
    ISBN-10: 1-59722-778-1 (softcover : alk. paper)
        1. Retired women — Fiction. 2. Dollhouses — Fiction. 3. Craft festivals — Fiction. 4. City and town life — California — Fiction. 5. Large type books. I. Title.
    PS3563.I4663M87 2008
    813'.54—dc22                                        2008012118

BRITISH LIBRARY CATALOGUING-IN-PUBLICATION DATA AVAILABLE

Published in 2008 in the U.S. by arrangement with The Berkley Publishing Group, a member of Penguin Group (USA) Inc.
Published in 2008 in the U.K. by arrangement with the author.

U.K. Hardcover: 978 1 408 41225 1 (Chivers Large Print)
U.K. Softcover: 978 1 408 41226 8 (Camden Large Print)

Printed and bound in Great Britain by
CPI Antony Rowe, Chippenham and Eastbourne

1 2 3 4 5 6 7 12 11 10 09 08

In memory of my dear friend
Geraldine Iorio
(1935–2006).

# ACKNOWLEDGMENTS

I'm most grateful to my loving husband, Dick Rufer, the best there is. I can't imagine working without his 24/7 support. He's my dedicated webmaster (www.dollhouse mysteries.com) and layout specialist, as you can see by the drawings at the end of this book.

Special thanks go to my dream critique team, Jonnie Jacobs, Rita Lakin, and Margaret Lucke; and to my niece and brilliant crafts partner, Mary Schnur.

Thanks also to my sister, Arlene Polvinen; my cousin, Jean Stokowski; and the many writers and friends who offered critique and inspiration, in particular: Judy Barnett, Sara Bly, Bob and Donnie Brett, Margaret Hamilton, Anna Lipjhart, Ann Parker, Sue Stephenson, and Karen Streich.

Finally, how lucky can I be? I'm working with a wonderful editor, Michelle Vega, and an extraordinary agent, Elaine Koster.

# CHAPTER 1

I picked up the mahogany-framed sofa with my right hand, and the gold balloon-back chair with my left. The seat of the sofa was royal blue, matching a hue in the busy pattern of the living-room carpet, which lay in my lap, along with a dining-room table and a chandelier. I held the furniture at arm's length and moved my head up and down to find the section of my glasses that brought the miniatures into focus. It didn't seem that long ago that I had twenty-twenty vision without glasses, let alone trifocals.

Finally, I assembled the tiny pieces in my shoe-box-sized Victorian shadow box.

"What do you think?" I asked my friend Linda Reed. She was seated one table over at the back of the old school hall. "Do these colors work together?"

The question was semi-rhetorical. In only two hours, at six o'clock sharp on Friday evening, the doors would open and the fund-raiser would begin — the Abraham Lincoln High School Dollhouse and Miniatures Fair, a decorative magnet for crafts lovers all over the county. I certainly didn't have time to reupholster my Victorian furniture, but I wanted my friend's approval.

I should have known better.

"The seat on that chair is pretty wide, even for Victorian ladies' skirts," Linda said. "I suppose it came as a kit?" She held a delicate replica of a Governor Winthrop slant-top desk in the palm of her hand. She'd made it from scratch, for the living room of her entry in Lincoln Point's celebrated Dollhouse Contest, a highlight of the fair. "And one of your buttons is loose." Linda leaned over and aimed her thin paintbrush at a tiny pearl bead, one-twelfth of an inch in diameter, one of a dozen I'd glued onto the chair back, to give a button-tufted effect.

"The chair needs to be this wide, not just to accommodate the ladies' petticoats, but to keep gentlemen at a suitable distance." I used my best imitation of a Victorian matron, then reverted to my normal, smooth voice, but with a touch of annoyance at the edges. "And how can you see a wobbly button from that distance?"

10

"I saw it an hour ago."

*And you didn't tell me?* Typical Linda. But I'd come to understand her moods and appreciate her good qualities, even as many called her the most disgruntled woman in Lincoln Point, if not all of northern California.

Linda's latest beef was with the city council and its proposals for making the area more attractive to tourists. Not that our small town could compete with its neighboring cities south of San Francisco, like Palo Alto and San Jose. We didn't have the advantage of a university (Palo Alto could boast about Stanford) nor a high fun rating (a national magazine had recently ranked San Jose the third "most fun city" in America).

Personally, I gave Lincoln Point a very high fun rating. Didn't we have an oratory contest every year, based on the Lincoln-Douglas debates? A parade on February 12, Lincoln's birthday, no matter what day of the week it fell on? Colorful and inspiring billboards along Springfield Boulevard with quotes from Honest Abe himself? In case you think Lincoln was not a fun guy, consider this quote from him, now the motto of our crafters' club: "Better to remain silent and be thought a fool than to speak out and

11

remove all doubt."

Linda Reed didn't care about fun ratings. She was against anything that would bring more people into her life.

"There's enough trash, trouble, and traffic in town already." Linda seemed thrilled with the alliteration she'd concocted, and repeated it whenever anyone mentioned the positive side of growth — that more visitors and real estate development meant more customers for our local merchants and more funds for city services.

I'd known Linda for many years, however, and had to admit she had enough reasons to be disgruntled.

Misfortune followed Linda like a string of melted glue from a low-end glue gun. She'd had two bad marriages and a shaky nursing career, often losing a position over hospital politics that were out of her control. And her teenage adopted son, Jason, had spent nearly as many of his school years being suspended or expelled as not. The most recent and worst accusation had come just this week when Crane's Jewelers, a town fixture for two generations, was robbed — the same morning that Jason cut summer school classes.

A lot on Linda's plate, as my younger friends would say.

Right now Linda was also nursing a grudge because I'd refused to go on a cruise with her.

"You'd go if Beverly asked you," she'd accused.

Linda had always been jealous of my close friendship with Beverly Gowen, my sister-in-law and — if I were forced to rank the people in my life — my best friend. Linda held on to that seventh-grade friendship-bookkeeping behavior: *You go shopping with her more than you do with me.* I'd tried to explain that I wouldn't go on a cruise even with Beverly. At fifty-eight, with bones becoming more brittle by the day, I couldn't see myself learning the samba. The same for any other dance ending in a vowel. Neither did I want to act my age and play bingo, or clap for an amateur musical comedy group, or lounge on a boat headed for an island that most likely did not have a library or a hobby shop.

"The best thing about cruises is the pampering," Linda had said. She patted the sides and top of her beehive updo, many shades of blond and a staple of Linda's look since her teen years in the midsixties, if the photos around her home were any indication. "A whole crew of people feed you, entertain you, turn down your bed, and tend to your every need."

That made sense — for her. Poor Linda had spent her life caring for others. She now worked as a nurse in three convalescent facilities, and as a mother to a problem child, with no support, let alone pampering.

A pushover for difficult personalities, I often found myself apologizing for Linda's petulant moods to one or another of our friends. My late husband, Ken, told me I was a pushover, period, and always the first one to volunteer when a need arose. Like helping to organize this fair, for instance, when the original chairwoman fell and broke her hip. Ken would have teased that I offered my services just for the glory of seeing my name on the program. In this case: Geraldine Porter, Dollhouse Committee Chair. Whatever his theory, it hadn't kept Ken from helping me with all my projects, and I had missed him every day of the last two years.

No time to reminisce, however. I had oversight duties to tend to and a Victorian chair to repair. I reached into the hard plastic crate at my feet, stocked with a myriad of ways to attach one material to another. Glue gun, glue dots, glue sticks, liquid glue, and two kinds of tack glue (both original and fast-acting) for starters. Plus a variety of tapes, string, needles, pins, staples, and Velcro. I chose a thin cyanoacrylate glue and went to work on the errant button.

"Here they come," Linda said. She announced the arrival of other vendors — and a few early-bird customers sneaking in — the way I would announce the appearance of knots in my thread, or a rash on my skinny arms (hers were chubby, another source of complaint). I wanted to remind her that the fair wasn't held for her own enjoyment and profit, but to generate revenue for the school. Each vendor had paid a fee to use a table and had agreed to contribute 10 percent of her or his weekend take to the school library. Linda wanted the best of both worlds — crowds of people buying her crafts, but no one actually talking to her.

"She's all bark," Ken used to say, and I had to agree. We'd been the lucky recipients of Linda's generous side through the years. She'd used her nursing skills to help both of us during Ken's long bout with leukemia, finding hard-to-get medical supplies, checking out the best deals on meds, even arranging a house call from a respected oncologist.

She'd waved away our effusive gratitude. "They all owe me," she said. "It's about time they did something useful for me."

We never asked who "they" were, and assumed she meant the medical profession in general, and her bosses over the years in particular. When I thought of the angel of mercy she'd been to Ken, I could forgive Linda many, many cranky days.

I set down my now-perfect chair — *So what if it started as a kit?* I asked myself. I'd added unique embellishments, like the tiny buttons Linda paid so much attention to.

The air-conditioning had been cranked up, so I pulled on a sweatshirt that read SEE THE WORLD IN A GRAIN OF SAND and hung my committee badge around my neck.

"I guess you missed your hair appointment again," Linda said, as she watched me struggle with my longish gray hair (I'd given up my easy-to-care-for pixie once Ken died). My unruly locks had become tangled with the black lanyard that held my badge.

I let out a resigned sigh. "I had a ton of meetings," I said. "To set everything up for the convenience of the vendors." *Like you.*

Linda didn't acknowledge my gibe. She was applying the last coat of dark stain to the drawers of her desk. A master at crafts, Linda built everything from scratch. She'd managed to squeeze a good-sized workbench into the one-car garage attached to her small house and outfitted it with the tools of the woodworking trade. Her miniature tables were fitted with carefully crafted mortise-and-tenon joints; her tiny desk drawers opened; her turn-of-the-century steamer trunks had operating hinges and fabric linings with faded flower prints.

Unlike most of my pieces. I managed to build one or two from-scratch items a month, but my real pleasure was in turning found objects into miniature furnishings. I enjoyed creating a table by the simple act of placing an olive jar cover on top of an empty spool of thread and painting them to match. The black wire top of a champagne bottle became a stool, and an old contact lens morphed into a lamp shade when I placed it on a colorful spherical or cylindrical bead.

For this fair, I had more items than usual on my table, the direct result of my ill-gotten windfall of free time. When Ken was diagnosed, I took early retirement from teaching English at this very school to care for him. In between doctor visits and hospital stays, while waiting for medical test results and resolving insurance issues, I distracted myself with my lifelong crafts hobbies.

There was nothing like entering the world of miniatures to take one's mind off the unpleasant realities of the macroscopic world. Nothing like rearranging furniture and tearing off wallpaper with the flick of the wrist. Nothing like studying a pair of wood screws, standing them on their heads, and seeing them as candlesticks.

Since Ken's death, I'd been spending more and more time in my crafts corner, which had spread to a crafts room, which some would say was now a crafts home. I'd built up a large inventory of miniature rooms, boxes, and freestanding scenes.

Now I unwound my apron ties from my waist, preparing to offer an official welcome and a helping hand to vendors just arriving to take their places for the fair. Technically, I was responsible only for dollhouse vendors, but I wanted to become familiar with all the specialties our craftspeople had brought for sale. The other cochairs were only too happy to have me spread myself around.

Not that there was a lot to spread, but I was working on it. Only two turns around for the apron strings tonight, meaning my waist was finally getting to a healthy measurement. My appetite had fled with Ken's, it seemed, and I had gotten much too thin — another source of consternation for Linda, who thought it unfair that she was the only one on the planet who gained weight so easily. "I just have to look at a doughnut," she'd say, "and the pounds pile up." I'd seen her eat three at one sitting, however, so I had little sympathy for her constant battle with pudginess.

"Keep an eye on my goods, would you, Linda?" I asked now, as I headed toward the front of the hall and my "greeting" duties. Geraldine on the job, Ken would say.

"What? Oh, no," Linda said, sounding exasperated.

I bristled, assuming she was responding to my simple request, but then saw that she was talking to herself. Something about her Governor Winthrop desk had disturbed her. A splinter? An uneven dab of paint? Either would be enough to send her on a verbal rampage.

"My table, Linda? Can you just keep an eye open?"

"Sure, sure," she said, back in the real world.

Her heavy tone had the enthusiasm of a ten-year-old asked to leave her toys and clean her room. I heaved a sigh. It was time for another heart-to-heart talk with my chronically out-of-sorts friend. To her credit, Linda allowed me to lecture her periodically on her people skills and always responded positively. Until the next crisis hit in her job or family life. I had an idea that the present crisis involved Jason and the jewelry-store robbery. For now, however, I was determined to enjoy the weekend, immersed in tiny ceramic bathtubs, wastebaskets the size of a thimble, and dinner plates with rims no bigger around than my wedding ring.

The school janitor, "Just Eddie" — he refused to tell us his last name — had done a little more than his minimal level of effort to spruce up the school's multipurpose room for the fair. The trash had been reasonably contained, the area around the heavy plastic barrels free of candy wrappers and greasy napkins. The usually sticky linoleum floor was relatively smooth, the price being the unmistakable scent of liquid cleanser, mingling with that of this noon-time's meat loaf.

Though I'd mailed a map of the hall to each vendor and stapled a poster-size layout on the wall by the entrance, I knew many would still not know their table numbers. I was there to help. Mabel Quinlan especially needed me — the eighty-something-year-old Queen of Beads couldn't keep the days of the week straight sometimes. Too much rubber cement, it was said. One look at the thousands of tiny glass beads she'd glued to items as small as one-inch coffee tables, and as large as a five-inch stained-glass window in a miniature Gothic church, would explain the tubs of glue she kept (some said sniffed) in her workshop.

"Table 8, Mabel," I told her, pointing to the first row. I'd assigned her a spot close to the restrooms and snack counter at the front of the hall, so she wouldn't get lost on her breaks, and far enough from the Children's Corner where the puppet shows and clowns would simply confuse her more.

"You're the best, Gerry," Mabel said. "Nothing miniature about your heart." She laughed at the line she'd probably rehearsed on the ride to the school. Linda's moods aside, most crafters were a good-humored lot, and I had many friends among them.

I smiled broadly as the room boxes and dollhouses rolled in, their satisfied architects behind them, pulling the structures on luggage wheels or staggering under their weight. Most of the ladies were members of our local crafts group, and I'd seen many of the pieces in formative stages — Karen's Cape Cod ("I'm all about symmetry this year"), Gail's split-level ranch ("My hipped-dormer idea failed"), Susan's Frank Lloyd Wright ("I'm in my low-slung, prairie phase"), and Betty's Tudor mansion ("Crown me now and have it over with").

All were for sale, and all were eligible for the big contest. They'd be displayed on the individual crafters' tables until Sunday morning, when they'd be moved to the annex and the final votes would be tallied. As chair this year, I wasn't eligible to enter my own pueblo dollhouse, and these masterpieces told me it was just as well.

I usually spent more money than I took in at crafts shows, and I could see that this weekend would be no exception. I wandered through the aisles, making a mental list of what I "needed." A half-scale red metal ladder that would be perfect for the garage scene I'd begun as a present for a neighbor. A floral ladies' desk set for my next Victorian shadow box. A decorator pack of wallpaper and a mahogany bookcase, to have on hand. A three-inch wicker porch swing, just because.

I flourished my clipboard and inspected each vendor's compliance with the rules. No more than two folding chairs behind any one table, no spreading of cloths or merchandise onto a neighbor's table, and nothing taller than eighteen inches, except for two-story dollhouses, which were assigned end tables so as not to block the view of other treasures. And a new mandate this year — no cell phones inside the hall.

"Thanks for all your work, Gerry," I heard repeatedly, as my friends-turned-vendors prepared their tables and cash boxes. Popcorn erupted from the giant machine we'd rented and filled the hall with an appetizing aroma, finally masking the stale, leftover odors of the summer school lunch menu. I basked in the fresh, salty smells and in the warmth of camaraderie.

When I reached the back of the hall, I was surprised to see that Linda had abandoned our corner, leaving both our tables unattended. Not that there was a big worry, but sometimes children could be careless and might knock over a tiny bowl of Fimodough fruit, or upset small pieces like the kuchibana, the lovely Japanese vases Linda crafted after lessons from one of our Asian American members.

Maybe Linda had had a bathroom emergency. I scanned our tables for a note. No message, but I noticed that the Governor Winthrop desk was missing. I had the crazy thought that Linda might have taken it to the restroom with her. It was her pride and joy, and she'd have been reluctant to leave it behind even for five minutes. She'd planned to add it to her dollhouse entry at the last minute.

I stepped over to the nearest occupied post, Table 29, where Karen Striker, one of our younger crafters, was repairing a shingle on her Cape Cod house. "Did Linda say where she was going?" I asked. "Or ask you to watch our tables?"

Karen looked up from her work and stared blankly at me, as if she'd been called back from a visit to the southern tip of Massachusetts. "Sorry, I'm totally not paying attention to anything but getting this set up," she said. "I didn't even know Linda was gone. Is there a problem?"

"No problem," I said, a bit annoyed at Linda's apparent unreliability.

For a distraction, and a moment of pleasure, I turned on the power to the rotating stand under my pueblo-style dollhouse. The building was roofless, all the rooms visible from the top, so the turntable was hardly necessary. Still, I liked the effect of the motion and let it roll.

I made one more pass up and down the aisles. I opened Mabel's bottle of water for her, exclaimed over a quarter-scale tea ceremony arrangement and a thatched cottage on adjacent tables, and used my thumb and index finger as a vise while Betty repaired the strawberry plant in front of her Tudor.

"Hard to believe the first real Tudors were in filthy, unhealthy towns infested with rats and flies," Betty said.

"Thanks for that," I said, with a smile.

A minute before six o'clock and all was well. Time for Just Eddie to open the doors. But where was he? He had a habit of "disappearing" even during normal work hours — we all wondered what was in his daily thermos. He was supposedly doubling as security guard for this event, but had clearly caved under the weight of the extra weekend work. I went up to the front doors and removed the rope across the opening myself. Crafts lovers and potential customers poured in.

I returned to my table, number 31, at the back of the hall, where I'd be stationed until it was time for the first raffle drawing.

Still no sign of Linda.

But out of the corner of my eye, I saw Chuck Reed, Linda's second ex-husband, head for the side door by the dining area.

Puzzle solved. Linda and Chuck were meeting in the parking lot, no doubt, to engage in one of their regular feuds. One week it was over money (neither had much), the next it was over their adopted son, Jason. The next it was back to money, and so on.

No problem. I dragged my chair three feet to my left, halfway between our two tables. It was quite clear which items belonged to Linda and which to me. Unwilling to admit that I didn't have the patience or the skill to be the miniaturist Linda was, I invented a theory that my furniture was more attractive to children and beginning crafters, since my pieces were clearly easy and inexpensive to make. This would attract more and more children to miniatures and keep the hobby alive. This theory had served me well for many years, and kept me from having to be the perfectionist Linda was.

I was ready to handle both tables. The only downside to Linda's absence was how humbled I'd be to admit that the exquisite pieces on Table 30 were not mine.

# CHAPTER 2

I felt like a one-fingered puppeteer. I did my best to manage Linda's table plus my own as people crowded the aisles. Even with the glow of a battery-lit stoneware lamp, Linda's magnificent room-box den seemed darker than usual. Its Shaker-style desk and bookcases appeared edgy, as if they were aware their true mistress had abandoned them.

"Please sign our guest list," I said, offering a beaded pen (I hadn't been able to resist an early purchase from Mabel) to a woman with a baby strapped to her chest. She'd just bought one of Linda's lovely nursery scenes and talked for several minutes about where she planned to put it. Usually I loved hearing customers' stories, but this evening I was distracted by the need to take care of twice as many items. I hoped the new mother didn't notice how little attention I paid her chatter.

The largest of the wares overflowing my table was the southwestern pueblo with its beehive hearth. I'd enjoyed getting my hands muddy with the earthy materials and keeping my fingers active with the colorful, woolly fabric of the rugs I'd hung on the walls and strewn over the bumpy tile floors. I was pleased with the final look — straight from the heart of Santa Fe — though today the hearth reminded me of Linda's hairdo. I felt a pang of worry at her absence.

I scanned the mass of people swarming around the tables, hoping Linda got involved in shopping on her way back from meeting (fighting with?) Chuck. I knew I'd soon hear all the details.

I estimated a hundred people had already entered the hall, talking excitedly, mostly women and children in summer clothes and clicking sandals. From years of crafts fair experience, I was pretty good at distinguishing among the various categories of visitors: the window-shoppers, the serious buyers, the collectors (even more serious buyers), and those looking for free advice and quick tips. And on an uncomfortably warm evening like this Friday in July, I suspected a few had come just for the air-conditioning.

"How did you get these blankets to drape so nicely?" a red-haired woman asked me, while her daughter, about eight years old, looked longingly at my ski lodge scene. "When I cut up real fabric, the small pieces are too rigid to fall realistically," she moaned.

Ken would always tell me not to give away all my secrets, but I was interested in sharing my craft and couldn't have cared less that someone might steal my idea and cash in on it in some way.

I pulled out a tip sheet on glue baths for my potential customer and explained how dragging fabric or paper towels through the bath resulted in just the right pliability for a realistic draped effect.

In between sales, I became more and more annoyed with Linda. I broke one of the rules I'd helped formulate — I switched on my cell phone and tried calling hers. No answer. Of course not, I realized — she probably forgot her phone was off. It also explained why Linda hadn't called me, either, to explain her absence.

That was a relief. Still, I queried Just Eddie (he had finally showed up again) when he came within shouting distance of my table.

"No sign of her," he said. "Probably had some emergency or she's off messing up her kid again." A reminder of how small a town

Lincoln Point was, and how Just Eddie was not the most sympathetic guy in the world. In spite of his weathered dark face, Just Eddie appeared to be a few years younger than Linda and me. He'd moved to Lincoln Point only a couple of years ago. Besides keeping his last name secret, the short, dumpy man also refused to tell us where he was from or where he lived now. There were rumors that his residence was in a trailer park farther south, toward San Jose. Maybe Just Eddie wanted to be closer to that fun city.

It had occurred to me that Jason was responsible for Linda's absence. I wouldn't dare call the police station and inquire, however (though my nephew, Beverly's son, was one of its finest officers), lest Linda be upset at what could look like sheer nosiness.

One of my own favorite rooms sold quickly. I'd taken a half-gallon tub from Sadie's, our popular local ice cream store, and formed an opening, cutting into about one-third of the curved surface. Inside, I had built a miniature soda fountain. Secretly, I'd hoped my granddaughter, Madison, who was visiting me for a month, would want it. But Maddie, like both her parents, was more into sports than dollhouses or anything remotely feminine. Served me right, I decided, wishing so hard for a little girl for my son and his wife. I'd neglected to ask for one who'd like pink. I had my first clue to her preferences when a beaded bracelet I'd made for her ended up wrapped around her soccer trophy. I blamed it all on the unisex name her Los Angeles–based parents gave her.

"Why name a child 'Madison'?" I'd asked my son, Richard. Subtly, I thought. "With parents named Richard and Mary Lou."

He gave me a trademark wink, learned at his father's knee. "That's why," he said.

And here was Maddie now, running toward me, her auburn curls tucked into a backward baseball cap. My sister-in-law, Beverly, who was entertaining Maddie (or vice versa) while I was working the fair, was several feet behind.

"Hey, Grandma! We came to see all your pretty stuff," Maddie said, barely containing a giggle.

"Nice try. I know how you feel about 'pretty.' If you think that's going to get you pancakes and strawberry syrup in the morning, you're right. I mean . . . mistaken." My turn to giggle as I held her close.

Beverly picked up a room box with a theme I knew she liked — a hat shop. "I

31

love this, Gerry. You're the best at fabric," she said. I hoped Beverly wouldn't try to buy the piece, since I'd made her an even more elaborate shop for her upcoming birthday. Beverly swung her arm, looking toned in a sleeveless dress, toward the un-staffed table next to me. "Where's Linda?" she asked.

"I wish I knew. Chuck was here and I suppose she's off dealing with him, but that was" — I checked my watch. A twinge of annoyance mixed with concern rippled through my body — "almost two hours ago."

One of the tiny lamps in my backyard barbecue scene flickered, and at the same time, I got a bright idea. "Bev, can you do me a favor? Do you think you could ask Skip to drive over to Linda's house and see if she's there?"

"You're kidding, right?"

I clicked my tongue. "No. I'm a little worried. I can't imagine what it would take for her to leave her station this long."

Beverly, one hand on her hip, ran her fingers through her short, curly hair, so much like her brother, Ken's, and now Maddie's. "You want my son, Lincoln Point PD's up-and-coming officer, to make a house call on Linda? What makes you think she's even there?"

"Couldn't he just zip by? What if something's happened to her?"

I was happy that Maddie didn't hear this. She'd wandered to the Children's Corner, where the town postmaster, Brian Cooney, was setting up for the next puppet show. He and Just Eddie were engaged in some battle over a shoddy repair job on the steps to the stage. The rumor was that the two of them had an ongoing feud that started when Brian wouldn't assign a post-office box to Just Eddie unless he gave a street address or phone number for the record. Unwilling to give in, Just Eddie had to drive ten miles to Middleboro, the next town, where apparently the rules were different, to get his mail. From what I could see, it appeared my handy-girl granddaughter was tacking the carpet to the stage while the men fought.

My focus returned to Beverly, whose response to sending her cop son to Linda's house was still less than enthusiastic. She gave me a look, raising her perfectly shaped reddish eyebrows. I knew what was coming and realized how foolish I sounded.

"Remember Easter . . . was it '81, '82?"

"When Linda skipped our brunch to meet ex number one, Peter . . . excuse me, *Dr. Balandin* . . . thinking they might get back together?"

Beverly nodded, her fingers in position to tick off other instances of Linda's delinquency. "Without ever letting us know. And then during that big rainstorm one winter . . . let's see, it was —"

"Valentine's Day, around '85, when Pete married his young student. Linda took a hotel room in Palo Alto and didn't show up until noon the next day. Zoning out, she called it."

"Exactly. This is Linda being Linda," Beverly said, pointing to the empty chairs behind Linda's table.

"You're right."

We didn't have to catalog all the other times Linda had "disappeared" during our lives together. She had a way of taking off when she felt she couldn't handle a situation. More than once, after looking all day for her, we'd found Linda in a movie theater or sitting on a bench at the Stanford shopping mall, reading a book, as if she hadn't put all her friends through trauma by not showing up where she was expected. Once she pulled into her driveway at three in the morning, to find Beverly, me, and a Lincoln Point black-and-white all pooling resources to search for her. She didn't understand what the fuss was about.

Beverly was right. This was another in a long list of Linda's dramatic performances. It just wasn't clear what the current impetus was for her bailing out. Something serious, I decided, like Jason and the robbery, to take her away from her precious crafts, but still, Linda being Linda. "Never mind," I said to Beverly.

Beverly rubbed my shoulders, and I leaned back into the welcome touch. "Why don't I have a seat and take care of her table for a while," she said. "Maddie seems to be doing well with Puppeteer Postmaster Cooney over there. I'm sure Linda will be back before our little girl gets bored."

"I think Maddie's the only one who gets along with the old curmudgeon," I said.

"Have you noticed — some people get along better with children than adults?" Beverly rubbed her palms together. "Now, let's sell some miniatures."

The voice of reason, and a helping hand. "Good idea. Thanks."

Beverly gave me a final pat and settled her lean body onto Linda's chair. I pictured Linda's returning momentarily, with a scowl at Beverly for moving her chair or wrinkling her tablecloth. I felt better already.

Even so, when Just Eddie came by, I gave him a questioning look. He seemed to understand what I was asking — he frowned and gave me a "who cares" shrug.

Our newspaper advertising and posters paid off and business was good, a peak coming just after the dinner hour, about seven thirty. Many newcomers to the hobby this year, I noted. Fortunately, I never tired of explaining the different scales to novices, especially children.

"We call it *full-scale* when one inch equals one foot," I explained to a little girl, about Maddie's age, but wearing an adorable pastel yellow shirt with embroidered flowers (something Maddie would wad up and use to wipe down her bike). I used my arms and fingers to demonstrate the scales. "The sofa in your living room is probably about seven *feet* long, so a 'full-scale miniature' would be seven *inches* long." I took out a ruler so the child could measure one of my sofas. I demonstrated half-scale from Linda's table. Much of her work was in half-scale, where each foot converts to only a half inch, so her sofas were only three or four inches long.

"These are cuter," said the little girl, not intending to insult me, I was sure. I agreed. Half-scale furniture was much cuter, but harder to handle and manipulate. Many crafters in our club worked in even smaller scales — one-twelfth, one twenty-fourth, and even one one-hundred-and-forty-fourth — which were nearly impossible for my old fingers.

Things moved along smoothly until the fight broke out in the back of the hall.

Postmaster Cooney had lost the cool one might expect of a puppeteer when Dudley Crane walked in and distributed flyers to vendors and customers. I glanced at the one that landed on my table and scanned the text, principally announcing a meeting at city hall on Tuesday afternoon. Red and blue bullets called attention to all the advantages of electing Dudley Crane to the city council and registering "a vote for progress."

Crane, who operated the town jewelry store (the same one now minus some cash and inventory after last week's robbery) was Mr. Pro-Growth for Lincoln Point; Cooney was one of the most vocal opponents of Crane's plan. Now, everyone in the hall who was paying attention was treated to the sight of Postmaster Cooney tearing up Crane's flyer.

There was nothing new in their arguments and name-calling.

"Why don't we go back to pony express? You don't do much better with our mail anyway," from Crane.

"Why don't we bulldoze every extra scrap of land and put up condos and fill them with people who need diamond rings?" from Cooney.

Just Eddie surprised me by assuming his security duties and breaking the men up. He was a good one to end the fight, being among those citizens who didn't care which direction the city took, as long as they didn't close any of the taverns or the convenience stores that sold discount cigarettes.

"It's not over, Crane," I heard Cooney say, as Just Eddie guided him back to the stage. "Don't mess with my family."

That was a new one, more personal, though not out of character for our postmaster, who never met a customer he liked. Curious, too, since as far as I knew, he had no family. Cooney, who never married, lived by himself since his mother died earlier in the year.

When we got back to normal bustle, Beverly and I were able to chat in between customers, some of whom had been my students a few years ago and a few buildings over on this campus. Beverly filled me in on her most recent volunteer project for the Lincoln Point Police Department — the monthly seat-belt survey. She wore her orange vest with pride.

"Ninety-three percent wore seat belts this month," she told me. "Too bad I can't arrest the other seven percent. All I can do is report."

"You and your son. There must be a genetic need to arrest."

Beverly laughed and pointed to the dwindling supply of Linda's miniature baked goods. "Use your own genetic talent and find more pastries and pies," she said. "They've been selling like hotcakes. Pun intended."

Obliging her with a smile for her pun, I reached into Linda's small canvas LITTLE THINGS MEAN A LOT tote and came up with a two-inch-high wedding cake, several one-and-a-half-inch loaves of crusty bread, a plate of éclairs, and a cookie sheet with gingerbread men attached. I needed one or two more items to fill in the empty spot created when a young woman bought a whole bakery counter assembly. I reached in again and pulled out a piece of fabric. Linda and I had both purchased inexpensive rolls of cheesecloth for workshop use, and this piece was a match to one in my own tote.

Except that Linda's had a red stain the size of a half-scale throw rug. My breath caught. I looked more closely. Not paint, not varnish. After all these crafting years, I knew the difference. This was blood.

I held up the cloth for Beverly to see.

"So she cut her finger," Beverly said, shrugging her shoulders. She smiled, keeping her (to me, charming) overbite in check. "No surprise, considering the tools you people use."

I felt my shoulders relax. Maybe giving up sleep in favor of committee meetings, with the added effort (delightful as it was) of grandparenting, was getting to me. I gave the patient Beverly a well-deserved grin. I opened my metal fishing tackle box, full of the referenced tools — knives, pins, hooks, needles, scissors, blades, and even a small hammer. "You mean these?"

"Exactly," Beverly said. "Or should I say Exacto?"

Maddie would have rolled her eyes at the crafts humor, but Beverly and I laughed.

While my sister-in-law was distracted by her own successful joke, I folded the cloth, blood spot turned in, and tucked it in my tackle box.

I had no idea why.

# CHAPTER 3

At eight forty-five, fifteen minutes before closing for the evening, I left Beverly with two tables to monitor and stepped up to the PA system at the front of the hall. Spotlighted in the center of the ticket table was the first of three prizes to be raffled this weekend: a large, cellophane-wrapped basket with treasures donated by Karen Striker. The lucky winner would take home a one-twelfth-scale milled plywood Cape Cod bedroom kit. Karen had included swatches of fabric for linens, draperies, and carpets, and a pocket-size tool kit with a pouch of finishing nails.

"Attention, everyone," I called, against a background of whiny feedback. Abraham Lincoln High School was not known for its state-of-the-art A/V equipment. Close to the front door as I was, I twisted slightly and looked hopefully toward the foyer for signs of Linda. Surely she'd return to pack up and cover her table for the night. I saw only fidgety children in strollers, up past their bedtime.

Several times during the last couple of hours, I'd left our tables on the pretext of visiting the ladies' room, buying popcorn for Maddie (who'd been happily recruited to assist Puppeteer Cooney in entertaining the younger children), or tending to a chairperson duty. I'd called all of Linda's phone numbers and left messages. I'd all but crept under each grimy restroom stall, as if a simple indisposition could have kept Linda from Table 30 all evening. I'd even called the number I had for Jason's cell, not on speed dial, but on a list of near and dear I kept in my purse.

Two or three times, I'd stepped out the side door near our tables and scanned the parking lot. Linda's dark green SUV was still in its spot, next to my berry red Saturn Ion (my son, Richard, had tricked me into buying the bright color, but that's what a mother's trust gets you). Linda and I had been among the first to arrive, so we had prime spaces up against the building. Just Eddie's formerly white, now rust-colored pickup had been two over from mine, but was now more like four spaces over. He'd taken another superlong cigarette break, I guessed, this time downtown. More often than not his breaks coincided with the happy hours at the local bars. As long as his truck wasn't right next to my car, I didn't care. I could easily picture Just Eddie carelessly opening his rusty door and slamming it into mine.

Now I wondered if I should have given a more careful look inside Linda's SUV, but no one was upright on the seats (I didn't know whether to be happy or disappointed about that), and the small red light on the dash blinked steadily, telling me that security had not been breached.

She went with Chuck, I reasoned, to take care of a Jason emergency. A quick calculation told me that, though the crafts fair circumstances made it seem like a long time, Linda hadn't been missing as many hours as some of her other AWOLs had lasted.

I brought my focus back to the hall, where it had gone quiet. I thought this might be a first in the multipurpose room: shoppers and vendors, popcorn makers and high-school-students-cum-soda-jerks had their mouths closed and their ears trained on me. I tapped the mike, read out a long string of numbers, and joined the applause when a woman and four children, from stroller age to about twelve, all waved their arms, declaring themselves the winners. I was sure everyone agreed they needed the boost. I hoped the twelve-year-old would take over and manage the kit project, giving Mom some free time.

I cast one last glance at the parking lot next to the side doors as I walked back through the hall to Tables 30 and 31, where Beverly had started to pack up the most fragile pieces, Linda's three-tiered wedding cake included. We'd take the delicate items and our cash home, and leave most of the larger, more sturdy items in the hall over-night. It was Just Eddie's job to lock up and guarantee everything would be there in the morning.

Just Eddie, his overalls streaked with grease from who knew where, gave me one more shrug as I queried him.

"What about Jason?" I asked him. "Have you seen Jason Reed around today?"

"Nope, but don't worry about him. Kid like Jason that grew up in Brooklyn has got enough street smarts for two Lincoln Points."

Brooklyn? Where did that come from? I remembered when Linda and Chuck picked up Jason, in Winona, Minnesota, on the Mississippi, not anywhere near New York.

We were all surprised to realize that the great river went that far north. Fifth-grade geography was a long time ago.

This was Just Eddie, taking a jab at my New York City roots again, and once more confusing Brooklyn with the Bronx, where Ken and I grew up. Furthermore, his grammatical error rankled me.

"Who," I said.

Just Eddie gave me a funny look, as if the hard work of the fair had addled my brain. *"Jason,"* he said.

"I meant, the correct form is *who* grew up in Brooklyn, not *that* grew up, when you're speaking about a person."

He shook his head and walked away, mumbling under his breath.

I couldn't help thinking Linda was to blame for all this aggravation.

*If she's eating room service somewhere,* I thought, *I'm going to kill her.*

Beverly might have convinced me that I shouldn't send the police to Linda's home, but nothing said I shouldn't make a stop there myself. Linda's SUV was still in the school lot, leading me to unpleasant theories. I had to at least make an attempt to check on her residence.

"I'm going to swing by Mrs. Reed's

house," I told Maddie. "I want to be sure she's feeling all right."

"Is she sick?"

"A little."

Everything seemed harder with kids around. My urge to protect Maddie was overwhelming, even when I wasn't sure there was anything to protect her from. I wondered if I'd felt this way when Richard was Maddie's age. Maybe my life wasn't so "exciting" then. Or maybe granddaughters, even those who played a mean game of soccer and wore backward baseball caps, seemed more fragile than sons.

The street Linda lived on was in an old part of town where new condos had been squeezed into what used to be spacious farm properties. The one-car garages guaranteed that the street would always be lined with vehicles (I'd read a statistic that California families had one and one-third cars per person), and this evening was no exception. I circled twice before getting lucky — someone pulled out and left a prime spot a few yards from Linda's small front porch.

Linda's house, an old stucco two-bedroom badly in need of a refresher coat of yellow paint, was between two new condo developments. Among Linda's complaints about the

growth in the area were boisterous neighbors and trash that spilled onto her property.

"If I could afford it, I'd put in a surveillance system and find out who was trashing
my lawn," she'd remarked.

All was clean and quiet now, however.

I unbuckled my seat belt, then hesitated. I
didn't want to take Maddie with me, just in
case. *In case what,* I wasn't sure. I wasn't
happy leaving her in the car, either. Not that
it was a bad neighborhood, just dark and
quiet. Almost creepy quiet.

Only a couple of minutes, I told myself.

"Wait here, sweetheart," I told Maddie. "I
won't be long."

I got out and locked the doors with my
remote, knowing Maddie was aware how
that worked: if she (or, heaven forbid,
anyone else) opened the door, the car alarm
would go off. No one else would pay attention, but I'd hear it and come running.

The street was lined with large, old trees
that cut out the moonlight and obscured
the light from the occasional street lamp.
With so many residential units in such a
small space, I'd expected some noise at nine
thirty in the evening. Apparently all the
rowdy barbecue parties Linda grumbled
about were over by now, and all the back-

yard chatting finished. There were no signs of life except for a lit window here or there in the large, all-beige condo structures.

I approached the house, not knowing what I wished for. If Linda was relaxing in front of her TV, I'd give her a piece of my mind; if she was in trouble . . . I didn't have a plan for that. A dim light that I recognized as Linda's hallway night-light shown through the porch window. I knocked on the solid wood door (the doorbell had been broken for some time, waiting for Chuck or Peter to fix it). A newspaper was still rolled up and resting on the brackets under the mailbox. I waited, somehow knowing there'd be no response.

I left the porch and walked around to the narrow side yard, thick with weeds (also waiting for attention from exes), waving to Maddie on the way. The windows were dark. I knew the layout well — I passed the combination living and dining room, chasing away images of Linda out cold on her seventies orange-and-brown-plaid couch, and of her body spread out on the dark brown wall-to-wall carpet.

The only window lit at all was the one in Jason's room, at the end of the hallway, in the back of the house. Light from the bathroom night-light filtered in through his open door. Once in a while I appreciated my height. I was able to gain a clear view of Jason's room by raising myself slightly on my tiptoes. I'd never seen such a mess. I picked out food containers, clothes, books, CDs, videos, and sports paraphernalia (a surprise since Jason seemed so lethargic and anti-exercise) strewn everywhere. On the bed, on the floor, under the desk and chair, on the metal shelving. Would Maddie grow into this lifestyle in a couple of years? I wondered.

Even the television set was . . . what? I zeroed in on it. The television set was on the floor, on its side. What I thought of as the disorder created by a teenager now seemed to be a room that had been ransacked. I shifted my position, partly supporting myself by the window frame, and looked more closely, as far into the corners of the room as I could. The chair was leaning back against the desk, and the bed linens had been stripped and dumped on the floor.

My heart raced. I wanted to run back and check on Maddie, but I needed to see more. I continued around the back of the house, and caught only one more glimpse inside, this time of the hallway, where nothing seemed disturbed, except a balled-up scatter rug. The phone books and a couple of pens or pencils were on the floor, but then Linda wasn't the world's most perfect housekeeper, so it was hard to tell normal disorder from a break-in.

I took a deep breath. I walked slowly around the house again, giving Maddie (for whom I needed a really good cover story) another wave. This time I checked for any sign of break-in. I checked the front and back doors (locked) and the windows (none open, none broken). The garage, set back from the house, had no windows at viewing level, but all was quiet (and no noxious gas poured from under the door). My imagination had turned a messy room into a burglary, I decided. If Jason's room was extraordinarily wrecked, it was because he was an extraordinarily difficult kid.

The whole time, I hadn't heard any sounds except sizzling electric wires, nor seen anything except a lone dog and its mistress. I knocked on the front door one more time, more for Maddie's sake if she was watching, then returned to the car and climbed in.

"I guess Mrs. Reed's okay. Probably sleeping already," I told Maddie, my stomach uneasy. "She has bad allergies this time of year."

"Wasn't her SUV still at school?"

50

I nodded. A casual gesture, I hoped, for my budding detective. "I guess someone drove her home."

Leave it to a ten-year-old to help you through a rough patch. By the time Maddie and I pulled up to my (life-size) house, we'd decided we were both too wound up (Maddie from puppets, candy, and popcorn; me from you-know-what) to go to bed anytime soon. We made a plan that included pizza and a board game.

My home — with four bedrooms, kitchen, and ample living space built around a large atrium — was a source of great pleasure for me. Ken and I had bought our Eichler in the midseventies. I'd recently received a letter from the Department of the Interior informing me that our Lincoln Point Eichler neighborhood, about forty miles south of San Francisco, had been added to the National Register of Historic Places. Impressive as that was for all of us property owners, for me the best feature was unlocking my front door and entering a beautiful natural setting. I never tired of looking at the magnificent jade tree and a border of cyclamen that Ken and I had planted in the atrium.

Sometimes I expected to open the door

and find Ken in his hospital chair, under the skylight, where he spent his last days.

Tonight it was Maddie who had my attention, however. While we waited for a large pizza with everything but anchovies, Maddie and I dug through the game cupboard to find the challenge of the night.

I pulled out a red box near the top of the pile. "Let's play Yahtzee," I said to my granddaughter, who always beat me at it.

"Why don't we play on the computer this time, Grandma?" Maddie said, covering her uneven-toothed smile with her fist.

I made a big show of walking to the table and pouring out the Yahtzee dice, and slapping the score pads on the surface, creating as loud a noise as I could. "I like to hear and touch things," I told her. I reached over and fingered her curls, moved to her underarms, and then to all her tickle spots until she was rolling with laughter.

We'd set up a card table in the atrium, under the stars, and had no sooner started the game when Giovanni's delivery truck arrived. I guessed we were well beyond the rush hour for fast-food deliveries.

I insisted on adding carrot sticks and milk to the menu, principally to assuage my guilt over not preparing a proper dinner. I was sure eating pizza at ten thirty at night was not what her parents pictured as they sent their only child off for an extended visit with Grandma Geraldine. I had only one week left to correct all my errors; Maddie was due to fly home next Friday.

Maddie must have read my mind. "This is what grandmas are supposed to do," she said. "I love late-night pizza."

"Still, let's make this our little secret," I said, chasing a mushroom across the cardboard box.

Maddie laughed. "When I call to say good night, I'll tell them we had tofu and broccoli." I tried to picture my tall, husky son lifting a forkful of bean curd to his mouth. His wife's influence, I decided, if not the overall spirit of Los Angeles.

Ken, who thought his O-type blood required him to eat red meat no less often than every other night, said we took Richard out of the Bronx a little too soon. Richard was a toddler when Ken's architectural firm offered him the opportunity to open a West Coast office. Beverly, six years younger than Ken, had already gone west to college, so it worked out nicely for the family.

Four phone calls interrupted our elaborate dinner party. The first was from Gladys Stephenson, the original Dollhouse Chairperson for the fair, thanking me for filling in for her and wanting a briefing on how things had gone. The second was from Mabel — she forgot her cash box in the school hall, and could she have Just Eddie's pager number. She wanted to be sure he kept an eye on it. I gave her the number, and hung up mumbling "lots of luck" under my breath. Call number three was from Roberto, my fifteen-year-old literacy student at Lincoln Point Library. He was writing a late-night letter to his girlfriend and wanted to know how to spell *longingly.* I obliged.

The fourth call, which came when I was moments away from being trounced, thanks to Maddie's third Yahtzee of the game, was from Peter Balandin, Linda's first ex-husband. Marriage number one had lasted only until Peter finished his doctor's degree in civil engineering, at which point he decided he and Linda had "grown apart." In truth, Peter had grown closer to one of his teaching assistants at the university. Linda still called on him for favors, working on his guilt.

"He owes me," she'd said. I pictured Peter's name on a debt list, with all the doctors and nurse supervisors Linda ever worked for, all the landlords she'd ever paid rent to, and probably all her friends, me included.

Evidently the favor this evening had been that Peter would take care of Jason for the evening.

"She was supposed to meet me for a late dinner to hand off Jason, but she never showed," Peter said, his telephone voice sounding irritated.

I wondered how Jason would feel, knowing he was being handed off here and there, as if he were a set of Peter's engineering drawings.

Peter's annoyance aside, I saw an opportunity to gather information. "Where was she supposed to meet you? What time? Is Jason still with you?"

Peter did his best to answer my questions, in order. He sounded too calm about Linda's failure to show up to suit me, but I realized that, for all he knew, Linda had been with me all evening and had simply failed to appear at dinner.

"Burger Heaven, at nine thirty. Jason is here. He's been with me since school got out. Linda was supposedly busy with something until nine."

"The crafts —"

Peter didn't care. "Jason says he doesn't know where his mother is."

I had the nasty thought that Peter could afford better than Burger Heaven. Unlike ex-husband number two, Chuck Reed, who did odd jobs and was always broke, Peter had a high-paying job as a consultant for a real estate firm. (I sensed another pro-growth vote.) On the other hand, Peter was not Jason's father, adoptive or otherwise, but Linda called in an imagined debt from him quite often. It was hard to know whom to root for, except for Jason, who'd had less than his share of quality family life.

Lately Jason was the scapegoat for all the mischief at Abraham Lincoln High School. He'd allegedly started a fire last week in the cafeteria kitchen when they ran out of his favorite pudding. A few weeks ago, he sup-posedly sprayed all the mirrors in the girls' lavatory with colorful graffiti. This latter deed for no good reason, other than his own willful disregard of authority, according to said authority. In all fairness, Jason wasn't always the culprit (in fact, that time it was the vice principal's own son who'd sprayed I LOVE YOU ALL in the girls' room), but whenever any monkey business happened, Jason was likely to be blamed first.

"Gerry?"

Peter, calling me back to the moment. "I haven't seen Linda since early this evening," I said into the phone. "She left our tables at the crafts fair and —"

"That's Linda being Linda," Peter said. I'd heard those words earlier from Beverly, but with an undercurrent of affection. I resented hearing them in Peter's cold tone. "Anyway, I'm taking Jason home with me tonight, so if you see Linda, let her know."

*Please* would have been nice, but clearly too much to ask.

When Peter hung up, I was only the tiniest bit more informed on the Reed family at least I knew Jason was not in jail.

You might think four bedrooms is a lot for one person, but not for a crafter, especially since Eichler rooms tended to be small, not like the enormous master suites and walk-in closets in the newer suburban developments. I still slept in the largest bedroom (twelve by fourteen) only because it provided a view of the patio, blooming with different plants each season. My crafts supplies and projects were barely contained in Ken's home office, spreading out into the two guest rooms.

Maddie always preferred to sleep in the corner bedroom nearest the street, which had been her father's, and which held my computer system, such as it was.

"You might as well just call this a plug-in typewriter," she'd told me on day one of her visit a couple of weeks ago. She spread her lips into the half smile she'd adopted when her teeth began coming and going. "You have no good software. You're two versions behind on everything. And you're still using dial-up for the Internet. It's an achromism."

"Close," I said, happy that she'd taken up my word-a-day challenge. A supplement to her sports-fact-a-day habit. "I think you mean anachronism. But remember, I have e-mail now."

She'd brushed the back of her hand across her forehead. "I know. Whew."

Tonight I found Maddie sitting on the floor in the bedroom next to her own. This was the overflow area, dominated by the one project I couldn't bear to finish.

Before he became ill Ken built a full-scale model of our first studio apartment on the Grand Concourse in the Bronx. The whole apartment would nearly have fit into our Eichler atrium. The door, of both the apartment and Ken's model, opened to a combination bedroom and living room. The kitchen was just to the right. When Ken and I were in the six-by-four kitchen together, there was much hip bumping, which at the time led to very late dinners.

No wonder I like miniatures, I thought.

But I couldn't bring myself to outfit and decorate the model apartment once Ken became incapacitated.

Maddie asked me about it every time she visited, and I made one excuse after another. Too busy ("but you've furnished four other dollhouses since Grandpa died"). Don't have the right materials ("you have piles of wood and fabric here, Grandma"). The weather hasn't been right ("how does that matter?").

Now I came upon Maddie peering into the model apartment. When she saw me, she walked her index and middle fingers up to the tiny front door.

"Let's work on this, Grandma. We can do it together. For Grandpa."

I felt my tears rush around inside my head, overwhelming my eyes and my nose. I breathed deeply. Maddie seemed to grow in front of me, from one scale to the next. Bigger, older, and wiser with each step. How could she be more adaptable than her grandmother?

I pulled myself together. "We'd have to make it all pink," I said.

Maddie's smile touched my heart. I leaned over and she put her arms around me. I felt her tears on my cheek. They reminded me that I wasn't the only one who missed Grandpa.

# CHAPTER 4

I took my cell phone to bed with me. In between reading and clipping articles in the latest issue of *Miniatures* magazine, I hit redial for Linda's number. I left the landline free for her hoped-for incoming call.

Which came at two in the morning, waking me from a sound sleep. In my experience, calls in the middle of the night never brought good news. My first thoughts were always of Beverly, who'd made more than one trip to the emergency room for episodes related to her childhood scarlet fever, then of Richard and his family, just because they were so far away.

The phone line was noisy. "Hello," I said, two or three times. I heard a faint female voice that I guessed was Linda's. I thought I heard traffic in the background. My caller ID box had no information beyond *Private Caller.*

"Linda? Linda, is that you?" I asked, now

fully alert in spite of the hour.

"Can you come and get me?" It was a scratchy communication, but definitely Linda.

"Where are you? What happened?"

I was aware of Maddie standing at my bedroom door, sleepy-eyed, in an oversize red-white-and-blue team shirt (basketball? hockey?) that must have been her father's. Of course, she would have been awakened by the extension phone ringing in her room, kept on for security.

I covered the mouthpiece with my hand and whispered to Maddie. "It's Mrs. Reed," I said, meaning, *Don't worry, it's not your parents.* I tried to control the concern in my voice.

I wondered how much Maddie had over-heard and what she thought of it. First I'd told her Linda was at home sleeping off an allergy attack, now Linda was calling at two in the morning and I was asking where she was.

Linda's voice again, in short bursts of speech. "I'm at a no-name gas station off 101, near the on-ramp to 87. My car's still at the school." Nothing so simple as a flat tire, which I suspected, and no answer to "what happened?" but my relief at the sound of her live, if shaky, voice overcame any curiosity for the moment. Then fear crept in, and I pictured Linda tied to a chair (not gagged, but maybe wounded and bleeding). My heart raced. "Are you . . . ?" What to ask — with Maddie now curled up beside me on my bed, questioning me with her eyes. There would be time later for explanations.

"I'll be there," I said. "I'll leave right away. Can you keep your cell phone on until I see you?"

"I don't have my cell phone. It must be in my car. I'm at a pay phone. I used all my change making this call. You can almost see the booth from the freeway. I think I'm near the San Jose airport." Linda's voice broke. I couldn't tell whether she was crying or there was static on the line. "I'm not hurt or anything, Gerry, so don't worry."

Don't worry, indeed, but her comment gave me a little relief. I wanted to grill her right then, hold her hostage, so to speak, until she told me where she'd been all evening, why she left her crafts fair post. But it wasn't the time. She clearly needed rescuing, not scolding. I knew Linda didn't have many friends, just one or two acquaintances among her colleagues at the convalescent hospitals; the patients there were in no shape to socialize. And Linda didn't belong to all the crafts clubs in town as I did, but rather treated her art as a solitary hobby. So, whom else could she have called?

I had a vague picture of where Linda was calling from. The San Jose airport was about ten miles from Lincoln Point, the area mainly industrial. I hoped we'd be able to stay connected by phone.

"I'll have my phone on," I told Linda. "You just stay right there. What's the number? I'll call you once I'm in my car." Maddie, who was paying rapt attention, leaned over and scooped up the pad of paper and pen I keep on my nightstand. She held the pad firmly across her bony knees while I wrote the number of the pay phone.

When I hung up, Maddie disappeared down the hall. I felt a nervous chill along my sweaty back. No question of being too tired to drive; I was energized by adrenaline (my layperson's interpretation of why I was more awake than if I'd had eight hours of sleep). I splashed water on my face and threw on the knit pants and sweatshirt I'd worn at the fair. I grabbed a pair of clean socks and my sneakers, then snatched my purse from the chair by my bed. Ready to go.

Then I stopped. What about Maddie? Should I leave her home or drag her out in the middle of the night? I thought of waking my neighbor and leaving Maddie next door. In spite of Linda's claiming not to be hurt, I had no clue how she would look (bruised? bloody?) or whether the trip might be frightening to Maddie. Nor did I know for sure that whatever danger Linda might have encountered was now over. I imagined someone standing over her, forcing her to make the phone call. *Call the police,* a little voice in my brain said, *why else do you have a nephew on the force? Let* him *go to a strange neighborhood and pick up a stranded citizen of Lincoln Point.* But then a stronger voice, Linda's, said, *Don't you dare.*

No option seemed good, but I didn't have to choose.

Maddie was at my door, dressed in her jeans and jacket, cap facing front, holding a package of breakfast bars and a banana.

"Mrs. Reed might be hungry," my granddaughter said. An amazing little girl. So what if she didn't like pink?

Maddie buckled herself into the backseat on the passenger side. If she had questions, she held them close.

"Sorry to get you out of bed, sweetheart," I told her, tucking a blanket around her wiry body. Her red-tinged curls caught the light from the bulb in the garage-door opener, and I ruffled them gently.

"Is Mrs. Reed all right?" I hoped that was her only concern, and not our safety, for example.

"Oh, sure. She sounded fine. Just stranded." I put a happy spin on it, as if Linda, miraculously recovered from an allergy attack, had been dancing all night with the owner of her favorite crafts store, who then forgot to take her home. I doubted Maddie bought it, but she didn't challenge me. "Why don't you try to sleep?" I suggested.

By the time I backed out of my driveway and started down the street, Maddie had nodded off. I heard her even breathing. Oh, to be ten, I thought.

I wished I'd listened to Skip when he suggested I get a GPS for my Ion. According to my techie-cop nephew, right now I'd be able to type "gas station" on some keypad and get addresses for all the pumps in my vicinity. Lacking that, I went by instinct and the scanty directions Linda had given me. I took 101 South, the Bayshore Freeway, toward the San Jose airport. A couple of miles down, I called the pay phone number Linda had read off. I was glad I kept a headset in the car, though California law still didn't require hands-free-only cell phones. The line seemed to ring for an eternity. I half expected an answering machine to click on, forgetting for a moment that the ringing phone wasn't on Linda's kitchen counter.

After an inordinate number of rings, Linda picked up.

"I'm back here," she said, sounding breathless. "I walked a little way from the phone, trying to see if I could get closer to a main street, but I don't think so. It's not that nice-looking around here, if you know what I mean. It's like a frontage road. It's . . . dark."

*Creepy* was probably what she wanted to say. Linda sounded like a lost child. Normally, Linda carried her extra pounds well, with excellent posture. The added height from her beehive hairdo gave her an overall air of confidence and command. This new timbre in her voice didn't fit that image. Also gone was the strident, bitter divorcée, able to make Christmas shopping at Michael's crafts store seem like a lost-time injury.

"I see signs to the airport," I told her, feeling hopeful.

"Keep going until you can exit to 87."

One good thing about middle-of-the-night

driving: there wasn't much traffic on the usually backed-up 101 freeway. Only a few cars and the occasional roaring truck or top-heavy RV. On the other hand, I wasn't looking forward to stopping in a deserted area. I wondered how I could be frightened of a neighborhood not a dozen miles from my home, but these were industrial streets and freight yards that I usually paid no attention to as I zipped past them on the freeway.

The Ion is a fairly quiet car; I was conscious of Maddie, sleeping in the backseat, and tried to keep the ride smooth by holding my speed down — maybe she'd sleep through the whole episode. Another part of me wanted to go ninety miles an hour and get myself on the California Highway Patrol radar. Then I could flash the get-out-of-a-situation-free card Skip had given me, and gain a police escort.

But the idea was to rescue Linda while keeping everything low-key for Maddie. I turned off at Guadalupe Parkway, still connected to Linda on the pay phone.

"Guadalupe, that's it," she said. "Now keep going, going . . ."

I saw it straight ahead of me on the left. A long row of overly tall billboards and signs, and then a gas sign with all of its lights out. I felt as though I'd been running on empty for many miles, and, though the station was closed (and looked like it would never open again), had finally found a place to fill up. I got off at the next exit and looped back over the freeway.

I heard Maddie stir. "Looks like we're here, sweetheart," I said in a light tone, stopping just short of singing a happy ditty.

Linda stood outside the broken-down booth, as far as the phone cord would reach. I figured the booth (the letters T LEPHO E were lit up on the top) was not the most pleasant-smelling miniature room one could spend time in. The neighborhood was flat, lined with cement buildings with battered metal washboard-type doors and what looked like a farmyard of containers. The ones that usually were attached to semis, barreling down the freeway.

I searched the landscape for signs of trouble. A suspicious car in the lot, close to Linda. (No.) Loops of colored wires and a timer wrapped around Linda's chest. (No.) Sounds of gunfire. (No.) Hooded men lurking in shadows. (No.)

I determined we were all clear, unless there was a sniper in the small, dark convenience store attached to the station office. As we approached, I heard Maddie rummaging in the snack bag she'd put together.

I tapped the horn though I could see that Linda had spotted me. I pulled up beside her and stopped briefly, not even putting the car in park, letting Linda fall into the front seat, then took off quickly for the freeway north.

I heard three deep exhales, including my own.

Something about the smell of a slightly overripe banana made the ride home seem normal. I suspected Linda wasn't the least bit hungry, but couldn't refuse a little girl's thoughtful gesture. (Linda was wonderful with children and with the sick; it was normal, healthy adults she seemed to have a problem relating to.) I nibbled on a raspberry breakfast bar, to show my appreciation. Maddie herself licked an orange Popsicle (not food to me, but simply a way to store sticks for crafts), having somehow managed to assemble a little picnic chest to keep it from melting completely on the trip down. A Popsicle at nearly three in the morning. A picture of Maddie's mother came to my mind. She had a questioning look on her face. *Don't ask, Mary Lou.*

Maddie fell asleep again, once she finished her snack. At a red light, I leaned back and added a jacket to the blanket covering her. I needed to keep the car reasonably cold to stay awake. And to protect any remaining Popsicles.

I looked over at Linda as often as possible on the trip home, but she didn't turn my way once. I knew she was taking advantage of Maddie's presence, sleeping or not, to avoid a conversation. When I told her Jason was spending the night with Peter, she responded with a perfunctory "Good."

The brief moments it took for her to enter my car didn't allow much time for close examination. I saw nothing obvious. No limp or visible bruising or bleeding. She was wearing the turquoise sweat suit she had on at the fair. Her beehive hairdo was disheveled, not easily accomplished since it was always heavily sprayed, but otherwise I saw no signs of distress.

We reached the school parking lot without incident. Linda refused my offer to drive her home and collect her car in the morning — make that a few hours from now. I wasn't awake enough to argue at full force. I expected — make that, required — Linda to talk as soon as we were free of Maddie. For now, she was safe from my interrogation skills (acute, according to my husband and son).

■ ■ ■ ■

Linda's SUV was the only vehicle left in the school lot. I got out of my car when she did and cornered her before she entered her vehicle, not quite pressing her against the door — impossible, since she outweighed me by the equivalent of several dress sizes — but a barrier nonetheless. Light from a cheap outside fixture over the door of the multipurpose room fell on her face and I saw the accumulated stress of the past ten hours. Her blue eyes were narrow, half-closed, and watery. Lines on her face seemed to have multiplied since I last saw her varnishing her Governor Winthrop desk. *Where is that desk anyway?* flitted through my mind, but escaped quickly as I focused on more significant matters. Up close, as bad as the thin light from the dirty bulb was, I could see that her running (not that she ran) suit was soiled and her jacket pocket torn.

"Speak, Linda." I wanted to sound like I was delivering tough love, but I never did quite understand what that meant in a practical situation.

"Please, Gerry. I'm very grateful to you. You know that. But just let me get home.

I'll see you tomorrow."

"Are you seriously thinking of sitting next to me at the fair as if none of this happened?"

She sighed heavily and I heard her exhaustion in her breathing. Linda's body seemed to slide down her car door, and I worried that she wouldn't be able to drive home. Not that I was all that chipper either at three thirty in the morning, now that my fear and excitement had waned.

"Please, Gerry."

Tough love faded, and I stepped aside so Linda could enter her SUV.

I didn't ask — I simply took it upon myself to follow Linda to her home, about a mile from my house, to make sure she got there without incident. Without disappearing again, really.

A few houses before Linda's, I passed a red sports car that I recognized as Chuck's, with an unmistakable weather-beaten Raiders flag attached to its antenna. Chuck, or someone with the same lanky physique, was in the driver's seat. I didn't see this as a good sign, but didn't have the energy to confront him or anyone else at this hour. I hoped he wasn't there to ambush Linda. More likely looking for Jason, who I hoped was safely tucked into Peter's guest bed.

I drove slowly by Linda's house and saw her enter through her garage.

Call me nosy. And frustrated. After a great expenditure of both emotional and physical energy, I still didn't have answers to a long list of questions. One more pass, I decided, in order to spy on Chuck. I drove around the block, and by the time I made a full circle, Chuck was pulling away from the curb.

Nothing left to do but take my granddaughter home to bed.

# CHAPTER 5

I'd fallen asleep just before five, having set my alarm for eight thirty, at which time I called my nephew, Skip. He'd already promised to pick up Maddie at the fair midmorning and take her to the softball game between the men and women of the Lincoln Point Police and Fire Departments. Sadly, I'd realized this was more of a treat for her than helping me make doilies for my dollhouses.

"I'd like to let Maddie sleep a little longer this morning, so can you come here and babysit while I go to the fair?" I asked Skip (happy that Maddie didn't hear the term *babysit*). I almost wished he'd ask me why Maddie needed to sleep late. Then I might have an excuse to tell him about Linda's strange evening. Maybe there was something on the police blotter that related to it. Is this nosiness or concern? I asked myself. A thin line, it seemed.

"Sure," Skip said. "When?"

"Now."

"Uh, sure. I can be there in about twenty minutes." I heard sleep in his voice, and a mumbling in the background. Either the TV or a bedmate. Skip, twenty-eight, was a handsome bachelor who kept his social life a mystery from me and his mother. Just as well, considering the above-mentioned *thin line* between nosiness and concern.

"Perfect. I need to leave by about nine fifteen. I'll make some sandwiches for you to take to the game."

"Sweet. Throw in some of those awesome ginger cookies you bake, and I'm there. Anyway I've been wanting to check out that decrepit furnace of yours. We may have to get you a new one."

How lucky could I be? With no family of my own, except for some cousins in Oklahoma, whom I'd never met, I appreciated being part of the wonderful Porter clan. The joke was that I was welcome in spite of my (once) dark, straight hair, with nothing like the eye-catching red that ran through all of theirs, in one stripe or another. (The highlights in my hair were old-lady gray.)

When Beverly lost her husband, Eino, in the first Gulf War, months from military retirement, eleven-year-old Skip, baptized

Eino Jr., became even more of a regular at our home and more of a fan of my ginger cookies. Having Skip around now made up a bit for Richard and his family's living four hundred miles away in Los Angeles.

Richard and Mary Lou constantly reiterated a standing invitation to me to visit them. They were also very good about sending Maddie to Lincoln Point often enough for me to be a real grandmother (*unlike this weekend,* I thought). I ran my finger over a drawing on my refrigerator. Maddie had done it when she was six years old, and desperately wanted me to remove it. I couldn't bring myself to discard the childish representation of Maddie, Ken, and me holding hands in front of our square-box Eichler.

Happy to be a homemaker for these few minutes, I shuffled between the kitchen and pantry (another very desirable feature of an Eichler home, along with floor-to-ceiling windows), making ham-and-turkey sandwiches on my homemade four-grain bread. Whole grains were a little lost on Maddie, but I was out of plain white store-bought. For all I knew Skip had the same white-bread taste but was too polite to tell me. I placed the cookie jar — a ceramic San Francisco Victorian house with a removable chimney lid — on the counter where no one could miss it, and filled my own lunch bag with a cheese sandwich and a thermos of Peet's coffee. I did all of this at about 70 percent wakefulness. Ahead of me was an eight-hour day at the fair. I looked back longingly at my bedroom.

But, as Ken always said, sleep is overrated.

I was never so glad to see Linda, and at the same time, never so put out with her. She refused to tell me why she'd had to drag me — and Maddie — out of bed in the dead of night to a phone booth in the middle of nowhere. I realized I'd turned out a set of phrases that sounded whiny even to me when I recited them to Linda, but I had to get the sentiment out.

"I'd do the same for you," was all she'd say as we sat, side by side, at Tables 30 and 31 on day two of the fair.

"That's not the point," was my weak comeback, since I knew she was right. "The least you can do is tell me if you were A, having fun or B, in trouble. And where is your Governor Winthrop, by the way?"

She raised her eyebrows. "That's not your concern, now, is it?" Then she bent her head to her work — tatting along the edges of a tiny linen towel. Her face, with more makeup than usual (to cover bruises?), showed nothing. There were no bandages on her fingers or arms from Beverly's postulated Exacto knife incident. I had half a mind to dangle her bloody cloth in her face (*explain this,* I'd say); it was still tucked at the bottom of my tackle box, which I hadn't reorganized from last night. I had no plans for the cloth, but somehow hadn't discarded it.

I tried different approaches during the day to get Linda to slip up and talk. Once, when I remembered the condition of Jason's room, I asked, "Was everything okay at your house last night?"

"Of course. What do you mean?"

I wished I could learn the knack of the poker face as Linda knew it. "Nothing," I said.

The Saturday crowd was lively, probably having slept more than I had. The piped-in music was loud and upbeat — happily, the committee had voted down one member's suggestion that we play Christmas music (today was actually Bastille Day) to encourage shopping.

By noon, I was barely keeping up with room boxes. I'd brought several to finish during lulls in customer activity. No sooner had I added gold leaf trim to the top of an

Early American dresser, than it was bought by a woman I recognized as Mabel Quinlan's beading partner. I'd also had a special request for a Passover table and finished just in time for my customer to pick it up. I had to warn her that the lacquer I'd sprayed on the one-inch matzah-patterned place mats was still sticky.

Linda, too, was busy and polishing up extras between customers. Not that it mattered inside the windowless, air-conditioned hall, but every time someone entered or exited through the side door, we could see that it was a bright, sunny day. Linda's mood seemed to match. Practically a first. She wore her hair in an upsweep today — one of her two standard dos — with piles of dry gray-blond strands at the very top of her head. I had a flashback to the younger, thinner Linda in a yearbook photo on her bookshelf. I wondered what her personality was back then, before adult struggles challenged her.

To give her a little credit — Linda was making an extra effort to be nice to me this morning. She offered to bring me back a snack or a drink from the concession stand at the front of the hall (every time she left her table, I felt a nervous twinge); she cleaned off my table when a bored little boy left potato chip crumbs on my tiny cherry-wood dresser; she gave me a cube from her new polymer-clay box, a lovely shade of red that would be perfect for miniature roses, and (definitely a first) complimented me on a set of "books" I'd made out of basswood strips.

Maybe she was feeling guilty about inconveniencing me last night. Or about not explaining why she'd needed to.

Or maybe last night was better for her than it appeared.

Beverly and Skip brought Maddie by after the softball game. Maddie's jeans looked like she'd been the one sliding into second base or skidding across the outfield to catch a fly ball. I wondered what had happened to all the frilly holiday dresses I used to send her before I knew her well.

I wanted to ask Maddie how she slept last night, whether she'd had any nightmares as a result of our spooky adventure. I supposed it was too much to hope for, that she'd think our trip was just a bad dream. I decided to wait and see if Maddie brought it up on her own.

"The cops won!" Maddie squealed, grinning broadly, apparently forgetting her zigzag teeth. She swung an imaginary bat against an invisible ball. Not thinking about anything creepy, I was relieved to see. "Skip roped it." She swung again. "Bam! A double down the left field line."

"Aw, shucks." Skip removed his LPPD cap, loosening reddish Porter curls, and held the hat against his heart. He bowed to Maddie, like a shy suitor, fully aware of how much Maddie adored him. "It was just a base hit. Nothing like last night, when yours truly, Officer Gowen, was on the job, rounding up bad guys, protecting and serving the citizens of —"

Beverly put her hand over Skip's mouth, and he pretended that it was enough to stop his flow of speech. "Sometimes I wonder what's the real reason why my son entered public service," Beverly said.

"Cops are chick magnets," Maddie said. I could tell by the flush that took over her freckled cheeks and the surprise in her eyes that the words were out before she knew it. The laughter that rose up from those who happened to catch her remark proved too much for her. Maddie giggled self-consciously and ran off to the Children's Corner. I reminded myself of my grandmotherly duties and resolved to talk to her later about where she'd picked up the phrase.

I caught Linda's eye a couple of times during Skip's visit, especially when Beverly followed Maddie to the stage, where Just Eddie and Postmaster Cooney were having it out over who-knew-what. Now it was just the three of us — Linda, me, and my nephew, the cop — during a lull, and in a rather separated little corner between the storage area and a single row of crafters' tables. Linda worked her jaw to one side and deepened her frown. "Don't say a word to him," her expression shouted.

For now, I wouldn't.

Besides, there wasn't time. We were called to attention by a tinny rendition of the tune "Hail to the Chief." Linda looked around with a questioning look, but Beverly and I recognized Skip's cell-phone ring (exceptions to the no-cell rule could be made for law enforcement, I decided on the spot).

"A what?" Skip asked, in a voice louder than normal to counteract the din in the hall. His eyes grew wide with disbelief. He plugged one ear against the drone of the fair. "A 187? For real?"

I'd learned a few police codes during Skip's career: 65 was a robbery; 65p a purse snatching. A 459 meant that a silent alarm had gone off somewhere, and I remembered

Skip's calling a petty thievery charge a 966. What was 187?

"A homicide," Skip said, clicking his phone shut, as if I'd asked the question out loud. Then, apparently realizing he was not in his squad room, he lowered his voice and addressed us. "For now, you didn't hear that, okay?"

We all nodded as Skip turned and all but ran out the side door.

The day passed quickly, with few breaks for dipping into my lunch bag and thermos. From time to time I thought of Skip, on his first homicide call. Not that he'd be happy about the violent act, but it was common knowledge around the LPPD that helping on a murder case was the first step toward earning a detective's badge. I knew he'd do well and felt conflicted that his success had to come at someone's (*whose?* I wondered) expense.

By midafternoon, Linda had recovered her old moodiness, and her frown lines were back. In all fairness, the instigating incidents might have been the appearance of her two ex-husbands, within minutes of each other.

Peter, ex-husband number one, showed up first, with Jason trailing him down what must have seemed interminably long aisles of crafts. Both males had their hands in their jeans pockets, elbows in, and shoulders hunched as they made their way along Tables 25 through 29, as though worried either that they might break something precious, or that a piece of satin ribbon would reach out and attach itself to their clothing. They rounded the corner, past me, to Linda's table.

Peter's tall, broad frame seemed to take up half of Linda's table front. Jason, on the other hand, was short for his age, and chubby, like his adopted mom. He seemed to shrink into his T-shirt. "Just dropping off your son," Peter said. "The one you abandoned last night?"

"I don't need dropping off," said a sullen, stringy-haired Jason, whose jeans had horizontal slashes from his knees to his ankles. He threw down his backpack, its camouflage design reminding us all of war. "I'm almost fifteen."

Peter removed his wire-frame glasses and gave him a glare that I felt sure wasn't the first of its kind in the last twenty-four hours.

Linda dragged an extra folding chair close to hers and pointed a stiff finger at its seat. "Jason," she said. Not a warm invitation.

Jason rolled his eyes. "I don't have to stay *here,* do I?" He pulled up the neck of his army green T-shirt until it covered most of his mouth. I figured he didn't want to be identifiable next to tables full of lace, beads, and tiny, cute objects.

"Hey, buddy." Chuck's voice. He'd come in through the side door a few feet from my table. Another tall man, but thin, with a preference for Western wear. Today's shirt featured two identical cowboys riding bulls (or very animated horses), facing each other across Chuck's skimpy chest. His sculpted ivory belt buckle was too big for his narrow waist and reminded me of a badly fashioned bathtub. "You can hang with me," he told Jason.

"Great," Peter said, and made as hasty an exit as I've ever seen, out the side door to the parking lot.

Jason let the neck of his T-shirt snap back, as much as jersey fabric can snap. "Oh, yeah, great," he said. "One freakin' picnic after another." But his behavior belied his outburst as he jumped off the chair and gave Chuck what might be called an affectionate look. Almost a smile, which was a lot for Jason.

Chuck frowned at Jason. "Watch your mouth," he told him, then turned to me. "Can me and my family have a private moment here, Ger?"

*Grrr.* I hated to be called "Ger," and Chuck knew it. I felt like asking him to reimburse me for the time I'd be away from my paid-for table, but Linda had been through enough. I held my tongue, bypassed Chuck, and addressed Linda. "Watch my table, will you, Linda?"

I walked away reluctantly, remembering the last time I'd left her in charge of my goods.

From my deliberately chosen seat at the lunch table along the east wall of the school hall, I could make out the body language between Linda and Chuck. It involved a lot of in-your-face movements from Chuck and retreating, cross-armed gestures from Linda. Then, vice versa. I was doing well, making educated guesses about who was winning each round until Betty (Tudor Mansion) Fine sat down across from me. There were few people in the dining area midafternoon, and I wished she'd taken her coffee to any of the six empty tables.

"How nice to have you to myself, Geraldine," Betty said, making me feel guilty about wanting to shoo her away. Betty had been making Tudor dollhouses and villages for as long as I could remember, and today her bouffant dyed-blond hairdo seemed as tall as the steeple on her country church. The elaborate coiffure blocked my view of Linda and Chuck, putting a severe damper on my spying.

I had no inclination to visit with Betty, but I knew that complimenting her work was often enough to keep her entertained and chatting unilaterally for a long time. I threw out a conversation starter.

"What a wonderful attic setting you have this year," I said, looking past her at Chuck, in the lead, with his finger pointing at Linda's chest.

"Oh, thank you, Geraldine. I made the little easel from some flat toothpicks I got at the dollar store."

"Really?" Now Linda was poking Chuck's chest.

"I used finger paint for the little unfinished landscape on the canvas, which is just a piece of muslin."

"Really?" Chuck had his hands on his hips. I thought I made out a frown to match Linda's.

"I noticed you're teaching a found-objects class at the adult school," Betty said.

"Really?" *Oops, wrong comment.* Of all days for Betty to reach out beyond her happy talk. "Yes, I am, Betty."

Chuck took off his hat, wiped his brow,

and paced the small area in front of Linda's table.

"I've signed up, but I wondered if you could give me a few little clues to get started ahead of time." Betty dug in her purse (giving me a chance while her head was down to see Chuck put his hat back on), and pulled out a plastic bag full of items she'd been saving (which I pretended to study, while actually catching Linda in the act of turning her back on Chuck and settling in her seat).

"Well?" Betty asked.

I had no idea what her question had been. I'd been following Chuck, who was rounding the aisle past Table 29, headed in my direction. The look on his face said he wouldn't call me *Ger* this time.

"Keep out of things that are not your business, Geraldine," he said. His voice had an underlying growl, which I supposed was meant to frighten me. But I couldn't take him seriously, perhaps because I had no idea what he was talking about. Perhaps because his breath reeked of alcohol. Or perhaps because of his silly cowboy hat.

"What was that all about?" Betty asked.

"Don't worry about it, Betty," I said. "Let's see what we can do with these old pillboxes."

If Linda was counting on a very busy last hour on Saturday evening so she wouldn't have to talk to me, she got her wish. Customers poured in for the raffle at five (Betty's granddaughter won a split-level ranch donated by Gail Musgrave, inexplicably making me feel better about my rude behavior to Betty), and the crowd stayed around until closing.

I had a new respect for the cliché, "we need to talk." The phrase was short and sweet, and with the proper tone, spoke volumes. I said it to Linda once when we happened to lean toward each other to get an item from our totes, and again when a mutual customer was distracted by writing two checks.

Unfortunately, an observation is not a question, and Linda could just give me that look and be done with it.

"Why is Chuck on my case?" I asked her another time. She treated the query as she did the cliché. Finally, I decided Chuck was right that I should mind my own business. Linda had a right to her privacy. Picking up a friend did not entitle one to know any more details than the friend was willing to share.

Once this fair was over, Linda and I would have a nice, leisurely lunch, and by then I would have forgotten about the irresponsible behavior, the strange trip to a questionable neighborhood, the missing Governor Winthrop desk, and the bloody cheesecloth.

Clearly, I'd forgotten nothing yet.

# CHAPTER 6

I loved coming home to a meal prepared by someone else, especially my family. After a grueling (a mini-exaggeration) day at the fair, I opened the door from my garage to my kitchen and was greeted by the smells of Italy. Or at least Beverly's version of Italy. Beverly and Ken used to claim there had been an Italian infiltration into the Porter clan a few generations back, and that a secret recipe for tomato sauce had been handed down by "Nonna Lombardo."

The feast was nearly ready. All I had to do was change out of my sweats, stained with drops of gold leaf and a smear of cherry-wood varnish, slip into a comfortable caftan, and show up at the table.

Saturday night's menu included an enormous escarole salad and the Lombardo special, spaghetti and beef *bracciola,* with a substitute of meatballs for Maddie. Wine for the adults, cola for Maddie, and warm bread for all. The glasstop patio table had been set with plates and napkins Beverly had brought me from Italy. I sat next to Maddie, facing my lovely two-toned blue home.

Nearly every home in our Eichler neighborhood was a pale color with a darker trim, a double rainbow effect that Ken and I loved. My heart swelled. If only everyone could have such moments with a loving family. But, *if only Ken and Skip's dad, Eino Sr., hadn't left us,* was always at the back of my mind.

Beverly, lean and fit herself, and without a heart episode for at least two years, kept telling me I was still too thin (I'd gained back only half the weight I lost while caring for Ken). She and Skip carried out their fattening mission in subtle ways. Like placing the breadbasket and butter closest to my place, scooping an extra serving of everything onto my plate, and being sure dessert was chocolate-based. Tonight I'd noticed a batch of Beverly's brownies on my counter, and she personally saw to it that there was always ice cream in my freezer and chocolate sauce in my pantry.

Even though temperatures had reached the nineties during the day, the evening was cool, with a slight breeze. One of the nice things about living in the Bay Area. I remembered summer nights in the Bronx when Ken and I would try to get relief by sleeping on the roof of our multistory building. Most often the air was not much cooler than inside our non-air-conditioned apartment. Steam rose from the tar and spilled from the bricks, and the humidity would hover around 80 percent through the night.

"Mmmmm. Smells good over there." The voice of our neighbor whose house was pale green with dark green trim, June Chinn. She'd hoisted her small frame onto a tipped-over crate (I'd seen it many times) and rested her arms on the fence between us. Eichler neighborhoods tended to be friendlier than most California tracts and subdivisions, as if sharing the same unique architecture bonded us all with the master builder, Joseph Eichler. "Don't you have a date tonight, Skip?" June asked.

"The night is young," Skip said, and gave her a wink.

"I'm here all night, Officer," June said, and disappeared into her yard, probably blush red at her boldness. Beverly and I shared a glance, both wishing we knew more about Skip's late-night adventures, both looking forward to the day when he brought someone home more than once. Beverly reminded him often that June, a tech writer at one of the few surviving dot-coms in Silicon Valley, was cute and single. We'd stopped inviting June to dinner for Skip's benefit, but I enjoyed the light flirtation they kept up.

Skip had another way of putting an end to his mother's and my nagging him to settle down. He'd turn it around and ask when we were going to date again. Enough said.

Tonight there was another country to hear from, and Beverly and I could remain neutral.

"June is pretty. Do you like her, Uncle Skip?" Maddie asked, just before squeezing half a meatball into her mouth. Leave it to the very young to come right out with it. She washed it all down with a long swallow of cola. Tomorrow night she'd have only milk to drink, I told myself.

*Dum dum dum-dum . . .* strains of "Hail to the Chief," from Skip's cell phone. I wondered if he'd called himself somehow to avoid his first-cousin-once-removed's question.

Skip raised his finger in an excuse-me gesture and stepped onto the grass past the patio bricks. He rested his black-sneakered foot on one of a ring of stones that surrounded my birdbath. We heard nothing but *uh-huhs* on our end.

"Gotta go," Skip said, clicking his phone shut as he walked back toward us, in the direction of the house. "A break in a case."

"My son, the detective," his proud mother said.

"Is this about the murder?" I asked.

"Or the jewelry-store robbery?" Beverly asked.

"Was there a shoot-out?" Maddie wanted to know.

Skip laughed at the enthusiasm his call aroused. He rubbed Maddie's red curls. "Maybe there'll be another cop in the family," he said. Her response was a wide grin. As much as I appreciated the law-enforcement profession, I'd been picturing Maddie as a doctor, like her father, or an artist, like her mother. If she was enamored of law enforcement, she could be a Supreme Court justice, but not patrolling the streets with a baton and gun, thank you. Not to worry, if she was like most kids, many ideas would come and go in the next few years.

"I can't say much right now," Skip said.

"I heard they took only the cash and some of the less expensive pieces," Beverly said, pursuing the jewelry track. "Crane is lucky they left the good stuff, though they did get away with something like fifteen thousand dollars."

"Wow, fifteen grand." Maddie whistled through a (happily) food-free mouth. "Any suspects?"

Another resolution: to monitor my granddaughter's television viewing more closely.

Skip caught my eye, and addressed me instead of his tiny interrogator. "Maybe a suspect." When he saw that Beverly and Maddie had left the table, distracted by a visit from June's cat (not needing a crate to overcome the fence), he leaned over and whispered, "Well, you'll find this out soon enough, Aunt Gerry. We think Jason Reed was involved."

A ripple went through me and the whole backyard shifted. "Jason? Involved in the murder?" I pointed to Skip's cell phone, as if a corpse lay there on the touch pad.

"No, no. Not in the murder. In the burglary." Skip had his keys out.

I sat back, took a deep breath and a long sip of red wine. Linda didn't have a murder to worry about, at least. There had already been rumors about Jason and the burglary, but I'd been hoping they were just that, rumors. I felt so sorry for Jason. And for Linda. She'd always wanted a family and adopted Jason late in her life, when she was forty-three and Jason was about three and a half years old. She did this without full support from Chuck Reed, her then husband. Linda had pressed the issue. Chuck relented and let Jason take his name, but left them both the following year. Lately, however, Chuck had been spending time with Jason, and Linda wasn't happy.

"Chuck never spent a minute with Jason when he lived with us and supposedly was his father," she'd complained recently. "Now he wants to be his buddy."

"Maybe a father figure is what Jason needs now," I'd ventured, then realized Chuck might not be the best model for that role. No steady job (currently, he was on the substitute list for when Just Eddie called in sick). A drinking problem, to put it mildly. And then there were those bandannas and belt buckles.

Peter was the ex Linda wished would pay attention to Jason. She'd talked her first husband into taking Jason once a month for bonding, but it wasn't working out as she'd have liked.

After one such day of togetherness, Peter reported, "The kid hates miniature golf."

(Occupational hazard — hearing the term *miniature golf,* Linda and I both confessed to picturing a very tiny golf course, on a twelve-inch-square tile, say, or a board with green felt, worked over to resemble turf. The golf ball could be a dried pea, painted white.)

I wasn't sure Peter was any better a model for Jason, just because he was an affluent career engineer. Peter was a braggart — "the kind of guy, if you've got a bottle, he's got a case," was Ken's description.

Thinking of Linda's life during the years I'd known her, my heart went out to her. She did her best, but it seemed not enough to earn her the happy family life she wanted.

I had one more question for Skip, who had gone into the dining room through the sliding patio door, with me trailing behind.

"Could a kid like Jason pull off something like that burglary by himself?" I asked.

Skip worked his jaw and jingled his keys. He was being overly patient with his nosy aunt, and I worried that he thought I wanted inside information.

"I mean, in general," I said. Now we were in the atrium, a few steps from the door to the street.

"Not likely," Skip said. "There's usually a mentor somewhere in cases like this." He leaned over, kissed my cheek, and went to work.

I was left pondering this new concept of "mentoring." I liked it better when it meant tutoring in English or math, or being a role model for a (legal) career.

"Where do you think the 187 happened?" Maddie asked, long after we thought she'd forgotten about her uncle's call.

*This little girl was too quick a study,* I thought.

"Far away from here, I'm sure," Beverly said, her long arms flung to their fullest extent.

"It might not even be in Lincoln Point," I said. "Maybe Uncle Skip is helping out the county, and you know how far that goes." (I didn't, but I felt it sounded good.) Beverly and I made a rush to clear the dishes, showing just how casually we were taking this turn of affairs in Lincoln Point.

"It's not that I'm scared or anything," Maddie said.

"Of course not."

That was Beverly and me, in unison.

Our cozy dinner party ended early, not just because of Skip's phone call and Maddie's too-curious state. As much as I wanted to tune into the local news on television and maybe find out more myself about the homicide — murder was very rare in Lincoln Point — I decided I could wait until I read about it in the newspaper. I still had a day to go at the fair, and Beverly had a long, hard day planned at the Oakland Zoo with Maddie.

Beverly's health was a worry to me. One of her heart valves had been slightly damaged from a strep-throat infection when she was a little older than Maddie. Ken remembered all too many details of the sandpaper rash that seemed to start it all. For the rest of the reading world, scarlet fever was the disease that took the beloved young Beth, in *Little Women.* For the Porter family, it was reality, not fiction.

Even now, every time Beverly was fatigued or complained of joint pain, I saw it as a sign of the disease, though she herself played it down. I'd suggested an activity closer to home than Oakland, but we both knew Maddie had her heart set on a return to the reptile room.

"Don't worry," Beverly said. "I'm not going to die on you."

I hoped not.

"A Ramona book," Maddie said when I asked her reading choice for the night.

We curled up on the bed in her father's room and delved into the boisterous, slightly rebellious Ramona Quimby's first day of a new school year. Quite a switch from the little girl whose daytime vocabulary included phrases like *chick magnet* and *fifteen grand.* I remembered the same back-and-forth behavior from Richard at that age. One moment he was The Too-Big-Now Kid, refusing to kiss his parents in front of his friends; the next he was hanging on to me or wanting one of us to stay by his bed until he fell asleep.

A girl after her English teacher grandmother's heart, Maddie had filled an entire tote bag with books for her trip. I was glad to see that the number of knock-knock joke books was down from last year.

My mind was only partly on Ramona's nemesis, Yard Ape, and whether he would dip her pigtails in the inkwell, or whatever the modern-day version was. (Dunking her cell phone into an oversize drink cup? Rubbing her iPod in a handful of neon green gunk?)

Most of my attention was on Linda's plight. I never thought of myself as having a great imagination. I preferred to enjoy other people's stories and poems. Yet now my brain seemed to be working overtime, creating links between Jason's alleged burglary and Linda's Friday evening/Saturday morning trouble.

What if Jason's mentor, as Skip called him, had abducted Linda and left her at that pay phone? A possible reason eluded me, but my number-one candidate wore an elaborate belt buckle and cowboy boots and drove a red sports car probably only 2 percent his, 98 percent some creditor's. On the other hand, I couldn't guess why Chuck would behave so dramatically with Linda. He seemed happy enough just to hassle her in the usual ways.

At eleven o'clock the phone by my bed rang. Linda's home phone number showed in my little ID box. I grabbed the receiver before the noise could wake Maddie, I hoped.

Once again I heard a voice in trouble. "The police think Jason robbed Crane's," Linda said.

I couldn't bring myself to tell her I wasn't surprised. "That's awful, Linda. Did they arrest him?"

"Absolutely not," she said, sounding as if that were the most preposterous idea she'd heard since someone suggested she spray paint her fine furniture pieces. "He's right here. In bed."

I bit my lip and rolled my eyes to the ceiling, tempted to hang up and unplug my phone. Instead, my pushover personality kicked in. "Do you want to come by for coffee?"

"Okay, if you want me to." That was Linda, making the whole thing my idea.

"Of course," I said.

It wasn't two in the morning at least, and it wasn't from a pay phone in the hinterlands. And I didn't even have to leave my home.

Things were looking up.

# CHAPTER 7

Crafts fair weekends always tired me out, even when all I had to worry about was smiling a lot, and keeping inventory on hand and my thermos filled. This weekend was over the top, however, with two nearly sleepless nights and the added responsibility of making sure Maddie was taken care of, and — very important — that she was spared the drama in the lives of her grandmother's friends.

At just after midnight, I poured second cups of coffee for Linda and me. We sat in the atrium, the heart of the house, where I kept a cozy arrangement of two chairs and a small table. I'd thrown a light robe over my mismatched cotton pajamas. Linda, who'd spent most of the evening at the police station, was in her crafts fair sweats, dusty rose this time. Her face was splotchy, her blue mascara streaked, and her hair limp. Nothing worse than a limp upsweep, but I didn't tell her that.

She'd briefed me on Jason's grueling experience "under the lights," as she called the interview.

"They treated my son like a criminal," she said in summary. "All they have is that he skipped school that morning and the newsstand guy — Armando or Alonzo or something — may have seen him near Crane's. Someone who doesn't even speak English right, Gerry. The police don't like Jason much."

"He *has* kept the police busy, with —"

"With what? You know he didn't do half the things he's accused of. Sometimes he falls in with the wrong crowd. He's a very impressionable boy."

The inconsistencies made my late-night head spin. He didn't do it, but if he did, it wasn't his fault. There wasn't a witness, but if there was, English was not his first language. It sounded like lawyer talk, which also made my head spin.

"I understand," I said.

"I think Chuck is involved. The police said he had a solid alibi for last Tuesday, the day of the robbery. But get this: evidently he started drinking early that day and was playing pool with his buddies. The bartender — you know, that loser Tom Baker — and four other upstanding citizens of Lincoln Point vouched for him." Linda took a cookie from the plate between us. "Yeah, right. A tight alibi. Anyway, Jason's fine for right now, until they decide they have something else on him, I guess." She took a breath. "But I'm all stressed out, and there was just no one else for me to turn to."

"Turn to for what, Linda? You're not exactly opening up to me." The delicate sounds from the waterdrop fountain in the corner of the atrium reminded me to breathe, to calm myself. Water poured from the uppermost vessel down to each of three others, in the aqueduct style that Ken loved, and cycled back to the top. I focused on lowering my voice — Maddie was only one room away. "What happened last night?" I whispered.

Linda folded her arms and blew out a breath, as if she'd just taken a drag on a cigarette, which would have been the case not too many years ago. "I don't want to talk about it right now, Gerry. Just be patient with me. I think it's all going to be over soon."

"And what might *it* be?" I asked.

Linda glared at me, as she often did when I pressed her for what she didn't want to give up. But this was my home, my coffee, and my sleep time that was dwindling away. I picked up my mug, nearly full, and carried it to the kitchen. I slammed the mug into the sink, making as much noise as I could without breaking it.

"I just wanted to see a friendly face, Gerry. Which I'm not getting. I guess I'd better go," Linda said. Her voice was huffy, which aggravated me more.

"I guess so."

Linda threw her purse over her shoulder and headed for door. She left her mug on the table.

I should have been relieved, but the feeling was more complicated than that. I thought of myself as a good friend. Maybe really good friends don't ask questions. Maybe the trendy, "I'm here for you," is what I should be willing to give, no matter how little I got in return.

It was too late and I was too tired to decide. In just a few hours I'd see Linda at the fair and apologize for essentially kicking her out of my house.

I locked the front door after her and stopped by Maddie's room. She was sprawled on her stomach, covers on the floor. Her left hand clutched something I couldn't make out. I moved closer and strained to see it by the moonlight streaming through the window.

She was holding two small pieces of foam board, the raw materials I'd pointed out to her for a bookcase in the Bronx apartment dollhouse. I could see that the edges were mangled, probably sticky with glue from her attempts to form a shelf. The room was warm, but still I covered her with the baseball-design afghan I'd knitted for her father many years ago. I kissed her forehead and slipped out.

I sat in front of my waterdrop fountain for a long time.

The fair was scheduled for only five hours on Sunday, ten to three. I hoped I could make it through without nodding off in front of a buyer. I made a quick plan. Beverly and Maddie wouldn't get home from the zoo until six or so. If I played it right, I could pack up my goods, help Just Eddie put the hall back to its normal configuration (his generosity in working on Sunday extended just so far), and be home by four thirty for a nap.

First, however, there were those five hours.

By the second hour of the fair, about eleven in the morning, everyone — vendors and customers alike — was talking about "The Murder." So much for Skip's admonition to keep quiet. Someone had not been so obedient as Beverly and I had. Not surprising that the word had spread. Violent crime was a rarity in Lincoln Point — the only murder I could remember was years ago, that of a seasoned criminal, whom the good citizens of the town seemed happy to be rid of. This new murder was big news.

The buzz filled the room as each new group entered the hall with more alleged information. The consensus was that the victim was an unidentified white woman, small frame, early thirties. One crafter said she'd heard the victim was shot, another that she'd been strangled. One customer surmised that she was a "working girl" who'd wandered over the line from the next town to the south, another that she was a drifter from the next town to the north.

Jim Quinlan, husband of Mabel, the Queen of Beads, came in all flustered, waving a copy of our local weekly newspaper, the *Lincolnite,* a morning paper put out by our editor who was also our minister.

We heard Jim's voice all the way in the back of the room. "Can you believe this? Mabel and I drove by that very spot not two days ago," he said, as if they'd been in imminent danger, and were still.

I paid only sight attention to the chatter

while I surreptitiously started to pack a few of my items in preparation for closing the fair. Surely I wouldn't sell more than one or two more knickknack shelves made from multiblade razor cartridges in the next few hours.

The news flowed past.

"I heard she had several different IDs on her."

"No, the paper said she had no ID."

"The cops are not telling us everything."

"They never do."

"Was she naked?"

"She was wearing a Raiders jacket."

"Where was the body found, anyway?"

Then Jim. The voice of authority, since he was holding the newspaper. "I told you, we just passed by there on our way to visit our grandson. The body was behind a gas station somewhere on 101, near the off-ramp to 87."

My heart skipped. I looked up at Jim, now walking away from my corner. Done with parading his story, he was heading back to his wife's table at the front of the hall.

I left a customer midsentence, with a quick *'scuse me,* and walked into the aisle. I caught up with Jim and kept pace with him toward Table 8. Not too difficult since Jim was older than Mabel, who'd admitted to eighty-one last year, then seventy-nine this year.

I steadied my breathing. "Are you sure about the location, Jim? How do you know exactly where the woman was found?" I asked him. I had to bend a bit to speak into Jim's ear. I thought I remembered a time when he was taller than me.

Jim slapped his hand on the paper, its headlines barking the story of the day. "It says so, right here. Do you know we almost stopped for gas at that station?"

"No, we didn't, dear. That station isn't even in business," Mabel said. We'd arrived at the bead table and I was momentarily distracted by yet another new item, a pair of tiny red pumps made out of Czech glass beads. "You're thinking about another ramp, the one at the 880 interchange."

"No, sweetheart, remember . . ."

I assumed Mabel and Jim had had a lot of practice working out differences like this, and didn't need my help. I took the opportunity to slip the newspaper from Jim's veiny hand. I sat on a chair in the dining area immediately neighboring Mabel's post and skimmed the story for salient features. The victim was indeed female, Caucasian, early thirties, and apparently not a local. A passing trucker had found her in the wee hours of Saturday morning. She'd been shot in the head and in the chest. It was not known yet how long the body had been there, but it seemed likely that the crime had taken place within a couple of hours of the trucker's finding her.

Reverend and Editor Stuart Edson had been kind enough to include a map with the article. I swallowed hard at the large X at the intersection of highways 101 and 87. One could get off many rounds of ammunition, I thought, before anyone would hear the shots in that neighborhood.

Though there was no detail on the newspaper map, I saw clearly the gas station, the deserted pumps, the pay phone. I saw my friend Linda, too, and tried desperately not to put a gun in her hand.

Mostly, I saw Maddie, in my backseat, sleeping as if she didn't have a care or a worry in the world. Now, it turns out that she was at the crime scene.

Tallying the votes for the dollhouse contest took longer than I thought, my distracted state being one of the reasons. I couldn't get the image of the *Lincolnite* X from my mind. I knew I had to say something to Skip eventually. But for now, I had to judge a dollhouse contest. It's not that you're withholding evidence, I told myself. Then gulped hard.

The group of judges I'd recruited, some crafters, some not, took their time, examining details carefully, grading on the basis of workmanship, originality, and a vaguely defined aesthetic appeal. I noticed that Linda's entry, an American colonial, was still minus its Governor Winthrop desk (I was almost beyond caring). We were ready with our results by one o'clock, only a little later than we'd planned. I took control of the PA system to announce the winner.

"Rosemary Hayes," I squawked. Thunderous applause greeted the mother of five-year-old twins who had found time to build and decorate a dollhouse. A sign of the times, in a good way, I thought: the winning dollhouse was "green." Rosemary had built a modern eight-room home constructed of soft wood and other earth-friendly materials, with replicas of solar panels on the roof. The walls were modular, slipping in and out of tracks, which allowed many different configurations of rooms. Lighting was meant to be natural, and many of the details were created from found objects, including an extensive use of game pieces. The prize was a generous gift certificate to a crafts store.

For as long as I could remember, the runner-up was always one form or another of a Lincoln-log cabin, this year's from Mabel's great-granddaughter. The young woman had re-created in full scale the cabin built by Abe and his father in Illinois in 1831.

When the applause died down, I was back at my table, exhausted, holding my head up with my hands. I snapped up when one of my former students stopped by. She brightened my day, except for the fact that her impending motherhood made me feel old.

"Mrs. Porter. Remember me? Melissa Consuelos? Well, now Melissa Fox." She pointed to her wedding ring and to her extended belly. "I thought I'd run into you here. I still remember that miniature scene you made while we were reading *Brideshead Revisited.* The ballroom?"

"Of course. I'm so glad you liked it." I'd spent a lot of time reproducing the ballroom of the stately Brideshead Castle — constructing chandeliers of tiny crystal beads and gilding pieces of foil to look like ornate mirrors.

Melissa held up a basket of purchases from the fair, mostly raw materials like balsa wood, small clamps, and paints. "That's what inspired me to be a miniaturist myself," she said.

"Wonderful." I hoped I'd also inspired her to read.

The time never seemed right for me to say anything to Linda, seated next to me at Table 30. But, I realized, the tension wasn't that much greater than it usually was when Linda was in a snit for one reason or another: I didn't invite her to coffee with Karen and Gail; I wanted to stop sharing birthday gifts, but I still shared with Beverly; I neglected to let her know of the sale at Joann's in the strip mall downtown (whereas, I *had* called Betty and told her about it).

I had a headache from imagined calls to Skip, calls I was able to talk myself out of until after the fair.

At one point, I came back from the restroom to see Dudley Crane, the wronged jeweler himself, talking to Jack Wilson, Gail (Split-level Ranch) Musgrave's brother and a candidate for office against Dudley. Whereas Postmaster Cooney was Dudley's pesky, verbally abusive opponent, Jack was the real threat, running for office himself.

Candidate Jack was at the fair ostensibly helping out his sister at the table across from Linda's and mine. No doubt there was self-promotion going on at the same time, as attested to by the several WILSON FOR COUNCIL buttons on his clothing and the piles of pamphlets on the table next to Gail's price list. Gail seemed embarrassed by the display, but there was no written rule against campaigning.

There weren't too many men in the hall, so Dudley would have stood out even if he weren't over six feet tall. Another Western-wear fan, I noted — but Dudley Crane was much classier than Chuck Reed, even in his beige weekend cowboy hat. He and Jack (also tall, but more muscular than Crane, and with a voice that matched Crane's in loudness) appeared to be arguing. From the few words I heard, Dudley seemed to be chewing Jack out for his scathing letter to the editor of the *Lincolnite,* stomping all over Dudley's latest growth proposal for the town and impugning shady practices regarding his estate-handling sideline.

It seemed strange that Dudley would venture into this den of women and their crafts to vent his anger, but he seemed not at all intimidated. I stepped by him to get to my table (admittedly hoping to catch more of their argument, but they'd stopped by now). Dudley turned to go. He tipped his hat — "Mrs. Porter" — and walked out the side exit.

All I'd heard from Jack was his testy question to Gail. "Can't you come up with a good cup of coffee for me?"

Gail didn't seem bothered by her brother's rudeness. She exited the area in the opposite direction from Dudley, toward her new best friend, Karen Striker, with her Cape Cod on Table 17. I guessed Gail was my age, considerably older than Karen, but the two had seemed to bond quickly when Karen joined the crafts group recently.

Before thinking it through, I asked Linda, "What was that all about? Did you hear anything?"

Linda's face brightened. She put down her small hammer and wood block, ready to chat. "Gail and Jack Wilson think Dudley Crane cheated them on their mother's estate. Same as what Postmaster Cooney's accusing him of. Remember both old Mrs. Wilson and Mrs. Cooney died a few months ago, and the children hired Crane to . . ."

Once I realized how thrilled Linda was to be gossiping about someone other than herself or her son, I tuned out. I had to curb this heightened curiosity I'd experienced lately. It was unbecoming a grandmother and a crafter.

# CHAPTER 8

I punched in Skip's cell-phone number on the way back to my table, breaking my own rule one more time. My mind was racing, one theory chasing another through my brain. I waited through four rings of Skip's line, then hung up without leaving a message. *Whew.* I needed to sort things out before I talked to an officer of the law, anyway.

I thought through the possibilities. The first was that, coincidentally, and unbeknownst to Linda, she had been in the same area as the crime scene on Friday night, and might have been a victim herself if I hadn't picked her up. If I could accept this, case closed, and I wouldn't have to talk to Skip.

It was also possible that Jason had been involved and had run off from Peter's and sent for Linda (then where was he when I got there?). Or that Chuck had been involved (I had no trouble picturing Chuck's abandoning Linda). I wrestled with my obligation to tell the police what little I did know of the weekend nighttime activities at the gas station. Surely not every citizen with a theory was obliged to share it. But I had been at the scene of the crime around the estimated time of the murder.

At one far end of my range of theories was that the poor woman had been murdered long before (then I'd driven right past her?) or long after (this was better) my picking up Linda. At the other far end was that Linda had intimate knowledge of the crime.

The intimate-knowledge theory was out of the question. Linda was not a criminal, let alone a killer, the worst of criminals. She was more likely a victim who might need my help.

Right now my table was lined with last-minute shoppers, so I had to put my curious mind on hold.

Like most vendors during the last hour of a fair, I'd put many items on sale to reduce the load we had to pack up and carry home. Crocheted throw rugs, any size from one-inch to four-inch diameter: three for one dollar. A set of one-inch books made from foam board, painted, spines lettered in gold with Jane Austen titles: three dollars for the set. Bedroom and kitchen curtains made from hem-binding lace, complete with (toothpick) rods and tiebacks: one dollar per pair.

I sold a whole shoe box of items in about fifteen minutes.

The murder was on everyone's mind, apparently. Each sale began or ended with a comment about the victim, or the crime scene, or crime stats for Lincoln Point. One popular observation involved civic pride.

"You know it was barely within the town limits," said one customer.

"It's just some technicality of zoning that makes that old gas station part of Lincoln Point," was another variation.

My favorite expression was one of denial, from Jim Quinlan, "She was probably killed in Mountain View and dumped here."

I was reminded about the effect the murder might have on our children when I heard a tense little girl.

"I hope the killer doesn't come after us next," she said.

"He doesn't know where we are, honey," her mother said, with a nervous look around the hall.

I hoped Beverly had an equally comforting comment ready for Maddie if the occasion arose.

I did my share of tsk-tsking and speculating on the crime, to placate my customers, not because my heart was in it. But it wouldn't have been good business practice to scream *gossipers!* to people who were supporting the fund-raiser and buying my wares.

I searched Linda's face every time the topic came up. Unreadable. She had her own crowd of admirers and buyers, and limited her conversation to negotiating prices (she seldom marked anything down) and information on crafts-supplies classes and stores.

I tried to engage her only once, when a customer asked what I thought about the murder (a silly question, but an opportunity to query Linda).

"Awful," I said. "What do you think, Linda?"

"Awful," she said. She gave a thin smile to the customer, and the same old look of annoyance to me.

This time, with my mistrustful thoughts and accusing theories, even for a second suspecting that my friend had any knowledge of the worst of all possible crimes, I felt I deserved it.

Just Eddie stood against the wall by the side

122

exit, flipping an unlit cigarette end over end, as he waited for me to make one last trip around the hall. My final tour of inspection. A criterion for our being able to use the multipurpose schoolroom for the quarterly fair was that we leave it cleaner than we found it. I could see that Just Eddie was itching to get out, get in his truck, and light that cigarette.

I filled a shopping bag with things vendors had left behind — a thermos, a plastic bag of beads, small scissors, and enough stray markers, tape dispensers, and staplers to outfit the entire incoming freshman class of Abraham Lincoln High. I'd wait a few days for their owners to make a claim, then would hand over what was left to the Mary Todd Elementary art teacher, another former student of mine. This one, to my delight, had led her students in a graffiti exercise, painting the walls of her classroom with quotes from Lincoln.

"I'm ready," I told Just Eddie. "You can lock up."

He pushed himself off the wall and muttered, " 'Bout time."

As if he weren't getting paid overtime. "Thanks for all your work," I said, unwilling to be dragged into his attitude.

*Linda and Just Eddie would make a good*

*pair,* I thought.

My house was quiet except for the trickle of water from the tabletop fountain in the atrium, and the low, moaning lawn-mower noise from my neighbor. I'd entered the house through the garage, not wanting to chat with June Chinn, or anyone else at the moment. What I wanted was that the murder had never happened and that Linda hadn't involved me in her adventure. Most of all, I wanted a nap.

The loud ring of my landline made that unlikely. I threw my purse on the kitchen counter and picked up the phone.

"Hey, Aunt Gerry. I see that you called this afternoon." A twilight-zone moment, until I realized that my phone number would have shown up on the display of Skip's cell phone even though I hadn't left a message. One more questionable by-product of the electronic age. "What's up? Or *'sup?'* as my last caller asked me." Skip was entirely too cheerful for my mood.

It was decision time. I laid my glasses on the kitchen counter, shut my eyes tight, and rubbed my forehead. As if that would result in a clear choice, a bright banner in front of me, telling me yes or no, talk or don't talk.

"Aunt Gerry?"

My head hurt. I'd been squeezing my eyes longer than I thought. "Skip, I, uh, just have a question about that murder. Was the newspaper accurate where it showed the location of the body?" My last-ditch effort to wish away the whole scenario.

"Yeah. There's an old gas station at that intersection, closed for renovation." *And a pay phone,* I added silently. "Some trucker stopped there for a nap in his cab, he says, then went out back to take a . . ." My delicate nephew cleared his throat. "Well, you know. Anyway, he found her."

"And the trucker's been cleared?"

"Oh, yeah, he's squeaky-clean, no connection at all to the victim, or to anyone in the state as far as we can tell. He's from Utah." Skip laughed. "Like, your textbook good guy."

"Oh." I wet my lips. "Well, I just wanted to be sure."

"What's going on, Aunt Gerry? Do you know something about the murder?" Skip paused for a quick, low-pitched chuckle. I assumed he expected the answer to be, *most certainly not!*

And that's what I would give him, I decided, as images of Linda came to my mind — helping me care for Ken, understanding my loss after he died. Just one more try, I told myself, to straighten this out with Linda first. I owed my friend that. "Most certainly not," I said.

The next pause was too long for my comfort. Skip cleared his throat several times. Stalling while he put some thoughts together? Weighing his next words? Finally, he asked, "You don't know anything? Not even, say, that there's a pay phone near where the body was found?"

My nephew's tone was serious. Not the Skip of softball games and a chick-magnet car. I pictured him sober-faced and attentive, probably wrestling with his own conscience about arresting his favorite (that is, only) aunt.

My mouth went dry. I uttered a series of *uh*s and deep sighs.

"I'll be right there," Skip said.

"Okay," was the sound that barely left my throat.

*There goes my nap time,* I thought, as if that would be my biggest loss once I spoke to Skip.

I paced the small loggia between my family room and the bedrooms, knowing I had to tell Skip everything I knew, little as it was, about my middle-of-the-night pickup at the crime scene. I told myself over and over that

I'd given Linda every chance to explain why she was there; it wasn't my fault that I now had to resort to what amounted to snitching. For all I knew, I'd been obstructing justice by not talking to the police sooner.

The door chime, ordinarily a pleasant set of notes, sounded harsh and startling, as if I knew the police were on my doorstep. Skip had a key to my house, to use in case of emergency, or when I called and told him the fridge had especially tasty leftovers. Otherwise, he rang the bell.

"You might have a date," he'd said, when I suggested he could come in unannounced at any time.

"Not in this lifetime," I'd told him. "And don't forget our deal." (Skip and I had an on-again, off-again agreement that we wouldn't try to fix each other up with dates. Beverly had refused to sign the "contract," even figuratively.)

I opened the door to my handsome nephew, in khakis, a summer blazer, and a soft yellow tie with red specks that seemed to match his hair. I knew he was following the "dress as though you've reached the next step" rule of business — in his case, going for that DETECTIVE GOWEN plate on his desk. Somehow, I thought law enforcement would have its own rules about dress, but the small-town LPPD might have been exempt.

"Coffee?" I asked.

"I'll get it. You talk."

"I see you're not going to make it easy on your old aunt."

Skip's smile said the opposite. "I'm here to listen," he said, and then pressed the coffee-grinder button so that neither of us could hear anything. That got the laugh he wanted.

"Skip —" I began, feeling my face sag into a pleading expression.

"Actually, I *am* going to make it easy on you, Aunt Gerry. Maddie told me about your trip to the crime scene. Well, not that you knew it was a crime scene."

I felt my shoulders relax even as my mind kicked into overdrive. "Maddie told you?"

"The next day. Neither one of us knew it might be this big a deal. It was an adventure to her." I pictured Maddie, thrilled to report to her cop uncle about her own exciting nighttime excursion. "Apparently she slept through most of the trip and still doesn't know exactly where she was, but when you called a few minutes ago, I put two and two together."

"That's what detectives do," I said, mimicking one of his favorite phrases.

Skip came to the table where I was slumped, with two mugs of coffee. He set them down, then leaned over and gave me a long, soft hug. "Before we talk, where's that private stash of ginger cookies?" he asked.

I loved my nephew.

Probably no other cop would have believed that I'd told everything I knew, that Linda hadn't revealed an iota of why she was stranded at the crime scene. But Skip took it all in, nodded appropriately, and then gave me another hug.

"I guess that's it. And, by the way, thanks for not asking me where my jeans are." Skip ran his hands down the lapel of his new, business-casual attire, a bit embarrassed, I thought. Not a cool outfit, I gathered.

"I'll bet they're not connected at all," I said. "Not your jeans. Linda and the homicide, I mean."

"We'll find out. But the time frame you're giving me is pretty close to the estimated time of death, and there's a chance she knows something, even if not consciously. Do you know if Linda's home now?" My look must have worried him. "Just for questioning. I'll try to keep you out of it."

"You don't have to go through hoops, Skip. I'm taking full responsibility for this."

Linda would know anyway, I thought. "Just, you know, take it easy. She's had to deal with Jason and the robbery at Crane's, and —"

"Not to worry, Aunt Gerry. I know this has been rough on you, too. I'll do my best. For everyone."

I knew he would.


I let Skip out and his mother and Maddie in at the same time. Not that I wasn't glad to have them home, but I'd been hoping for at least a bit of quiet time, if not a full-fledged nap.

"Uncle Skip!" Maddie jumped up into his arms, not as easily as on her last visit, a few months ago. I noticed Skip reel a bit, and I wondered if it might be from the distinctive zoo smell I caught, as well as from the inches Maddie had grown.

Beverly gave her son a peck on the cheek. "I'm surprised to see you, dear," she said.

"Gotta go," Skip said, letting Maddie down gently and leaving the rest up to me. With any luck I wouldn't have to share the fact that this was actually a professional house call by Skip.

"We brought dinner," Maddie said, pointing to the sagging plastic bag in Beverly's hand.

"It's just deli, but I thought you might be too tired to cook," Beverly said.

"You don't know the half of it."

"Is everything okay with you, Grandma?" Maddie asked, sweet-smelling after a long bath in green bubbles.

*Uh-oh.* That was the trouble with smart kids. They're all-over smart, not just in arithmetic and spelling. I wondered if Maddie had put it all together. She was, after all, a coconspirator in picking Linda up. I hadn't had a chance to learn if Beverly had talked to Maddie about the murder. Dinner conversation had revolved around potbellied pigs, tortoises, lemurs, and whether we still had time this summer to arrange an overnight stay with the zoo's special camping program (only if I didn't have to chaperone).

"I'm just tired, sweetheart," I told her now, and noticed her eyes already at half-mast. Thank you, Beverly, I said to myself, for wearing her out.

"Let's skip reading tonight, then, and you can go to bed," Maddie said.

"Maybe I will, if you're sure you don't mind missing a chapter in the book."

Maddie put her arms around my neck. "I'm pretty tired myself," she admitted.

She was out before I got to the door.

I had a couple more things to do before I called it a day.

I pushed Beverly's number on speed dial.

"I've been waiting for your call," she said. "I just read the paper. That place where the body was found, isn't it where you and Maddie went to pick up Linda?"

This was the first I heard that Maddie had told Beverly about our adventure, too. Wouldn't you know — in spite of all the day trips, movies, museums, and kids' programs I'd squeezed into my granddaughter's visit, the late-night trip to a dilapidated phone booth was emerging as the highlight.

With all the fair activities, plus taking care of Maddie, the usual daily chats between Beverly and me had been curtailed. Now, tired as I was, I gave her the whole story, starting with the call from the pay phone and ending with her son's visit to my house.

"We were right on the X," I told Beverly.

A low whistle, then "Wow," was her response.

"Yes, wow. I guess you could say we turned Linda in. She's not going to be happy," I said.

"Is she ever?"

"Thanks for pointing that out." I blinked my eyes, trying to stay awake. Even in this stupor, I thought of another of Ken's favorite Lincoln quotes: "Most folks are about as happy as they make up their minds to be."

Beverly continued. "Just to let you know, Maddie hasn't heard anything specific about the murder. Needless to say, it was not the hot topic in Oakland. She may have forgotten about it."

"You're probably right. She was more interested in the jewelry-store theft that night that Skip got the call."

"Kids have their own coping mechanisms, don't they? They have ways of not focusing on something as horrible as murder. So I wouldn't worry, as long as it's not someone we know."

"And as long as someone we know didn't do it," I said.

"Wow."

Well said.

I debated about making the next call, but in the end, punched in Linda's number. I didn't know what to hope for. The cowardly thing, I supposed — that there would be no answer and I'd get credit for a caring call, but wouldn't have to speak to her.

I got my wish. I spoke to Linda's answering machine.

"Hi, Linda. This is Gerry, just checking in to see how you are."

That sounded dumb. But there was no way to edit, so I said a weak, "See you soon. 'Bye," and hung up.

I slipped into Maddie's room and unplugged the telephone extension, just in case. Then I made my way, half-asleep, to the end of the hall and to my own full-size bed.

# CHAPTER 9

On Monday morning, I slept until almost ten o'clock, close to a record for me. Maddie had made her own breakfast, increasing my guilt over not paying enough attention to her for the past few days. In fact, she was ready to serve *me* breakfast and jumped off the chair when she saw me trundle into the kitchen.

She poured orange juice, propped the box with my favorite crunchy cereal against a bowl, and pushed the button on the emergency coffeemaker. I kept a standard all-purpose coffeemaker for mornings like this when I was hung over (from chocolate or overwork, that is) and it would have been dangerous for me to operate the electric coffee grinder. Sliced banana on my cereal, and toast with butter and strawberry jelly rounded out the meal. More than I usually ate, but I didn't leave a crumb of food or a drop of liquid.

As soon as I was fueled and awake, the events of the weekend flooded back to me and I wondered how soon (if ever) I'd hear from Linda. I decided to give it until afternoon and then follow up with Skip.

To my relief, Beverly was taking a recovery day. She'd announced the plan at dinner on Sunday night.

"I'll be at an all-day party tomorrow," she'd said during cookies and ice cream, so please don't disturb me." If Maddie hadn't been present, Beverly would have used "orgy" or "date with a hottie."

Her family and friends understood this pattern: after a particularly long day or a couple of busy days in a row, Beverly would retreat to her bed. She'd spend the day on her back, with eyeshades and soft music. I'd tried to convince her to let me find someone else to take care of Maddie this weekend, but she'd insisted she had everything under control, loved the Oakland Zoo, and adored Maddie (I knew this at least was true). I'd learned to trust her judgment.

The valves of Beverly's heart were forever scarred from her early scarlet fever, forcing it to work harder to pump blood. She'd been receiving special antibiotic treatment on and off since she was about thirteen years old, at times on a monthly basis.

Beverly had an especially bad episode when she was in her late teens, shortly after Ken and I were married. We'd all been present when the doctor showed us a clunky plastic model of the human heart, demonstrating what happens when its valves are unable to open and close easily. I remembered surreptitiously placing my hand over my own heart at the time, grateful for my smooth-running valves and amazed at the quiet mechanism that kept me alive.

None of us at the time would have guessed that the Porter who would meet an early death would be her brother, my husband, Ken.

Having Maddie, alive and healthy in front of me, was a good reminder to avoid that path of memory.

"What shall we do today?" I asked Maddie. My only commitments for the rest of the week were a tutoring session with Angela, an older woman studying for a high-school equivalency exam, at the Lincoln Point Library, and balancing the accounts from the fair. I knew the treasurer of Abraham Lincoln High School PTA would want his check as soon as possible, but we could all wait a day or two.

Maddie had apparently already given today's schedule some thought. "I haven't used any of my spending money yet. Everybody keeps treating me to things. Mr. Puppeteer even bought me and Jason snacks. So maybe we can go shopping today?"

My heart skipped, or maybe the wrong valve jerked open. "You were with Jason?" *Just a friendly question from Grandma.*

"Only for a couple of minutes when Dr. Balandin brought him to the fair."

I remembered Peter Balandin's "handing Jason off" errand.

"On Saturday?" I asked. *Still casual.*

"Uh-huh."

Maddie had retrieved her neon orange wallet from her pocket and was laying out her money on the table. There was no earthly reason for me to be concerned that Maddie had been in Jason's company, I assured myself. Just because he *might have been* involved in a robbery. And his mother *might be . . .* I stopped the runaway train. Maddie and Jason had spent time together when both were younger and had a little more in common. It was natural that they would have talked if they ran into each other.

"Did you have a nice chat with Jason?" I asked her. *Very calm.*

Maddie nodded, carefully neatening her pile of bills. "Jason said he'd buy me an ice cream from the truck across the street, but Mr. Puppeteer said not to go that far. Then Mr. Puppeteer bought us both potato chips right in the hall, even though Jason didn't do any work for him."

"Well, you would never have left the school hall without telling me anyway, right?"

Maddie rolled her eyes and clicked her tongue against her teeth. "Of course not." She fingered her bills and lined them up in her wallet, then swept the coins into the pocket of her LA Dodgers (I remembered when they were the Brooklyn Dodgers) sweatshirt. She'd brought all of her team clothing with her, equally balanced, I noticed, between her mother's favorite teams and her father's.

"So, can we go shopping?"

"Sure." I was thankful that Maddie didn't seem to notice my overreaction at the mention of Jason. I relaxed my breathing. "What kind of shopping would you like to do?" I hoped she wouldn't ask for anything having to do with sticks or balls unless they were crafts-store size.

"I need some souvenirs. For my mom and dad and Devyn." I'd been hearing about Devyn, Maddie's longest-running friend, for a couple of years. Devyn, with a y, was a girl in Maddie's class. (I suspected her parents were named Sue and Bob.) "Then we can come back and work on the doll-house, and then cook spaghetti together."

"A great plan. Let's get dressed and put it into action."

We high-fived with palms and fists (Maddie had taught me the rhythm on her last visit) and headed for our respective rooms to dress for the day. I slipped a phone call in between donning layers of clothing — I was too much a coward to call Linda, but left a message for Skip. I was sure he wasn't going to make detective grade by giving his aunt special treatment with personal calls and visits, but I couldn't keep my curiosity and concern in check.

I hadn't planned on a visit to yet another crime scene, but Maddie wanted to stop at Crane's Jewelers.

"Maybe I can get some earrings for my mom," she said.

"They'd be kind of expensive here," I warned her. Crane's was one of the larger stores on Lincoln Point's main shopping street, short as it was. Crane's was known even in the county's larger cities as *the* place to buy an engagement ring. Or a twentieth-anniversary emerald, or thirtieth-anniversary pearls, both of which Ken had given me.

"You won't be able to afford this store until you're a heart surgeon," I told Maddie. I believed in conditioning the young. It had worked with Richard. Not a heart surgeon, but close enough, in orthopedics. Or maybe he'd gone to med school *in spite of* my carefully planned brainwashing.

After a couple of minutes of window-shopping, Maddie tugged me in the direction of Crane's front door. "Let's just look inside."

The shop was empty except for Dudley Crane himself, who was wiping the display cases with glass cleaner and paper towels. Without his Western dress and no hat to cover his bald spot, he looked older than his forty-something years. The shop had been in the Crane family for several decades, and Dudley seemed to have grown into the name and reputation.

One of the new aspects of his business was handling estate sales that involved a significant amount of high-end jewelry. I thought of Gail Musgrave and her dissatisfaction with his management of her mother's estate, and the same complaint from Postmaster Cooney. Dudley must have a difficult job, I thought, making deals in the emotionally charged world of family legacies. Not that I had been handed one. My parents died with only modest savings, barely enough to cover their funeral expenses.

"Morning, folks," Dudley said, with a smile in our general vicinity. "Anything I can help you with today?"

Maddie ignored the many cases with diamond earrings, pendants, and watches laid out on dark blue velvet. She didn't seem to notice the array of wedding sets in satin-lined boxes or the tennis bracelets hanging from Lucite holders.

Instead, she pointed to a vaultlike area behind the counter, with a floor-to-ceiling metal door. "Is that where the jewelry and money were locked up? The stuff that was robbed?"

I was mortified. First, at her grammatical error (we'd deal later with robbed vs. stolen), and second, at the precociousness of her question.

"Madison! Is this why you wanted to come in here?"

"Maybe just a little," she said, not the least bit intimidated.

I could blame Mary Lou, her mother, for reading Nancy Drew mysteries to Maddie even when she was a baby, but I had to claim some responsibility for passing on the curiosity gene. Maddie was now two for two as far as recent Lincoln Point crime-scene visits.

"It's not a problem, Mrs. Porter." Dudley looked down from his six-feet-plus height and addressed Maddie in a fatherly tone. "Some very bad people came in here and took what wasn't theirs."

"Do you think they'll catch them? My Uncle Skip is a cop. I'll bet he gets the guys."

"I certainly hope so, young lady. Now, can I offer you a lollipop?"

Maddie chose a yellow sucker from a sterling-silver container by the cash register. Also near the checkout point was a pile of flyers for a meeting tomorrow afternoon. It was the same flyer Dudley had distributed at the fair (to the consternation of some) — calling everyone to a town meeting on the new growth plan for Lincoln Point. Dudley was at the forefront of the development effort. I confessed to feeling ambivalent. I loved the old joke, edited to apply to our town. Q: What's the difference between a developer and a no-growth person? A: A developer wants a home in Lincoln Point; a no-growth person already has a home in Lincoln Point.

I wandered along the rows of Crane's

Jewelers display cases, feeling I should show some interest in the inventory, having barged in with Maddie, like a miniature SWAT team.

I ran through my birthday calendar in my head. Mary Lou would be thirty-five at the end of the summer. I found the case with miscellaneous items — pillboxes (my daughter-in-law didn't need one yet), a carousel-shaped ceramic jewelry box, ID bracelets and other gifts that could be personalized. Nothing struck me as particularly Mary Lou's taste.

I turned to collect Maddie from a case in the corner with sterling-silver sports charms, and say my thanks and farewell to Dudley. At that moment, the door chimes rang, and I turned to see who else might be shopping for jewelry on a Monday morning, or who else might have come to query the shop owner about the recent burglary.

Not the first person I would have predicted. Very nearly the last: Just Eddie. He was wearing his gray cotton work clothes; that at least was predictable.

The open door obscured a view of the corner case where Maddie and I stood. Just Eddie stormed up to Dudley. "Where did you put it, Crane? Where is that —"

Dudley's eyes popped, his chin jutted out,

and his palm shot up. *Halt.* His splayed fingers might as well have been knives, they were so effective in cutting Just Eddie off.

Just Eddie turned in the direction of Dudley's gaze.

"Good morning," I said, as nonchalantly as I could.

Eddie's face, already flushed, seemed to get redder in front of me. He didn't say a word, but walked between two cases to a curtained-off area behind the cash register. Dudley's office, I assumed. I caught a whiff of the awful half-cigarette, half-cigar sticks he smoked.

Dudley wrung his hands, then passed one hand over his bald spot. At times it was nice to be tall, I thought, to be able to see the whole picture, as it were. "Eddie moonlights here . . . cleans up a couple of times a week, and he doesn't want it known all over town. It's possible that there's an income-tax issue." Dudley's voice reached a whisper at *income tax.* I looked through the large windows and checked the curb outside. As far as I could tell, there was nothing like a paneled van with an IRS agent and a listening device.

"I understand," I told him.

Maddie, who I thought hadn't heard any

of this, made a zipper motion across her lips.

We exited the store, a more interesting stop than I'd envisioned.

# CHAPTER 10

As soon as we left Crane's, the venue of who-knew-what kind of business dealings between Dudley and Just Eddie, Maddie lost interest in shopping. Was this child really my biological granddaughter, or had Richard and Mary Lou adopted her?

"My feet hurt," she told me. She pointed across the street at the enticing SADIE'S HOMEMADE ICE CREAM sign. "Can we just have ice cream and go home?"

I looked down at her skinny body, her bony knees. How can feet and ankles get tired holding up so little weight? I wondered. Would she be as tired standing in right field (or whatever position she played) for two hours?

But what kind of grandmother wouldn't grant a worn-out ten-year-old's wishes?

"We'll have more time to work on the dollhouse," Maddie said.

We both laughed at that pitiful attempt to

bribe me.

One hot-fudge sundae (Maddie) and one mocha shake (me) later, we were in the "project room" next to the bedroom Maddie was using.

Ken had painted the whole apartment dollhouse before he got sick. The inside was off-white throughout, the outside red brick. He hadn't gotten to outlining the bricks or painting the window frames, but the brick color was perfect, almost weather-beaten, like its real-life prototype.

"I found something we can use in the bathroom," Maddie said.

Then my heart flipped as I saw that she'd already found the perfect material for a shower curtain: a plastic bowl cover from my food-storage drawer.

The moment when you look at an everyday object and envision it on a different scale, as something else entirely, is thrilling, and I could tell by Maddie's face that she'd experienced that. Selfish as it was, I wanted her to have a hobby that we could share, and also one that would give her the kind of pleasure miniatures had given me through the years.

Maddie trimmed the elastic edge from the bowl cover and smoothed out the plastic.

She laid a ruler on it, then whisked it off the table. "Uh-oh. I guess we'd better iron this first," she said.

We were on our way.

I was strangely comfortable working on the project I'd avoided for two years. Because it was Maddie's idea? Or was I finally ready to move into another phase, honoring my husband by not using him as an excuse to be self-pitying? Probably a little of both.

With her tiny fingers, Maddie worked well with Fimo dough. I showed her how to roll a small piece of the dough on a hard surface, first one way and then the other, to create a rounded bar of "soap."

As much as I was enjoying the afternoon, the project didn't have 100 percent of my attention. I was waiting for a call from Linda or Skip.

I sat with Maddie as she watched a parent-approved video (she'd brought slightly fewer videos than books) in the living room. My interest in animated movies went only so far. I'd started leafing through back issues of *Miniatures* magazine and hobby builders' catalogs as soon as the popcorn ran out. Also, believing family sources that both Maddie and I could use a few extra pounds,

I'd put a batch of chocolate-chip cookies in the oven.

The call came during a stampede where a seemingly innocent lion was killed. I wondered how this had cleared Richard and Mary Lou's suitable-movie criteria.

I was glad to hear Skip's voice.

"Hey, Aunt Gerry. I have a status report for you. If you want one, that is." I caught the tease in Skip's voice and wished I could tease back by sending the smell of melting chocolate (his second-favorite cookie, after ginger) over the wires. I'd answered the ring on the kitchen phone, tucking the receiver between my neck and shoulder so I could check the cookies while Skip talked.

"Linda's story is that a guy dumped her at that location after a date gone bad."

"Linda on a date? That's as likely as *my* having a date."

Skip laughed. "Not because you couldn't have one, Aunt Gerry. I told you about Nick, this guy at the station, just about to retire and —"

My fault for starting us on that track. "Back to Linda, please."

"In fact, Mom has worked with Nick on this seat-belt project."

"Then maybe she wants to date him. Now, Linda?"

"Yeah, well, Linda's date was a stranger she picked up at a bar, and she doesn't know where he can be found to corroborate her story, and she doesn't remember the name of the bar where she met him, and so on. He 'got fresh in the backseat' — her term. Isn't that from the fifties?" I didn't respond. "Anyway, she 'refused his advances' — isn't that fifties, too? So he pulled over and left her out there."

"That's quite a story. It doesn't make sense, Skip. Linda leaves the fair, goes to a bar —"

Skip picked up the rhythm. "Someone hits on Linda. Like that's going to happen." Again, no response from me. My nephew didn't need the encouragement of a laugh. "Guess I shouldn't say that. Sorry."

It was clear to me that Linda was lying. Not because she was guilty of a crime, but for some other Linda-reason that I couldn't quite put my finger on. Still, I thought I'd get an expert opinion, with no jokes. "Seriously, Skip. Do you think she's telling the truth?"

"Frankly, no. But that's all she'll say right now, and I can't prove her story isn't true, so we let her go. Besides, although I think she's hiding something, I really doubt she killed this woman."

Here I felt a comforting wave flow through my body. "Do you know who the murdered woman is yet?"

"We've identified her as a Tippi Wyatt. She has a long sheet in Brooklyn, so her prints are in the system. She moved to the Midwest somewhere and then picked up another sheet there. She doesn't seem to have any ties to Linda or anyone else in town for that matter. She's been staying the last few nights at that fleabag Motel Some-Number-or-Other a few miles outside of town."

"So it was all just random?"

"Well, if you believe that some random killer happened to kill the random person passing through town, and the body happened to be found where Linda's random so-called date dumped her."

"Well, when you put it like that. But it certainly could have happened that way. Coincidences happen all the time, and —"

"Take it easy, Aunt Gerry." I could almost see Skip's hand go up to stop my runaway speech. "We're still just in the check-everything-out phase."

I cleared my throat. "Sorry. How's Linda?"

"On the warpath."

*Ouch.* Not that I was surprised, but I'd hoped for that miniature-size chance that Linda would understand why I'd had to talk to Skip. As I was ready to move on and ask Skip for a report on Jason and Crane's burglary, Maddie came into the kitchen, spots of white liquid glue and paint all over her T-shirt. She'd changed from her LA Dodgers sweatshirt to a San Francisco Giants T. (I remembered when they were the New York Giants. I sensed a pattern.) Maddie's face, hands, and legs also showed signs of serious crafts work.

"What about the other matter?" I asked Skip. I handed Maddie two pot holders she'd made for me in an arts-and-crafts class and turned away from the oven.

"Huh?"

"The . . . uh, never mind." No need to bring up Jason now, in Maddie's presence. "Thanks for the warning about Linda."

"Sure thing. Talk later."

"What happened to Mrs. Reed?" Maddie asked. Her words were muffled as she tried to juggle the bite of hot cookie in her mouth. "Is this about the other night?"

Sooner or later, my brighter-than-average granddaughter would put it all together. She might as well hear it from me. "Let's talk over a drink," I said, pulling a carton of whole milk from the fridge.

Maddie seemed to take in the information

about Linda's plight calmly enough. I had to use all my vocabulary skills to explain that someone had murdered a woman right where we had picked Linda up. I used some innocuous philosophical tidbits, like "sometimes people do bad things," and a euphemistic "a lady lost her life." Maddie nodded a lot; I suspected she had a better grasp of things than I gave her credit for and was trying to make it easy on me.

I was relieved Skip didn't think Linda was a killer any more than I did. I hoped that was the view held by the entire Lincoln Point PD. I tapped the side of my glass of milk with my fingers. If only I could do some investigating on my own. I wished there were some way to track Linda's movements the way television cops did, sifting through phone records and credit-card receipts. Had Linda stopped for coffee or gas? (Of course not, she was apparently on foot, without her purse. Her SUV was in the same spot in the school parking lot as when we arrived midafternoon.)

"I remember that place really well," Maddie said. "I told Uncle Skip and Aunt Beverly about it."

I jerked out of my mental detective work. "I know you told them, but I thought you were asleep for most of the trip."

"Not the whole time. I remember the phone booth, all broken-down. Really dirty glass, too. It was pretty scary."

"It certainly was." Did I really want Maddie to relive the fears of that night? "More milk, sweetheart?"

"And the big sign with the spelling mistake."

"What sign?"

"It was tall and it said 'Bird's Storage — Cheep Rates' " She rolled her eyes, as only a ten-year-old can, with intensity and full-face participation. "I got it — like, birds go *cheep cheep,* with two *e*'s, but really the right *cheap* has an *a*. Don't you hate when they do that? Like, they have Kid's Korner in the bookstore near us. They spell *corner* with a *k*." Maddie clicked her tongue: *tsk-tsk.*

I felt another shiver, of the good kind. My granddaughter loved to read, had found joy in miniatures, and even cared about spelling. So what if she was also a tomboy? The future was secured.

I pictured Route 101, the road we traveled on the way to Linda. I'd been concentrating on the exit signs — to the 237, the 85, and minor streets — and on staying connected to Linda by phone.

An idea crept forward in my head. I

couldn't recall the sign Maddie mentioned, but if there was a storage facility, they'd most likely have video surveillance. While I was thinking this through, Maddie had gone to the computer in her bedroom. She called me in.

"Here it is, Grandma," Maddie said, showing me the computer screen. "It took a while with dial-up, but I finally got through." She grinned and wiped her forehead, pretending to be stressed by the effort in this low-tech house. She'd researched the address of Bird's Storage, then gone to a map site and, sure enough, there was the graphic stickpin identifying the location of the storage facility. The map was nearly identical to the one in the newspaper. I thought of the *Lincolnite's* X — not a happy association.

A path was opening up. The police would certainly have confiscated any video the storage facility had, so Skip would have access to it. If I could view the video, I might be able to see something the police missed. Not that my nephew and the LPPD crew were incompetent, but they didn't know Linda as well as I did and might not know what to look for.

I checked my watch. Nine thirty. Which mattered only because it was past Maddie's bedtime.

"Very nice work, Maddie" — she blushed, as most redheads do, in a charming way — "but we need to watch the clock more carefully so you can get your beauty sleep."

As soon as I could leave Maddie, I punched in Skip's number. When he picked up, I launched immediately into my idea.

"I don't know, Aunt Gerry," he said. "You've already given your statement. Maybe you should just let us take it from here. Anyway, the tape is pretty useless. I saw it all and there's nothing of value on it."

"But I was *there,* Skip. Something might jog my memory."

He gave in more easily than I expected. "You'll have to view it here at the station, and then amend your statement."

"Great. I can be there in about fifteen minutes." In my excitement, I'd forgotten about leaving Maddie, but it turned out not to matter.

"Aunt Gerry, don't you ever sleep? Or take a day off?"

"Well, you're working tonight, too."

"Nuh-uh. You called my cell. I wasn't working until you called."

"Oh, no. Are you in the middle of a date?"

"More like the beginning. Unlike you and Linda —"

No wonder he hadn't spent a lot of time arguing with me. "Never mind me and Linda. Just go back to your date. I'll see you tomorrow morning. Will your date be over by nine thirty? That's about twelve hours from now."

I heard a sigh, then a dial tone.

# CHAPTER 11

Not wanting to bother Beverly for at least one more day, I'd planned to drop Maddie off at a bookstore near the Lincoln Point Police Station. The owner, Rosie Norman, had been a student of mine. (It occurred to me that the percentage of Lincoln Point's population who were my former students was very high; perhaps I hadn't retired soon enough?) I remembered Rosie's class as the year I'd built a model of John Steinbeck's stately Victorian boyhood home in Salinas, California. As a result (I could only hope), Rosie was a huge fan of Steinbeck, *Grapes of Wrath* and *Cannery Row* being her favorites. I knew I could safely leave Maddie in her care.

Not surprising, Maddie didn't like the plan. "Please, please, please," Maddie chanted. "I'm the one who saw the sign."

I made a quick call and got assurance from Skip that there was nothing grisly on the tape, like a live murder, for example.

"I wish," he said. "I'm telling you, there's nothing on it. An occasional blurry image of a vehicle, plus some parked cars, but that's it. The body was not in camera range."

"Got it," I said. "It will be boring. We'll be there in a few minutes."

By nine forty-five on Tuesday morning, Maddie and I were in a small A/V room at the police station. Skip had paperwork to catch up on and would check in with us later.

The police station was the oldest building in town. As you would guess, a quote from the man we thought of as our town's founder, Abraham Lincoln, was carved in bas-relief at the entrance: "I must stand with anybody that stands right, and stand with him while he is right, and part with him when he goes wrong."

The department was currently in competition with the library for grant money from the city council. I had mixed loyalties since I tutored at the library and used it extensively, but, through Skip, realized the need for a more modern police facility. At present, no one was receiving funds. The money was being held hostage until the development proposal went through, and that in turn was hostage until the coming election. I was very glad I wasn't involved in politics any more than as a reasonably well-informed voter.

Skip had mentioned that a second trucker had come forward and reported that the lot had been empty when he stopped there a few minutes before midnight. (Evidently the spot was a popular "rest" stop for truckers, thus accounting for one component of the odors I'd picked up on my rescue mission: Linda's phone booth was downwind.) This helped determine at least the earliest poor Tippi Wyatt could have been killed — the time of death had been narrowed down to sometime between midnight on Friday night (the time of Trucker Number 1, with no body) and three in the morning on Saturday (when Trucker Number 2 found Tippi). Long after Linda's 2:00 am call to me. That still left the possibility that Tippi Wyatt's body was only a few yards from . . . I gulped and sat down next to Maddie.

The video had been cued up to midnight on Friday night. I pushed play and Maddie and I started our watch. Inch after inch of tape went by as we shifted around in uncomfortable chairs, in front of an inferior video display, with no popcorn. Maybe Maddie would take this low-class environ-

161

ment as a point against a career in law enforcement. I took it as reason to join the pro-growth people and have a chance at a new police station.

Not that I had any expertise in security, but the surveillance system at Bird's Storage seemed quite primitive. A single camera offered a distorted view of the area, covering some of the garagelike openings in the building, a large section of the parking lot, and part of the gas station. Only the very edge of the phone booth was visible at the top left of the image, looking past the roof of the station and the gas pumps. There was no way to tell if the booth was occupied or not.

I knew only enough geometry to lay out templates for wallpaper and carpeting in my dollhouses, but I had some sense of how a lens worked from shopping, at Skip's insistence, for the fish-eye peephole in my front door. I drew a rough sketch on a little notepad I kept in my purse. I figured the camera was located on a wall or fence on the side of the property, looking north, with a ninety-degree sweep. Much too high, it seemed, but probably to keep the camera from being vandalized in that undesirable neighborhood.

It was clear also that there must have been

storage spaces not on video at all, in the triangles on my drawing just under the camera.

After more than thirty minutes of watching nothing but what amounted to a still frame of Bird's Storage's metal doors and two sedans that never moved, Maddie stood up and stretched.

"I'm bored and hot," she said, fanning herself with her loose T-shirt.

"Me, too. Do you want to quit?"

"No way."

I knew she wouldn't. *That's my girl.*

If the murder had taken place in Bird's lot, it was by someone who had scoped out the security system. Or who was very lucky. As Skip said, the person managed to stay out of camera range. Not that it would be that difficult, however. The owner (of the "cheep" facility) had most likely installed the minimum equipment to meet some regulation or to avoid a lawsuit by the renters.

It would be hard to say who fidgeted more on the stiff chairs, but we stuck it out for almost another hour, aided by corn chips and soda from the vending machine, delivered by Skip in a thirty-second visit. I tried to open a window (not that the air outside was terrific, but at least it wasn't stagnant) and found the two small windows had been nailed shut. I wondered if we were in a holding cell.

When the video read 1:24 am, a van drove across the frame. Maddie and I leaned forward simultaneously, but there was nothing revealing about its appearance or its trip into and then out of camera range. We settled back on our metal chairs.

At the 1:33 am mark, a light (everything was in shades of gray) pickup drove into the lot. Maddie jerked up. I thought it might be because it was at least another sign of life in the session, but she'd reacted to something more specific.

"It's Just Eddie's truck," she said. "See the big carton in the back?"

I peered at the screen, adjusting my trifocals. Maddie could be right. I couldn't tell either way. The image on the television screen was too blurry. Maddie's judgment was either better because of her excellent eyesight, or worse because of her eagerness to find something.

All I remembered about Just Eddie's truck were its rust spots and not wanting to park next to it in the school lot. Nothing as subtle as rust spots would show up on this video.

"Are you sure?" I asked Maddie, rewinding and pausing on the blurry vehicle.

Maddie was right at the screen now, a half inch from touching it. "I'm sure. I'm sure, Grandma. See this big box? I think it's from a refrigerator. I saw it in Just Eddie's truck."

It finally clicked. The battered carton marked REFRIGERATOR in Just Eddie's truck bed. How could I have forgotten that eyesore on top of eyesore in the school parking lot? Because I was too worried that he'd scrape my car and I'd need a new paint job, I decided.

We scanned through the last twenty minutes of the tape. Seeing nothing else, we wound back and studied what could have been Just Eddie's truck. The flatbed vehicle entered from the right, moved relatively slowly down the side of the parking lot in front of the lockers, then out of view, into either the southwest or the southeast corner of the lot, out of camera range. Skip and his buddies wouldn't have been alerted since the vehicle made no suspicious moves and there were no special markings visible. Even if they wanted to trace the vehicle, they wouldn't have had anything to go by. Until now.

Maddie was no longer bored. Her legs swung up and down so furiously I was sure they'd be bruised from the metal chair rungs.

The tape segment ended shortly after 3:00 am, about fifteen minutes after I picked up Linda. Given the angle of the camera and the quality of the video, there was no way Linda or my car would have been discernible. I rewound the tape and clicked off the television set.

"Let's go tell Uncle Skip," Maddie said, with new energy.

My head was dizzy with new possibilities. I took a deep breath. "Maddie," I said. *Uh-oh. What was I about to do?* Be a very bad role model and ask my granddaughter to join me in obstructing justice?

Apparently, that's exactly what I was about to do.

Maddie dumped our soda cans and corn chip bags into a beat-up wastebasket (how special that it matched the chairs) in the corner of the room. I made a note to tell Richard and, mostly, Mary Lou about their excellent training. Unlike the training I was providing.

"Not yet," I told Maddie. "Let's not get Uncle Skip all worried until we're sure."

Maddie's eyes widened. "I'm sure."

Not making it easy. I checked my watch. A little after noon. With any luck, Skip would be out to lunch, if cops were ever that regular. "Let's return the tape to the

166

front desk and see," I said.

See what, I didn't know, but Skip had indeed stepped out. Maybe finishing last night's date.

"I'll make sure he gets the tape," the young, rotund desk officer said. "Unless you want to wait?"

"No, no, just tell him I'll talk to him later."

"Grandma . . ." Maddie started, then stopped.

We hurried out the door of the police station and down the steps to the street. I had my keys ready and beeped the car doors open. Maddie followed silently. She didn't ask any questions.

I was glad I didn't have to share my feeling: that some twist of good fortune had worked in my favor and kept me from having to talk immediately to Skip.

My next thought was: maybe Linda did have a date. With Just Eddie.

My mind worked hard on the way home to justify my skipping out (so to speak). Not that I was technically withholding anything. After all, Skip wasn't around when we finished viewing the tape.

Maddie got out her iPod and put on her headphones. She drummed her fingers to something I couldn't hear. I drummed the steering wheel, concocting scenarios that would put both Linda and Just Eddie at or near the X.

Once or twice I nearly laughed out loud (LOL, in e-mail and text-messaging language, Maddie had taught me) at the image of Linda and Just Eddie on a date. Easy to understand why it might go bad. If they were seeing each other, however, there was no reason for either of them to carry on in secret; both were unattached. If Friday night's episode was simply too embarrassing for Linda, I didn't want to make her more uncomfortable by telling the cops on her. Hurting Just Eddie's feelings or protecting him in any way didn't make my list of reasons to keep it all confidential for now.

I planned to call Linda as soon as I was home. And away from Maddie, who looked at me as if she were my conscience. I hoped she was simply disappointed at not being able to tell her uncle she'd cracked the case, and not because she thought her grandmother was breaking the law.

It should have been an easy commute home from the police station, usually a ten- or fifteen-minute trip. Except that today a huge traffic jam had Maddie and me stopped behind a long line of cars on Springfield

Boulevard. We strained to look out the side windows to see what the problem was. Large posters on sticks gave us the clue: today was the scheduled rally for Proposition 22, drafted by Dudley Crane and his followers, the special referendum on growth for Lincoln Point. Protesters and supporters of the growth proposition had lined the street in front of city hall, in the same civic-center complex as the police station. Too late to turn around and take the back streets that ran behind the complex. This tie-up went a long way toward a vote to reject anything that would bring more of the same, I thought.

I caught glimpses of the slogans, taking one position or the other. I read that 22 IS BAD FOR YOU, that 22 MEANS JOBS FOR YOU, that GROWTH EQUALS GRIEF, and one I couldn't quite place on the political spectrum: TIME MARCHES ON. I recognized some stragglers at my end of the traffic line and tried to match the person with her or his view on the issue.

Jack Wilson (the brother of sister craftswoman, Gail "split-level" Musgrave), who was running against Dudley Crane for a seat on the city council, led an unsurprising contingent of KEEP LP GREEN marchers. Postmaster Cooney shuffled by and, though

I couldn't read his sign (he held it over his shoulder, as if he were marching with the Abraham Lincoln Brigade), I knew he was also *con* Prop 22. The Lincoln Point teachers' organization held signs cut in the shape of books, with TEACHERS DO CATCH 22. I assumed that was *pro,* since school upgrades were part of the proposition, but wished I could have a word with the grammarian in the group.

The voting was nearly four months away. I could only imagine what it was going to be like closer to Election Day.

I admired the energy of the people gathered, but didn't feel swayed one way or the other by their rhetoric or their methods. I thought of one of my favorite Abraham Lincoln quotes: "When the conduct of men is designed to be influenced, *persuasion,* kind, unassuming persuasion, should ever be adopted." I'd never seen that quote on a public building.

"We have rallies like this all the time at home," Maddie said, more disgruntled than I'd seen her since she was two years old. Though I tried to blame her mood on the traffic jam, I suspected it had more to do with me and my rush to avoid presenting her detective work to the LPPD.

I took the opportunity to engage (read:

distract) her. "What kinds of things do they rally about in your neighborhood?"

"I don't know exactly. But Mom says it's what makes this country great." Maddie didn't catch my eye in the mirror as she usually did, but had her eyes down, as if she couldn't bear to look at me. I had some work ahead of me to win her back, I knew.

In spite of the traffic hassles, I was proud of Mary Lou and her point about the benefits of being able to have rallies like this. My daughter-in-law put her time and energy into causes she felt strongly about. During one visit to Los Angeles, I was recruited to help her distribute information on the inadequacies of the art program (or was it that there was no art program?) at Maddie's school.

In general, I tried to stay out of politics. As with this issue, there were complexities that no one ever talked about. Certainly the politicians didn't explain them in their colorful, boilerplate brochures. Case in point: if I wanted a new police department or library, I had to endure enormous condo complexes, lose the city's green spaces, and, for all I knew, favor some clause in fine print that took away funding for after-school music lessons.

This fall, we'd be voting for new city

council members, who would in turn appoint the planning commission. Although the council was the deciding body, the commission had great influence over how much attention any referendum received, whether it passed or failed. And that would be determined by who was using this as a stepping-stone for an office at the state or national level, and other political factors beyond my comprehension. So what was the point? It was always the voters who had to compromise.

Stopped at a light, my car and all the others I could see were approached by the ralliers. All were very polite, probably following strict city guidelines against harassing the public. Leaflets from both sides were slipped through open windows, with "May I offer you some literature to help you decide on the issues?" When windows were closed tight in air-conditioned cars, such as mine, the marchers knocked politely and held up the flyers, mouthing a request to open the window.

I rolled down my window and took a leaflet from the first person to approach. After that, I had Maddie hold it up and shake her head. Something like, "I gave at the office," I thought.

"Are you cool enough back there?" I asked

Maddie. "Shall I crank up the fan?"

"Dad says that's not the way it works. You don't crank anything."

I looked in the rearview mirror. Maddie's frown said she hadn't forgiven me yet for denying her a moment of glory with her Uncle Skip.

My only grandchild would be leaving in a couple of days to return to her Southern California home. We needed to talk. This was one debate I couldn't avoid.

I turned left down the next unblocked side street, Gettysburg Boulevard, and headed home.

# CHAPTER 12

Maddie had gotten into the habit of pulling my cell phone from my tote and plugging it into the charger as soon as we returned home. Partially as a thoughtful gesture, and partially because she didn't trust me completely to remember such a high-tech chore. Today she went straight to her room. I did the task myself and decided to give her a little time to cool off, in all respects, before our heart-to-heart.

I knew Linda worked a seven-to-three shift on Tuesdays at the Mary Todd Home, one of three care facilities where she was employed as a nurse. Linda hadn't been able to get a full-time job at any medical establishment, so she put together what amounted to one and a half jobs, splitting her time among three locations. All the facilities were within county limits, at least, but still Linda had a tough working life, often pulling double shifts. The Mary Todd was closest to Linda's own home. She went straight home from there as a rule and, when she could, took a nap until dinnertime.

When to call? Later in the evening, when she'd be rested, or while she was tired and vulnerable? Something in between? Nasty as it seemed, I wanted her to get my message as soon as she arrived home. I punched in Linda's number, ready to leave a message, turning on my air conditioner at the same time. I hadn't quite recovered from the oppressive heat of the police station, and had a new desire to vote for progress if it would get us renovation funds for the LPPD. Talk about an easily swayed voter. An uncomfortable morning sent me one way; a small traffic jam another.

"Hello." Linda's dull, tired voice.

Now what? I had prepared myself only for a cryptic voice message. "Linda! I thought you'd be at work."

"Then why did you call?" Still tired, but also grumpy.

Flustered (Ken said I always let her get to me), I came up with, "To . . . uh, leave a message so I wouldn't forget."

Could I sound any dumber?

"So? What's your message? Shall I hang up and let you talk to my machine?" There was not the slightest touch of humor in her tone.

All at once, Linda's bad temper got to me. She had asked a lot of me lately, told me nothing, made no effort to sound friendly or tell me why she was home on a scheduled workday. After I had practically committed a felony or two (I wasn't sure about this, but so what?) to protect her privacy. I gathered my wits and found my voice.

"This whole thing has gone on long enough, and —"

"What *thing?*"

I hit the air-conditioning panel again, for two degrees lower. "The *thing* with Just Eddie."

A long silence. Which I interpreted as *her turn to be flustered.*

I tried to wait her out, but couldn't. "I'm worried about you, Linda. Can't you understand that?"

"Can I come over?" she asked, subdued.

Interesting. No denial of a *thing* with Just Eddie. And a measure of humble pie in her voice.

"Of course. I'll put on some coffee."

"Iced tea would be better. And I'll need about an hour. I'm in the middle of something."

Apparently the old Linda hadn't disappeared completely.

Maddie's door was closed. I had a sinking feeling that she had written her grandmother off as deceitful, dishonest, corrupt, and five other synonyms I hated to think of. I remembered her father at that age, more likely to be angry with Ken than with me. He'd close his door and crank up (I still liked that obsolete phrase) the volume on his stereo. Nowadays, with all the new electronics, at least the loud music went directly into the child's ear. Better for parents, and possibly for the hearing-aid manufacturers of the future.

I thought about my next move. Maddie and I needed that heart-to-heart, but first I had to talk to Beverly.

"Wow," was all my sister-in-law could say when I caught her up. Then, "Wait. You think Linda and Just Eddie . . . ?" We laughed as if it were junior high and we'd found out two unlikely friends were kissing in the schoolyard.

I figured Beverly had an image in her mind similar to mine: Linda and Eddie were both on the chunky side, with Linda at least a head taller. I was immediately ashamed that any of that would matter if they really were dating, and was glad I hadn't said it out loud.

"It's a theory. I don't want to get Skip involved yet," I said.

"Understood. Good for them, I say. We all deserve a little . . . something." We laughed again.

"I hate to do this, Bev, but do you think you could take Maddie this afternoon while I talk to Linda? She'll be over in about an hour."

"No problem. I had a good rest this morning and I feel great. We can go to the pool and I can rest some more."

I sighed with relief. "Have you had lunch yet?"

"Not if you're offering to pack one."

Two tuna-salad sandwiches, two apples, two bags of potato chips, a bag of celery sticks, and four cookies later, I got the courage to knock on Maddie's door. "Maddie, are you ready for some good news? Aunt Bev is going to take you to the pool."

I heard a few computer sounds, then her shuffling to the door. She opened it, stepped out, and hugged me. I smelled something vaguely nutty and chocolate and guessed that Maddie had picked up a snack on the way to her room. "I'm sorry I was mad at you, Grandma."

My heart lifted at the feel of her warm body and tight embrace. "Were you mad at me, sweetheart?"

She nodded, her head rubbing up and down against my waist. "I wanted to be the one to tell Uncle Skip."

So that was it. No felony charges forthcoming, at least not from Maddie. "Did you think I would take the credit for your amazing detective work?"

"I know you wouldn't. I don't know why you have to talk to Mrs. Reed first, but it's okay, I guess."

We hugged for a long moment. I drank in the smell of the grown-up non-baby shampoo I'd let her use. With each visit, my granddaughter seemed smarter, but this time she was more than that. She was mature.

It often occurred to me how bright most kids were these days. Their parents talked to them and included them in conversation almost as if they were adults. Not the way I was brought up, living a kid's life apart from my parents, probably barely knowing how to count and sing the alphabet when I entered first grade. Whereas, at four Maddie could name the planets and all the dinosaur species; at five she was reading a child's guide to anatomy (from Richard) and a child's guide to fine art (from Mary Lou). I doubted there was a school or museum program in greater Los Angeles that Maddie hadn't been enrolled in.

But I'd wanted more for her. I wanted her to be pleasant to be with, understanding, and forgiving. Now she was all of those, putting me to shame.

I thought of the politicians rallying in town. Maybe instead of trying to groom Maddie for a career in surgery, I should be looking at her as a future president. I hoped she'd be able to skip over the planning commissioner step.

I put out a pitcher of iced tea and a platter of Linda's favorite Brie and crackers on the atrium table. I'd showered and changed out of my police station clothes, and into shorts and a Stanley Elementary T-shirt from Maddie's school in LA. Whatever Linda did before her arrival, it wasn't changing clothes. She was in her nurse whites (still required at the Mary Todd), except for bare legs and tan huaraches. Wisps of her beehive had escaped their perfect V formation on her forehead and threatened to obscure her vision.

After a few nibbles, I got the ball rolling. "I know Just Eddie was involved with that trip on Saturday morning, Linda. I saw his truck on a surveillance tape. And we both know that the murdered woman was found close to where you and he were. So you might as well give me your side of the story."

I didn't quite say that I wielded some influence over the police investigation, but I hoped that's what would come to her mind.

"What do you want from me, Gerry?" Obviously the intervening hour had given Linda time to recover her reticence and defensive attitude. "I'm doing my best. I work very hard, I have Jason to take care of, I'm barely making ends meet with three jobs, and I'm all alone."

"That's just it, Linda. You don't have to be alone. You could ask for help." But that would take trusting someone, I added mentally. "Now if it's just a coincidence that you and Eddie had a date in the same area as the —"

Linda's loud, sudden cough took ages to subside. She got up and helped herself to a glass of water from the door of my refrigerator. "A date?" More coughing as she came back to her atrium chair. "Me and Just Eddie? Oh, Gerry, I should get up and leave right now if you think me and Just Eddie are an item."

*Just Eddie and I.* But who was keeping

track? Evidently my theory was off the mark. "Okay, then enlighten me. What was Just Eddie's truck doing at the crime scene, a few yards from the phone booth?" I tried to give *phone booth* all capital letters with my inflection.

Linda fanned her throat with a paper napkin, as if to preparing to talk again without choking. "I'll tell you what happened, but you have to promise you won't talk to Skip."

"I can't promise that, Linda." (She didn't have to know I already had practice in the withholding-information arena.)

A deep sigh. "First, I don't know anything about the woman or the murder." She looked me straight in the eye, pleading. "You know I could never kill anyone." Then she gave me a rare smile. "Not that I haven't fantasized about an ex or two."

Linda was grumpy, yes. A chronic complainer, hard to get along with, never satisfied. But not a murderer. I smiled back, and took her hand (another rarity, since Linda and I were not touching buddies). "I know you couldn't do this."

The moment passed, and we were back to arm's length.

"It's all about Jason. Remember that robbery at Crane's a week ago? I think Jason was involved." Linda whispered the last sentence.

This was the closest Linda had ever come to admitting a wrongdoing by her son. I felt sorry for her and tried to smooth over the embarrassment she must have felt. "Are you sure? I know he cut his classes that morning, but —"

Linda held up her hand to stop me. "I found a gemstone, a very pricey sapphire, in the drawer of my Governor Winthrop desk. I knew Jason must have put it there." My slight gasp didn't stop her. I felt Linda needed to get a great deal out in the open, without interruption, so I let her talk. "It was the same day as the burglary. He was in my workshop, around my crafts table, which he never is. I walked in and he said he was looking for some glue or something. I didn't put it together until I was working on the desk at the fair and I found this beautiful sapphire." She held her hands in the shape of a globe. "So I went out to the parking lot to call Jason."

Linda stopped for breath. She used both hands to lift her glass, as if it took all her strength to get a sip of tea. The fact that she hadn't touched the Brie (Linda could eat more cheese and crackers in one sitting than anyone I knew) was another sign of her distress.

If this were Beverly telling me such a story, we would now embrace for a long time. But it was Linda, and our relationship was not the hugging kind. I did the best I could to encourage her, to remain nonjudgmental.

I cut off a thin wedge of Brie, placed it carefully on a plain water cracker, and put it on her plate. I gave her my calmest voice. "Take your time, Linda. I really do just want to help you."

I saw a slight lowering of her shoulders as she took another breath. "When I went out, that was right after you left the table to work up front." She took a bite of cracker and Brie. *Progress.* "I never would have left the tables, Gerry. You know that."

I believed her. I put my hand on Linda's arm. Her eyes teared up. I responded by spreading another slab of Brie onto a cracker and handing it to her. I also moved a box of tissues closer to her.

"Thanks," she whispered. "I couldn't reach Jason. When I got back to my table, Just Eddie was going through my things. I knew he must have been looking for the gem. I had no doubt he was involved in the robbery and probably lured Jason into being his accomplice." Another sniffle and a

184

bite of Brie. "I tried to push him away and accidentally cut him with my Exacto knife, which made him madder."

The bloody cloth. Another loose end taken care of (if I believed all this, and it was just outrageous enough that I did). "How could all this have gone on in a crowded hall?"

Linda blew her nose. "Everyone was distracted and busy setting up. You were checking people in. He kidnapped me."

She'd slipped in that information so simply, I almost missed it. "Kidnapped?"

"Well, he told me if I didn't go with him, he'd go straight to the police and tell them Jason pulled the Crane job on his own. He poked my ribs like with a gun. I remember thinking maybe he just wanted me to *think* he had a gun, but I wasn't going to call his bluff. He's too crazy. Then he drove me out to this disgusting trailer he lives in."

"Near that phone booth?"

"Not exactly. I got out eventually — the lock was as rickety as Eddie's brain — and walked a ways to the phone."

"I don't understand why he would drive you all the way out there."

"Well, first he's not the best-lit room in the dollhouse, if you know what I mean. I think the idea was to get me isolated while he went through everything and looked for that sapphire. He got into my house somehow. I guess he's had a lot of practice."

I remembered the mess in Jason's room, the view I'd gotten when I snooped around the Reed home on Friday after the fair. Things were falling into place, but just barely.

"He probably wanted to scare you, too," I said, without thinking.

Linda shivered, though the air-conditioning was barely holding its own against the hot day. "Well, it worked."

A light went on in my own rickety brain. "Couldn't you just hand over the stone?"

She shook her head. "I didn't want to do that. I figured he'd just use it against Jason anyway. It was damned if I do, damned if I don't."

Something about Linda's story was not making sense.

The gemstone, for example. "I read the papers, Linda. Crane's didn't report the loss of an expensive gemstone. Just cash and some costume jewelry."

"I know my gems, Gerry." That much was true. Linda had worked part-time at a gem shop in Palo Alto before landing her third care-facility job, and now sometimes helped Dudley Crane with estate sales. "This was a

186

deep Ceylon blue, no matter how you turned it. Perfect shape. Untreated. I'm guessing at least forty or fifty thousand dollars."

More than my last two cars put together. Who would pay that much for a stone? Rock stars? Donald Trump? We had neither in Lincoln Point. But that wasn't the point of the story. "Why wouldn't Dudley report it? Maybe it's not from his store."

Linda crossed her arms across her ample chest. "You mean it's from another robbery Jason pulled?"

"No, not at all." Although it had crossed my mind. "What does Jason say about it?"

"He hasn't told me anything," she whispered. I guessed I'd be embarrassed, too, in this situation.

"What's happening now?" I looked around my atrium and checked that the dead bolt on my front door was in the locked position. "Has Just Eddie given up looking for the stone?"

*Chirp. Chirp. Chirp. Chirp.* Linda's cell phone rang. I got up to refresh the iced-tea pitcher and to give her some privacy. I heard only mumbles from her end.

"That was Chuck," she said after the very brief call. "He's actually being nice. He wanted me to know he picked up Jason after detention." She paused, seeming to regret applying the word to her son. "It was for nothing, Gerry. Just that he was tardy four days in a row. That school has it in for Jason for some reason."

"Just Eddie and the stone?" I asked, getting back to the pre–phone call topic.

"I think I convinced him I don't have it. But I'm worried about what he'll do to Jason. The police let Jason go — they really have nothing if Eddie doesn't talk — and I thought Jason would be safer with Chuck, and maybe would open up to him, you know. He is his father."

Such as he was. Once again, it was Jason I felt sorry for.

One more loose end. "Where's the sapphire now?"

Linda swallowed hard, then bit her lip. She took a sip of tea and cleared her throat. "You have it."

The shock of the surprise rippled through me. "Wha — ?" The last thing I expected to hear. I leaned toward Linda. "Wha— ?"

*Rrring. Rrring.*

My phone. Not good timing. I rushed to see the caller ID on the box in the kitchen. Unless this call was critical, it would have to wait until I found out what Linda was talking about. I looked at the display: *Private*

*Caller.* I was tempted to let it ring through to my answering machine, but I was never comfortable doing that while I was responsible for Maddie.

I grabbed the receiver, annoyed at the interruption.

"Hello."

"Mrs. Geraldine Porter."

"Yes." A wary affirmative. I hoped I hadn't connected myself to a telemarketer. I was anxious to find out what Linda meant. That I had the stone?

"This is Dr. Woodkin from Lincoln Point Hospital."

A wave of fear coursed through my body. Maddie? Beverly? "What's happened?"

"Nothing urgent, ma'am. A small accident with your granddaughter, and we need you to go to the hospital as soon as possible." A strange, uneven voice. Not the smoothness I remembered from all of Ken's doctors. Images of Maddie in a fatal dive, or lying at the bottom of the pool, or bleeding from a wound, flooded my brain.

"A small accident? How small? What's wrong?"

"Please go to the main desk."

"Is Beverly there? Beverly Gowen?"

The line was dead. It wasn't the first time I had become frustrated with hospital personnel, but this was over the top. I thought of many such summonses during Ken's illness, being called back to the hospital, on those rare occasions when I came home for a couple of hours of sleep.

Linda had come into the kitchen. I answered the question in her eyes. "Something's happened to Maddie. I need to go." I swung my purse over my shoulder and scooped my keys from the counter.

"Do you want me to drive you?"

"No, thanks. I'm fine."

"I could follow you."

"No, really. Just lock up, okay?"

In my car (right after rolling through a stop sign) I had the fleeting thought that it might have been more sensible for me not to drive. Why didn't I take Linda up on her offer? She probably would have liked to do something for me, and I refused out of hand. Not my most sensible hour. I thought only of Maddie and rushed ahead.

# CHAPTER 13

Lincoln Point Hospital was the highest structure in town, sprawled around the slightly flattened top of our only hill. The complex had a radial configuration that Ken admired, with five wings coming off a central core. I marveled at the way he could look at this building as an architect; for me it was simply the place where Ken was sick.

I hadn't been here in two years. I had no good memories of the neighborhood. What should have been a friendly café across the street reminded me of the endless black coffees I drank when family and friends forced me out of the hospital. The large pharmacy next to the café supplied needles, pills, and bottle after bottle of Ken's medications. The lovely flower shop on the other side of the café was where the wreaths were assembled for Ken's funeral.

I wound my way up the long driveway, a familiar tightness in my chest. I knew exactly where to park for easy access to the main desk. I crossed the asphalt, imagining I could feel the heat through the thin soles of my sandals. Once I was inside, images crossed my mind — Ken hooked up to constantly beeping machines; Beverly standing behind me in the waiting room, rubbing my neck and shoulders; Richard and Mary Lou taking turns coaxing me out of Ken's room.

I couldn't bear the thought of Maddie's tiny body in a hospital bed, with the same robotic machines. But that would be better than . . . I couldn't go there, either.

The hospital budget had allowed for a new coat of paint in the last two years, I noticed, but the smells were the same, and even worse than those from the school's multi-purpose room and cafeteria. New signage and blue-stenciled footprints led me along the corridor to the main desk, which was more accurately the main window. The admissions staff were protected by a glass partition like the ones used by bank tellers. I'd always wondered if the design was a response to an ages-ago shoot-out in the hospital lobby.

I got in line at the desk. The chatter around me was roughly half in Spanish, half in English. Without much effort, I'd learned a little Spanish through my GED students at the library. I recognized some of the same phrases that were going through my head. *I hope she'll be better. I hope the doctor tells me more. I just want his pain to go away.*

My hands shook as I tried to find tissues in my purse, which was already a tangled mess from when I'd rummaged for my cell phone on the trip to the hospital. I wanted to call Beverly, wherever she was, but quickly realized I'd left my phone in the charger on my counter. I breathed heavily. Why wasn't there a special window for those of us who had been summoned? Where was Beverly? If she were at the hospital, she would have been waiting for me at the entrance. Had Beverly also been involved in the accident? The *small* accident, I reminded myself.

By the time my turn came, I needed answers badly.

"I'm here for Madison Porter," I told the very large woman, "KIM," in the circular reception area.

The computer was off to the side (out of gunshot range?). I watched as she worked the keyboard. She shook her head. "No Madison Porter."

"I got a call to come here. She's ten years old. My granddaughter. She might have come in with Beverly Gowen. Maybe it's under Gowen?" I spelled it for her, my mouth dry from the few words I'd spoken.

Another head shake from Kim.

"The call was from a Dr. Wood-something. Woodkin, I think."

"I'm sorry, ma'am. There's no name even close to that on our staff."

I tried to ignore the throat clearing and the shuffling of feet from the couple behind me. "Can you check once more? It could be under Porter or Gowen. Maybe there's a special list for new admissions. I got the call at home only about twenty minutes ago."

Kim gave me a look that said she was through with me. "Maybe you should just try to calm down."

I nearly shouted, *I am calm!* but I knew my extreme anxiety was all too obvious. I had one more request. "What's the nearest hospital from here? Can you have someone call there? I don't have a cell phone."

Kim warmed up. I was glad I hadn't lashed out at her. Not unheard of when I'm in desperate straits. "Okay, take a seat, and I'll have someone help you in a few minutes."

I knew that phrase. Even with the best intentions, a few minutes could run into two hours, easy. I thought a minute and remembered where the pay phones were. Down one flight, next to the cafeteria. At least that's where they were before the proliferation of cell phones.

I made my way down the hall and through the heavy doorway to the stairwell. A distinct, mashed-potatoes-in-a-box smell overwhelmed my nose; the clatter of unbreakable dishes attacked my eardrums.

My plan was to call Beverly first, then, if there was no answer, start in on neighboring hospitals. I knew there was one in Mountain View, a few miles away.

I breathed a sigh of relief when I saw three phones, right where I remembered them. The old-fashioned equipment was out in the open, but I needed information, not privacy.

I punched in Beverly's cell-phone number. Not an easy task to remember all the digits, since she was number one on my speed dial.

"Hello?"

Beverly's voice. I could hardly believe it. "Bev, are you all right? Where's Maddie?"

"Gerry? What's up? I didn't recognize the caller ID and almost didn't pick up."

The matter-of-fact tone did wonders to calm me. "I'm at a pay phone. Is Maddie there?"

"Sure. She's right next to me, working on

her second bag of chips. The one that was supposed to be mine. And she's trying to tickle my feet with her thongs." The sound of Maddie's laugh and "Hi, Grandma," in the background brought my breathing back to normal. "You sound flustered. Is something wrong?"

"Not anymore."

On the way home I tried to figure out what happened. A wrong number? I sincerely hoped not. That might mean that some other grandmother was unaware of a child's accident. I was almost positive the doctor — if he was a doctor — had said my name.

On further thought, I realized all the things that were off about the call. The doctor's voice. Not professional sounding, and with a vaguely familiar ring. Also, my English teacher's ear picked up an error: He'd said, "go to the hospital" instead of "come to the hospital." A small thing, but possibly not an error, if, indeed, he wasn't at the hospital. I wished I'd recorded the conversation.

But so what? Maddie and Beverly had not been in an accident; that's what mattered. When Beverly had been briefed (in truth, briefly, since Maddie was by her side) on my last frantic hour, she was of the opinion that it was a prank. Neither of us could think of who would do such a thing, but there seemed no other explanation.

I pulled into my garage, exhausted from the tension. My tote bags and boxes from the crafts fair were still in the trunk of my car and scattered over the front and back-seats, but I couldn't summon the energy to bring them into the house and begin the sorting process, going through pieces of finished and half-finished furniture, piles of fabric, tools, and supplies. I had a box filled with glues and paints, another with sales receipts and vendors' checks for their 10 percent donations, and on and on, it seemed, throughout my vehicle.

I braked mentally. Checks. What if someone had called to lure me away so he could break in? To get me out of the house to steal the checks? I shook my head, at no one in particular. True, the total was probably well over three thousand dollars, but the checks were all made out to the Abraham Lincoln High School PTA. Not easily cashed by your average thief.

I decided to take at least a couple of bags into the house, starting with the one with the checks. I grabbed the tote with fabric swatches, and a small one with beads and stones.

*Stones.* I did another mental rewind. Not checks, which were useless to anyone except the school-district treasurer, but a gemstone. Before the false alarm about Maddie, Linda had confessed that a rare sapphire, stolen by Jason, was in my possession. The trauma of thinking I might lose my granddaughter had pushed that admission to the back of my brain. It didn't take much to go from smart to dumb when loved ones were thought to be hurt. But now things were clearing up. Linda must have transferred the stone during the fair. The gem was in one of the boxes or bags in my car.

From this realization, a theory flowed: the fake hospital call was, indeed, to get me out of the house. Whoever made the call wanted the sapphire. They couldn't have known that I hadn't unloaded the baggage from the fair.

I ruled out Linda. I knew in my heart that she was incapable of inflicting such pain on me, even if temporary. Anyway, she'd already told me I had the gem. She could have simply asked for it back. That's probably why she came over in the first place, why she gave me any information at all about last Friday night. Still, I thought it was worth a try to confront Linda about the fake call. If nothing else, it might jog her into telling me more.

First, I needed to search all my bags. Suddenly, I had enough energy to unload the car. But not before I closed my garage door and did a sweep of my house.

In the movies, I'd be carrying a baseball bat, going from room to room, looking for a prowler. I made the search, but without the bat. I checked that the front door was locked (Linda had done her job), the windows were in place, and nothing was obviously upset. Except me. I walked into every room. I pulled back the shower doors, opened the closets. With each new step, my heart moved from my chest to my throat and back again.

All clear. If someone had been in my house while I tracked down a fictitious emergency, he'd taken care to hide the evidence. It didn't make sense, but I tried to focus on the fact that Maddie was fine and so, apparently, were my worldly goods.

My emotions ran toward annoyance, that I'd fallen for the prank and that it had sent me into a paroxysm of fear. I lugged my bags into the house and set to the search for a gemstone. I carefully unwrapped and inspected every item. A tedious task. The cover of a small jar of fabric paint had come loose and the paint had flowed freely through a canvas tote bag filled with wooden blocks of various sizes. I took a break to wash off the dozens of small pieces, but many were permanently stained. Even in my agitated state, I came up with an idea to make a wall of graffiti out of the colorful accident.

Two bags to go, and I struck it rich. A gemstone, a sapphire to my untrained eye, wrapped in tissue, was lodged in the corner folds of one of my larger totes. Linda must have reached under my table at the fair and dropped it into the nearest bag.

I placed the stone on a scrap of white silk. I was dazzled by its size — a flattened sphere, about a half inch across — and by its clear blue color. Linda had called it Ceylon blue.

Beautiful, yes. But worth someone's life? I wondered. I wondered also who was the true owner. And how it might be connected to the events of the past few days.

I needed to find out.

# CHAPTER 14

"What a miserable thing for someone to do, Gerry." Linda was quite upset by the "sick joke," as she termed it. "But what are you thinking?" she asked. "That I would know something about it?"

"Not that you knew ahead of time, of course, just that you might be able to connect it to something else you know and haven't told me." I was flailing around. I wanted to take the sentence back and edit it.

"I honestly have no idea, Gerry."

Her voice on the phone was convincing. I wished I could see her face, always a giveaway as to her level of sincerity.

"I found the sapphire, by the way. What were *you* thinking?"

I heard a loud sigh. "I know you never unpack right away, so I figured it would buy me some time until I talk to Jason." A pause, then, "What are you going to do with it?"

Surprisingly, I hadn't given it much thought. For one thing, I hadn't fully recovered from the trauma of the call from the hospital. And I was still processing the news Linda had given me before the call — the kidnapping story, the logistics of which had become fuzzier and fuzzier in my mind over the past couple of hours.

I knew what I should do — forget about having things clear in my mind, and go to the police. Let them sort it out. I walked around my house, portable phone in hand. My thinking mode. I stopped at the patio door in time to watch two chestnut-backed chickadees land on my birdbath, splash together (they always seemed to travel in pairs) for a second or two, then take flight. Now, that was the way to spend a hot July day in California. Not obstructing justice for no other reason than to rescue an ungrateful friend, over and over.

The phone line was silent. I thought Linda might have hung up.

She hadn't. "That gemstone is worth a lot of money, Gerry."

"So? What are you saying? We take it to a pawnshop and buy ourselves a new outfit?" I was beyond caring if I sounded harsh.

"More like a couple of years of college for Maddie. I told you. It's about fifty thousand dollars. But I'm not a crook, Gerry." I bit my lip to keep from reminding her that her son most likely was. "It's not about the money. Can't you see? It's about Jason. If you give that stone to the cops, it will all come out. Jason could end up in prison."

Linda's voice cracked. I felt myself caving, though I firmly believed that crooks should be in prison. I paced the house, seeking the coolest spot. The air conditioner was no match for temperatures near one hundred degrees. I leaned on the ironing board in the laundry room off the kitchen, on the east side of the property. I seemed to have gained twenty pounds this day, all of it pushing down on my shoulders.

I fingered a small, frayed towel that would soon be cut up, its pieces to be draped around the bathroom in my miniature Bronx apartment. "What do you suggest we do, Linda?"

"How about giving me a little time? Let me talk to Jason. Find out exactly what he . . . what happened."

*Nice switch to passive, Linda.* In Linda's mind, things *happened* to Jason. He wasn't the active agent, responsible for choices. Poor Jason, I thought, but not the way

Linda would mean it.

"Did you say you haven't talked to Jason yet?"

"Not since we came back from the police station. You know, it's not that simple for me, Gerry. It's not like you and Maddie. Jason is a difficult child."

"But this is not just childish behavior, like playing with his food, or —"

Linda cut me off. "I don't want to assume anything. It might turn out that Just Eddie planted the gem on Jason."

"Then Jason planted it on you and you planted it on me?" Even Linda couldn't resist a chuckle at that. "Why on earth would Just Eddie plant a fifty-thousand-dollar gem on Jason? If he wanted to frame him, he could have planted a fifty-dollar pendant, or a bracelet, or —"

"Well, we already know Just Eddie is not the —"

"Not the brightest gem in the case, I know. But still —"

"Twenty-four hours, okay, Gerry? What if it were Maddie in trouble?"

My eyes landed on a photo on the mantel (even Ken had a hard time forgiving Joseph Eichler for including fireplaces in California houses, though it was a common practice in the Bay Area). A silver frame, matching the silvery marble of the hearth, surrounded a photo of Skip in a Santa hat, holding Maddie in front of a long-ago Christmas tree. They were about nineteen and one, respectively. Maybe it was the good-old-days syndrome, but I couldn't remember much stress in my life at that time.

I wished I could drop the phone, sit outside, relax with a cup of chamomile, and listen for the lovely songs — chick-a-dee-dee-dee, chick-a dee-dee-dee — of the black-bibbed birds that visited me almost daily.

"Gerry?"

I turned my back on the photo, shutting out the voices of my conscience.

"Okay."

I hoped Maddie would never put me in this position. If I'd keep possession of a stolen gem (grand larceny?) for twenty-four hours, to give Jason Reed the benefit of the doubt, what would I be willing to compromise for my granddaughter?

It felt like a stampede through my atrium, but it was only Maddie and Beverly coming home from the pool. They'd let the large cooler drop to the floor, rattling my chair. If that hadn't awakened me, Maddie's wet beach towel tied around my arms, or her loud laughter would have done it. Remarkable that I'd fallen asleep, considering the tangle of thoughts in my head and the shards of guilt stabbing at my conscience.

"I'm supposed to be the one who needs naps," Beverly said. "But I know you've had a tough day."

"You could say that."

Enough said. At least while Maddie was around.

I'd rewrapped the sapphire and put the stone back in the tote where I'd discovered it. I didn't know what my rationale was, other than I could always claim that I hadn't found it.

Maddie was in rare form, even cheerier than her usual good mood. And why not, with another pizza dinner on the horizon?

"It's too hot to cook, Grandma," she said.

"Tomorrow night —"

Maddie interrupted, shaking a finger at me, her face wrinkled in mock sternness. "We're having tofu and broccoli."

Every time I glanced at her, I had to remind myself that she'd had a wonderful day splashing around the pool at the high school, being with kids her own age, and having lunch with her favorite almost-grandmother. There had been no accident; she had not been at Lincoln Point Hospital.

The trauma was all mine.

The doorbell rang while we were putting out silverware and napkins on a side table in the atrium. Maddie and Beverly had had enough of the outdoors for one hot day. An atrium dinner was a nice compromise, a natural environment with man-made cooling.

Maddie ran to the door (I expected any year now she would stop running short distances), yelling, "Pizza, pizza!" Followed quickly by, "Uncle Skip!"

My heart lurched. Not because I was disappointed in Giovanni's slow delivery, but because I couldn't face my beloved nephew. I inadvertently looked in the direction of the pile of totes in the corner of the family room. *In a cartoon or comic strip,* I thought, *the bottom of the large bag would throb and glow a cornflower blue.*

I felt my guilt turn to anger, at Linda for putting me through this, at myself for letting her. I heard Ken's voice, gently scolding, reminding me what a pushover I was. Then, teasing, "Lucky me," he'd say. "I'm the one who got you; you're my very own pushover for life."

Too short a life. Tears welled up. I faked a cough so I could disappear into the bathroom for a tissue. For a moment to myself.

I had to get my priorities straight. Loyalty to Linda and Jason should not take precedence over other obligations. Skip deserved to be working with the entire truth, as I knew it, and — although there was only a remote possibility of personal danger — Maddie needed to be protected from whatever criminal element was running amok among our friends and neighbors. What if the call from the phony doctor was a warning? Not quite a horse's head at the foot of my bed, but a sign that "they" could get to me if they wanted to.

I might be overreacting, but enough was enough. I'd make a date to talk to Skip first thing in the morning, Ceylon blue sapphire in hand.

I heard Beverly. "Hi, Skip. I'll bet you tapped the phones and knew that Giovanni was on his way."

Skip started to respond, then looked at Maddie and appeared to change his mind. *Uh-oh.* "Right," he said, with what I knew to be false cheeriness. "You're absolutely right."

"It's not here yet, Uncle Skip. We thought you were it."

"Well, maybe we should just go and pick it up."

"Yeah. Let's go," Maddie said, tossing

knives and forks on the table, producing an uproar of clanging metal. Her domestication went just so far.

"You know, I was hoping you and my mom would stay here and make that special lemonade that I love. Grandma does not — and I mean, does not — know how to make it the way you do, with that extra flavor."

Busted, and not about my inferior lemonade, either.

"I put in a little strawberry flavoring," Maddie said, in a slight whisper. In case a nonfamily member was listening, I guessed.

"Mmm. That must be it. So, is it a deal? Grandma and I will pick up the pizza, and you'll have that lemonade ready when we get back?"

Maddie acquiesced, though she was clearly not too happy about the arrangement.

Neither was I. Except, in a way, relieved.

I picked up my purse and started out the door with Skip.

"I need to get one more thing," I told him. I turned back into the room and headed for my glowing tote.

Giovanni's minivan was rounding the corner of Rutledge, my street, as we pulled away from the curb in Skip's unmarked sedan.

Not his personal car. This was clearly police business. Skip drove right past our pizza dinner and parked on a side street a couple of blocks away. He reached back to the floor behind him and came up with a small brown paper bag.

His demeanor was so somber, I expected him to read me my rights. Maybe he felt it unnecessary, in that I hadn't said a word since we left the house.

"Does this look familiar to you?" he asked. He opened the top of the bag wide enough for me to look inside without removing the object.

I peered into the bag and saw pieces of wood. I recognized tiny drawers, a slider, and ornate table legs — all broken apart, their ends in splinters. The largest intact piece had a double scroll design, like the top of a slant-top desk. A Governor Winthrop desk.

"It could be" — I paused — "Linda's desk for her Colonial."

"I thought it might be. The bottom piece has the initials LR on it."

"Where did you get this?" I asked.

"When did you see it last?" Skip used a button on the driver's side to roll down both our windows. I felt he was controlling more than my window.

No question who was in charge, in or out of an interrogation room. I thought back to the first evening of the fair, in the school's multipurpose room: Linda's putting finishing touches on the desk, placing it on a piece of newspaper to dry. When I went back to our tables after my greeting duties, both Linda and the desk were gone.

"At the fair, on Friday evening, before the doors were open to the public," I told Skip.

"Was it in Linda's possession?"

"Yes. How did you get it, Skip?"

"Was it in one piece at that time?"

"Yes. Skip, please —" *I'm not one of your perps* (did they use that term outside of television dramas?), I wanted to say.

"The desk was in Dudley Crane's hand. His dead hand."

I gasped. "Dudley Crane is dead?"

"Murdered."

"Murdered?" I was barely aware that I'd lost the power of intelligent speech.

I needed time to process the facts. Two murders in less than a week. It was one thing when the victim was a stranger, an unknown woman with no connection to Lincoln Point. A drug dealer from New York City, if I remembered correctly. Or the Midwest. That was still a tragedy, to be sure. But Dudley Crane? A longtime citizen of

211

the town. A respected merchant and a candidate for public office. That was another story. The breeze blowing across the front seat seemed to stop short of the edge of my window. The car was stifling.

"He was found this morning, in the parking lot behind his store. He'd been shot. His safe was open and empty, so it could have been another robbery, that this time he walked in on." Skip pointed to the bag. "This is all we have."

"Not exactly," I said.

Skip looked at me and shook his head. "Not again, Aunt Geraldine. You know, I had a feeling you might know something more than you've been telling me, but I hoped not."

Full name, relatively speaking. And no smile. Not good signs. Skip was very much in cop mode. A wonder he didn't call me Mrs. Porter.

I pulled the sapphire out of my tote, and placed it, on its bed of tissue, on the armrest between us. Skip had parked facing east; the sun streamed in over our shoulders, hitting the stone for maximum brightness. The armrest might have been the velvet background in a fine jewelry store. Like Crane's. I swallowed and cleared my throat. "This might be a long story," I said. "Do you want it now? Before pizza?"

Skip nodded, his eyes opened wide, focused on the sparkling gemstone.

"Maybe we should let your mom and Maddie know —"

"Just talk, please. I'm sure Mom will come up with a cover story."

Skip was right. Beverly had surely picked up on the ruse to get Skip and me together, alone, and would invent a story so Maddie wouldn't worry.

I spilled out the events in order, starting with seeing Just Eddie's truck on the videotape from Bird's Storage (making it clear that it was Maddie who ID'd it first). I told Skip Linda's story — how she found the very pricey sapphire in her Governor Winthrop desk, and dumped it into my tote to avoid giving it to Just Eddie, who then "kidnapped" her.

"That's how she got to that phone booth," Skip said.

"Right. And she did all this to protect Jason. What I don't know is whether Jason did anything wrong in the first place, or whether he's been framed." My mouth was as dry and irritated as if I'd sat all day in a field of South Bay pollen. "I want you to know I didn't realize the stone was in my possession." My voice was probably as weak

213

as that of his most guilty suspect.

"Until when?"

"Just a couple of hours ago." At least, I didn't have to say, "Twenty-four hours ago." For all Skip knew, I was on my way to show him the gem when he showed up. In truth, all I'd done since finding the sapphire was take a nap and order pizza. "This may be too little, too late, but I really was going to contact you tomorrow. I was giving Linda a day to straighten things out with Jason."

I dug a bag of cough drops out of my purse and offered one to Skip.

He laughed and relaxed his shoulders. "No, thanks. I'm more used to this kind of" — he made quotation marks in the air — "conversation than you are, Aunt Gerry. Sorry if I came on too strong, but I was feeling that Linda had the upper hand in the intimidation department, and I had to get it back."

He was right. I'd been letting Linda call all the shots. I was impressed at Skip's insight. Police training? Or simply the culture of young people today, almost every one of whom either had or was in therapy?

In my day (which was receding rapidly into history) "therapy" meant someone was severely maladjusted, even mentally ill. Now it was part of the education and maturation process from an early age. Skip went to a therapist at age eleven, when his father died, and it occurred to me that he might still have regular sessions, just as a part of getting along in the world and dealing with life.

I remembered a recent crafts club meeting at my house. Thirtysomething Karen Striker was trying to get old Mabel Quinlan to commit to a certain number of items for a Mother's Day display. Mabel told her she'd be sure to bring "enough."

"How many?" Karen asked.

"Enough so we won't run out," Mabel said.

Finally, exasperated, Karen said, "You need to work on your definitives, Mabel."

We all gave her a questioning look. Karen explained that it was a therapy term for *be specific.*

During my mental wandering, Skip had rewrapped the gemstone. "I'm sure there are so many overlapping sets of fingerprints on this by now that nothing will be useful, but we'll give it a try."

I gave him a sheepish look. I hadn't exactly protected the stone while it was in my custody. I felt a surge of annoyance at the way Linda had dragged me into her out-of-control life. At the same time I worried for her, about how it all looked to the police, especially the fact that her desk was found in Dudley Crane's hand.

It was out before I knew it. "Are you going to arrest Linda?"

"I was thinking of arresting you."

I searched my nephew's face for a sign of humor. He kept me waiting at least three seconds before giving me a token grin and head shake. "Just to be thorough, here — technically all you had was a guess, about Eddie's truck, from the detective work of a ten-year-old. And you had a gem that no one has reported stolen. Jason could have found it walking by the railroad tracks."

"And I didn't know about Dudley Crane's murder." Just to keep the good spin going.

"Right. But don't ever do this again. Okay?"

"Okay." *Whew.*

I was relieved, and maybe had learned a lesson, but I wasn't ready to completely abandon the case to Skip and the LPPD.

"What reason could Linda possibly have to murder Dudley?" I asked. "Chuck, maybe. Peter, maybe. Even the vice principal of the high school and a few nursing home administrators. But Dudley Crane? Unless Dudley also threatened to expose Jason, which would mean Dudley knew who committed the robbery, in which case, why wouldn't he just go to the police?"

"I can't give you a motive right now." Skip scratched his head. "They disagreed about growth/no-growth, didn't they?"

"Yes, but Linda wasn't as vocal or as powerful in the community as even Postmaster Cooney, for example, and certainly not as much as Jack Wilson, who's running against Dudley. Linda wasn't that political outside her own little interest in keeping Lincoln Point cozy."

I thought about the day Maddie and I dropped into Crane's Jewelers. I was sure Maddie would always remember being able to see Dudley's vault, and perhaps the lollipop he gave her also. I remembered one more thing. "In fact, the last person I noticed having issues with Dudley was Just Eddie."

"What issues, do you know?"

I tried to remember Just Eddie's words. "He was looking for something, demanding that Dudley tell him where he put it." I snapped my fingers. "I'll bet he was talking about this sapphire."

I had to admit that the idea of Just Eddie as a murderer didn't strike me as too fanciful, and the idea of him in prison would not make me weep.

"You might be right about the sapphire, but why are we talking about this, Aunt Gerry? You are not a cop. You do not need to know or figure out anything more."

"Just tell me this. Is there a report of a stolen sapphire of this description? There was nothing in the newspaper, but Linda says it's worth about fifty thousand dollars."

Skip gave a low whistle. In his younger, pre-cop day he would have made a remark about how that would go a long way toward getting him a hot date.

"Not everything went out to the paper, but I can tell you nothing like this is on the official record of the stolen inventory."

"Was any other store robbed recently? In a nearby city?"

Skip shook his head. "Could be, I suppose. We're always on the lookout for stuff like that. Robberies with the same MO, known associates, that kind of thing. But nothing jumps out at me."

I was stuck.

Skip, the professional, wasn't. "My best guess about this is that the last owner wasn't supposed to have it. It was stolen from him, or her, and couldn't be reported because it shouldn't have been there in the first place."

"Then it could have been from Crane's private collection, so to speak. He does estate sales. Maybe he skimmed off the top of an estate inventory. I know he handled Gail's mother's estate — that would be Jack Wilson's mother, too, of course. Can I have a list of all the estates he's handled in the last — ?"

"It's been nice chatting with you, Aunt Gerry," Skip said, turning the key in the ignition, for our long, two-block ride home.

"Okay, that's your job. I get it." For whatever reason, the image of a murdered stranger came to me. A woman who apparently had no one to grieve over her death. "One more thing, Skip, and then I'll quit. What about Tippi Wyatt? Do have anything new on that case?"

Skip put the sedan in gear and made a U-turn, heading back toward Rutledge. "Nothing's turned up. Still on hold. Doesn't seem to be connected to anything at the moment."

I had no reason to think the two murders were connected except for Just Eddie and his truck. And Linda at the phone booth. In other words, nothing.

"Well, I guess I'm through for now."

"You're through, period. This is a police investigation, a homicide, and I want you to back off. I know Linda's your friend. I know you have a curious mind and that your granddaughter is just like you. But, really, I don't want to see you or Maddie anywhere near this case. It could be very, very dangerous. Don't you have dollhouses to decorate?"

"Will you at least thank Maddie for noticing Just Eddie's truck? She wants desperately to impress you."

"If it was his truck."

"It was. There was this refrigerator box —"

"So you said. It's not exactly unique, Aunt Gerry. A large box on the bed of a pickup."

I saw his point.

Skip parked in front of my house. He turned to me. "Before we go in, is there anything else I should know?"

I shook my head. "No."

"You're not hiding a fugitive in that pretty blue house, are you?"

I laughed. "Of course not."

"No little side trips? No other confessions from your friend?"

"None."

"No other stolen goods?"

I shook my head vigorously. "None."

Not that I knew of, anyway.

Maddie was not a happy little girl when Skip and I returned.

Her skinny legs were moving as fast as I'd ever seen them go, under the atrium table. She put down her glass of milk (thank you, Beverly) and greeted us with, "The pizza's cold."

"Mmm, I love cold pizza," Skip said, downing half a slice in one bite.

"There's lemonade in the fridge, in case you want to know."

"And I've been dying for that lemonade. Can you pour a glass for me?"

"I guess." Maddie walked to the refrigerator, frowning. Playing hard to get, for sure. "I know what you were doing. You were talking about the murder case, and you didn't want me to hear."

"We were actually talking about you. Grandma told me how you picked out that truck on the videotape, Maddie, and that was very good work."

A little brightness. "Thanks."

"But from here on, it's too dangerous for you or Grandma to do any more work, and that's what Grandma and I had to discuss. How I would take over from here."

I knew the speech was as much for me as for Maddie.

"It's going to be tough without your help," Skip said, ruffling Maddie's curls.

221

"Nuts," Maddie said.
I felt that way myself.

# CHAPTER 15

By Wednesday morning, I longed for a normal day. No strange rescue calls, no secrets from the police, no items of questionable provenance in my possession, no news of murder. I didn't ask much.

I hadn't spoken to Linda since I promised to keep quiet about the sapphire. I wondered how things were with Jason, whether she was any closer to knowing what her son was up to. The last word (which we managed to tease out of Skip, once Maddie went to bed and his mother and I could gang up on him) was that Linda would be brought in for questioning. Not arrested. At least, not right now.

I knew in my heart that Linda had not murdered Dudley. I was fairly certain Linda didn't even have a gun, and there were any number of reasons for her desk's being in Dudley's cold hand. (Well, I could certainly think of one — Just Eddie, whom I now thought of as The Great Framer, could have planted it.)

It was a good thing I didn't have to worry about any of it. Skip was on the case and I was off. I should be able to trust the fate of my friend to my very capable nephew. Another very good reason for my giving up any involvement was Maddie — she would be leaving on Friday, and I wanted to make the rest of her time with me as happy as possible. I'd told her this morning, briefly, that the nice man who gave her the lollipop had a bad accident.

I had a ten o'clock appointment with my literacy student, which I thought would help get me back on a normal track. I'd been working with Angela Agusta for nearly a year, and she was closing in on taking her GED exam. Angela's story was inspiring: After she'd helped put her three children through college, she decided she wanted her high-school equivalency diploma, before she turned fifty. She worked part-time in the library and studied harder than any teenager I'd taught at Abraham Lincoln High School during my entire career.

My role in Angela's education was to tutor her in three of the five areas necessary for the high-school equivalency diploma — reading, writing, and social studies. I left mathematics and science to those more inclined. Looking at the study guides for those topics, I felt certain I would never pass either one if I had to take the test this year.

Maddie was in shorts and yet another sports team T (periwinkle blue with a yellow ball, the team name worn off), ready to leave by nine thirty. She seemed to have recovered fully from the disappointment of last night. A forgiving little girl, all she'd required was a Popsicle and an extra chapter of a Ramona book at bedtime.

Now she dragged her backpack, filled with books, toward the door to the garage.

"We're going to the library, you know. There will be books there," I teased.

"I might not like any of them."

We were almost out the door when the phone rang.

I stopped in my tracks, car keys ready, and looked at Maddie. "Should we or shouldn't we?" I asked with raised eyebrows and a tilt of my head toward the phone.

Maddie dropped her backpack and skirted around me. "It might be Uncle Skip. Maybe there's some news on the investigation."

What had we created here?

"Hi, Dad. Yeah, everything's fine." I hoped Richard didn't sense that his daughter had been hoping for another caller. I supposed he'd better get used to it, come to think of it. Maddie-the-teenager was just around the corner. "I made a new friend at the pool yesterday. His name is Scoop." A pause. "No, not Skip. Scoop. Like ice cream scoop. And Uncle Skip says I can't help him anymore with police work. Do you think I could help the police in Los Angeles, Dad?" Another pause. "Sure, she's right here."

*Uh-oh.* "Good morning, Richard."

I spent the next five minutes convincing Richard that Maddie was quite safe (he'd already read about the Crane murder on the Internet) and that all we'd done was watch a videotape in the safety of the Lincoln Point Police Station. For better or worse, my son trusted me, and we moved on to another topic.

"I want you to think about coming to LA in the fall, Mom."

That again. Richard and Mary Lou were on a personal mission to get me to visit their Los Angeles home. I hadn't been there since Ken and I made the trip together every month or so.

"You know, we were just leaving for the library, Richard."

"A likely story. No pun intended."

"Really —"

"Listen, Maddie's class is going to produce a play this year. *Hansel and Gretel.* Wouldn't you love to see it? If you come early enough, you can help us with the publicity."

Then Mary Lou's voice, on the extension. "I was thinking you could make a miniature stage set and we could raffle it off," said my conniving daughter-in-law.

"See why I married her? Brilliant idea, Mary Lou," Richard said.

"I'll think about it," I said, trying not to be lured by an enticing project. I could take apart a broom to construct a thatched roof, for example.

"You haven't been on a plane in three years." Richard was referring to the year that Ken was sick, plus the two years since his death.

"Is there some rule about that? So many plane trips per year?" I tried to lighten things up, and change the subject.

"I'm just saying — you need to move on."

Another popular therapy term. Someone should come up with a glossary. At least he hadn't told me to get on with my life. "I assure you I'm busy enough, Richard. Is there some reason you're picking this particular moment to bring this up, because we really are out the door. I have a literacy student waiting. It's one of many things that keep me busy these days."

I didn't quite hang up on my son, but I knew I'd have to apologize later.

"They just want you to visit, like you used to, Grandma," said Maddie, the eyes and ears of the world (now, there was a meaningful expression from the old days).

"I know, sweetheart." I picked her up — a few inches off the floor, with my arms around her waist, was all I could manage lately. "We're going to be late. Let's move!"

I couldn't explain my issue with flying, not to Richard and Mary Lou, not to myself. It wasn't as if Ken had died in a plane crash. Maybe I didn't want to have too much fun without him.

Maybe I needed some therapy.

While Maddie listened to her iPod tunes in the car, I allowed myself to draw up a mental list of suspects in the Dudley Crane murder. No harm in that; there would be no paper trail; it was all in my head. In spite of Skip's admonition, I couldn't give up the idea of helping to clear Linda. I felt I owed her that much after breaking my promise of a twenty-four-hour reprieve on the sapphire.

My favorite candidate for the killer was Just Eddie. Chances were excellent that he was behind the robbery, with or without Jason. Say, Crane stole the sapphire from an estate he handled, Just Eddie found it when he was robbing the jewelry store. He noticed that Crane didn't claim it, and then . . . what? This was a great scenario for Crane's killing Just Eddie, but not vice versa.

I turned down Rutledge and made my way to Gettysburg Boulevard. No marchers today, and no litter, either, making me proud of the city's cleanup crews.

Maddie tapped her knees and nodded her head rapidly — I had to assume that her iPod tunes had been vetted by her parents. Maybe this was a good day to check out some audiobooks from the library.

Next to Just Eddie on my list was Postmaster Brian Cooney (one of the dullest personalities I'd ever met, and obsessed with the importance of his job), who had two motives. He was fiercely opposed to Crane's growth platform and had implied that Crane had somehow cheated him on his mother's estate. Could a boring, fifty-year-old man, who lived with his mother until her recent death, be a murderer? I supposed no particular personality type could be ruled out.

I moved on to Jack Wilson, Gail Musgrave's brother. Not only was he running opposite Crane as candidate for a spot on the city council (I wondered if he were now running unopposed), but in Crane's plan, the county would be able to buy certain lots of land for much less than market value. Wilson stood to lose millions of dollars if the proposal went through.

I knew Gail pretty well from the crafting community. I admired her energy and constant striving to better herself — she'd started taking classes to get her real estate broker's license. I'd met Jack Wilson only in large groups. I tried to picture him — a tall, well-built man who lived on a ranch with his family and loved his horses — wielding a gun. It wasn't that far off that he'd own a gun, but I saw him more as shooting critters, not humans.

Chuck Reed was always a good scapegoat. A loser, in Linda's words, and for valid reasons. Try as I might, however, I had no way to connect him with Dudley Crane in a way that might motivate him to commit murder.

I recalled all the loud arguments that had broken out at the fair: Just Eddie vs. Postmaster Cooney; Cooney vs. Dudley Crane; Reed vs. Reed; Dudley Crane vs. Jack Wilson and Gail Musgrave. Now that I thought of it, the fair had been more of a war zone than I realized at the time.

I felt I'd covered all bases for suspects, and the only other possibility was that some drifter — perhaps the same one who killed Tippi Wyatt — had decided to rob Crane's store on his way out of town and ended up getting caught and shooting Crane.

Why Crane would be found grabbing hold of Linda's Governor Winthrop desk in any of these scenarios was beyond me.

I wondered if the police had compared the bullets used in the two murders. And what would they do with the sapphire? Dust it for fingerprints? Mine were on it, and also on file with the school district, so technically I could pop up as a suspect.

I wished I had some answers. How ironic that with my intimate connection to the LPPD, I didn't know some basic facts of these investigations. My only nephew was a cop, and my sister-in-law a civilian volunteer for the police department. (Beverly was off today, resting for her Thursday morning job of tagging abandoned vehicles along the streets of Lincoln Point.) Maybe I'd chosen the wrong hobby.

It had been an unproductive drive except to get us here to the converted railroad station that served as the LPL. The library loomed in front of me, in the civic-center complex that included the police station and the senior center.

Today, I knew that Angela, with her enthusiasm and positive outlook, would be as much help to me as I'd be to her.

With Maddie settled in the children's room (story hour was about to begin), Angela and I headed off to a storeroom behind the information desk. I was sure this room had once been a tiny ticket office. Now it held a card table with two folding chairs, and a garage-style metal shelf with office and restroom supplies. Unopened cartons under the table left little room for my long legs, but did provide pint-sized Angela with a footrest.

It was slightly cooler outside, decent enough inside the library, but sweltering in the storeroom (we needed a city council, whoever might be on it, that would give us a new library).

Angela didn't seem to mind the cramped, airless conditions; she had news that made her spirits soar.

"Guess what, Mrs. Porter? They tell me . . ." A pause. "They *told* me when I am a high-school graduate, I can start to take classes at Foothill and Mrs. Schafer says she'll let me help at the reference desk. And also, Carlos, my oldest, will pay for my tuition."

I was thrilled that Angela was thinking ahead to a community college. I reached over and gave her a hug. "That's wonderful, Angela. You must be very proud of your son, too." I knew Carlos, a business major, had earned an internship at a major financial center in Palo Alto.

Angela grinned broadly, then turned serious. With the four fingers of her right hand, all of which had silver rings, she tapped the stack of GED guidebooks on the table between us. "First, I have to pass this test, though."

"I have no doubt you'll pass if you keep at it the way you have been."

Bad sentence. I was always more conscious of my own grammar around Angela, not wanting to give her bad habits. As a result, I often sounded stilted.

Angela's current library job entailed routine tasks like shelving books, mailing overdue notices, filing and duplicating, and (her favorite, she said) retrieving reference books from stacks that were not accessible to regular patrons. Her goal of helping at the main reference desk (definitely attainable in a small-town library) seemed modest to me, but to her it was a life's dream.

I thought about how lucky I had been,

taking college for granted. Not that my family was among the superrich, but there was never a doubt that my parents would be able to help me with college. Maddie was even more fortunate, with more affluent parents, private school, informed counselors, and all the extracurricular advantages she could stand.

The young Angela, on the other hand, had had no one to guide her. It gave me pleasure to be part of the support group she had now.

Today's lesson was in advanced reading and comprehension. Angela would read an essay out loud, and then answer multiple-choice questions. I admired how Angela didn't seem to mind going through texts obviously meant for younger students.

"The first potatoes were grown by the Incas of South America, more than four hundred years ago," she read, sounding as if the information really mattered to her quality of life. She answered all the questions correctly, and moved on to the next passage.

"Mary Cassatt, like the Impressionists who inspired her, preferred bright paintings, picturing a lively world bathed in light. Her technique was to use rapid brushstrokes and thick coats of paint."

*A little closer to Angela's life,* I thought, and

resolved to bring a set of Cassatt "mother and child" cards for her next week.

I visited Maddie during our restroom break and treated her to the junk food of her choice from the vending machines. She chose a packaged pair of chocolate cookies (candy? crackers?) that I'd never seen before, nor heard of. A point in favor of the days when no food, drink, or conversation was allowed (including "study groups") in libraries.

The current lack of rules did allow Maddie to make a new friend during the story hour, however, and I was glad she wouldn't be bored when Angela and I went back to work. I predicted there'd be a new Lincoln Point–to–Los Angeles pen-pal duo in the season ahead.

As Angela and I headed back for one more hour in the roasting storeroom, I saw an excuse to dally. Gail Musgrave was in a reading corner by the reference desk, gazing intently on a large book of some sort. Like a teenager, she sat on one leg. It had been a while since I had such agility. When she saw us approach, she closed the book quickly and shoved it under some magazines. Odd, but none of my business. If she enjoyed some exotic form of adult entertainment, she was welcome to it.

"Will we see you at the crafts meeting tonight?" I asked.

"Yes, yes," Gail said, unfolding her leg and bringing her upper body, short as it was, to attention. She fingered the edges of the book she'd (apparently) hidden from us, nudging it farther under the magazines. "We're making books at your house, right?"

I nodded. "Books, magazines, leaflets. Anything you find in a library."

"Movies on DVD," Maddie said.

Gail laughed and relaxed her hold on her pile of magazines.

"If you'd like to join the crafts group, you can make the DVDs," I told Maddie.

She gave me the look of one who has lost a round.

"That was funny," Angela said, settling her tiny body onto the uncomfortable metal chair.

"What was funny?"

"How Mrs. Musgrave didn't want us to see the book."

So it wasn't my imagination. "I wonder why," I said. A rhetorical question.

"I don't know. She uses those books all the time. I get them for her. The ones on jewelry and gems."

I was glad I hadn't yet explained the nature of rhetorical questions to Angela.

# CHAPTER 16

A few times a year, the members of my crafts group work together on a project, to be donated to a charity. The timing now was perfect. The fair was over; no one was under a deadline. A new one would come around all too soon, for the fall fair at the end of October. We'd decided to build a miniature one-room public library as a raffle prize for a library fund-raiser.

Karen Striker and I had already provided the main structure, using a storage box from the local discount store (the kind where you can buy everything from a prescription drug to a patio table, with umbrella). The box, set on its side, would be turned into a "room" twenty-two feet (inches) long, with a ten-foot (inch) ceiling. We laid the carpet (a piece of mottled felt), wallpapered three walls with a subtle beige-on-beige leaf-design wrapping paper, and installed book-cases (a series of compartmentalized Lucite trays meant for organizing a jewelry drawer).

We needed books. Many books, to fill the shelves (the sides of the organizer box) along half of the long, back wall and one side wall. The other wall space would have a newspaper rack, an information desk, and other library furnishings. We'd had a heated discussion over whether to include a row of computer terminals. The compromise was that we'd have a computer at the reference desk, but no others.

"No one knows how to make one of those things anyway," Mabel had said.

During dinner — stir-fry tofu and veg-etables, finally — before the group arrived, Maddie and I talked about her contribu-tion: the DVD cases.

Maddie knew how to access pictures of movie posters online. After a few standard complaints about the slow modem she had to work with in my house, she explained how she would set up the printer to get the correct size. She made a list of her favorite movies, most of them animated, with color-ful covers.

We did the math. A boxed DVD set mea-sured five and a half inches by seven and a quarter inches.

"Looks like we'll need covers that are about a half-inch square. That'll be close enough," I told her. We picked out half-inch balsa-wood pieces from my stash.

Maddie rolled two tiny blocks between her fingers. "These aren't very big."

"That's the idea."

"How many do you think we'll need?"

I could tell that the tediousness of the task ahead was dawning on her. Making two or three DVDs, or any item, was fun, but producing them in large supply required discipline. It was worth it in the end to see row after row of fabric bolts, for example, in a miniature fabric shop, or shelf upon shelf of glassware in a tiny restaurant, but crafting dozens, even hundreds, of identical pieces could be tiresome. Wasn't that why our group had decided to do the bookmaking (not the illegal kind) together?

I wanted Maddie to experience both the disciplined work and the final satisfaction. I wasn't sure it would happen in the little more than twenty-four hours before Friday, when I'd put her on a plane to Los Angeles, but we could get started.

More math was needed. We figured that one rack would hold about one hundred DVDs. Maddie's eyes popped. I considered comparing this activity with one hundred swings of a bat during practice, but, in truth, I had no idea how many swings of a bat were involved in a game, nor did I want to turn her off by disparaging her beloved sports.

"But not all of them will need covers, only the ones on the ends. For the rest, you just need to cover the spines." I avoided saying: "the very, very tiny spines," but she was smart enough to get it.

"Maybe I'll just make one of those racks like they have in the video store, where they're all facing out."

"Good idea," I said, then gave in to the temptation to give her an even easier way out. "Or, you could look in magazines for a picture of a row of DVD spines, print it to size, and . . ."

Her face lit up. I could see that, as a miniaturist, she was going to be more like me than Linda.

*Who was where by the way?* I wondered, but I pushed that question aside.

Maddie set herself up in my office. There was more modem grumbling and a snide remark about the age of my printer, but otherwise a quite satisfactory arrangement for both of us. She didn't have to sit around with a gaggle of old women (until it was time for dessert), and I didn't have to worry about the nature of the conversation, which

I felt sure would be talk of murder.

Which started immediately.

Betty Fine and Mabel Quinlan, who arrived together, gave barely a nod toward the tables I'd arranged in the atrium, loaded down with raw materials — wood, colored papers, scraps of fabric, leather, and felt. They tripped over themselves to tell me their theory of the murder of Dudley Crane.

"Just Eddie did it," they said in unison.

"What makes you think so?" I asked. The morning paper had very little information, stating the simple fact that Crane's body had been found in the lot behind his store.

"Just Eddie works in Crane's part-time, you know, and I can't believe he wasn't behind the robbery," Betty said, patting her bouffant hairdo (not a strand of hair budged). "Crane must have figured it out and Just Eddie shot him."

"There is no way that Just Eddie could work in a store like that and not be tempted," Mabel said.

So the first votes were in, sans evidence.

Susan Giles was next. A Tennessee native, Susan still had her Southern accent after three decades in California. "The Postmaster," she said. "Where do y'all think the expression 'going postal' comes from? Besides, Crane handled the estate when cranky old Mrs. Cooney died, and Brian confided to me that he would never, ever recommend Crane to anyone."

That would be "nay-evah, evah." A duet of "ahas" went up from Betty and Mabel. I didn't contribute a sound.

Karen Striker and Gail Musgrave were close behind, standing on the welcome mat when I answered the doorbell.

"I'm glad for the company," Karen said. "Imagine, a friend murdered, right in our own town. Very scary."

Not one, but two murders in a week, but somehow the first one, of a stranger, didn't have the impact on the citizenry.

With two votes for Just Eddie and one for Postmaster Brian Cooney, Karen checked in.

"I'm all Just Eddie," Karen said. "Had to be."

"If it wasn't Just Eddie, it must have been someone from Los Gatos or Menlo Park. I can't believe a citizen of Lincoln Point would do such a thing," Betty said.

I was glad no one had mentioned Jason — until Mabel slipped.

"What about that Reed boy, the adopted one? I heard he has no alibi for the day of the robbery."

"How would you ever know that, Mabel?"

Betty asked. "I think it's a shame when a child is automatically blamed because he's adopted."

"He has been trouble, though," Karen said. Tonight her hair was swept around her face, looking remarkably like that of a model from a magazine she'd brought. "It's those Brooklyn genes."

Another jab at New York. Like Just Eddie's. "Lots of good things come from New York," I said, with a smile, hoping to remind my friends of my roots in the Bronx, a couple of boroughs north of Brooklyn.

"No one knows where Jason was born," Susan said.

"I do," Karen said.

We all looked at her. Karen put her hand over her mouth. "Oops. I probably shouldn't have said that."

Too late. Karen worked at city hall, which gave her enormous credibility over, say, a rumor. I could pretend to be uninterested, since I knew Betty, Mabel, and Susan would pounce on her.

As they went at her, I felt sorry for Karen, whose youth put her at a disadvantage among seasoned rumormongers.

"Okay, let's just say that at one time Linda came to city hall — she was interested in knowing about Jason's parents. She thought his acting out might be due to some physical reason, and she asked for disclosure."

"And?" Susan asked.

"She couldn't get most of what she wanted, but she did go away with some bits, here and there."

"So, was Jason really born in Brooklyn?" Betty asked.

"I can't say," Karen responded. But she already had.

We moved off Linda's son, though Jason's delinquency was legendary and his lineage would be fascinating to us. Possibly her fellow crafters were being respectful to Linda, even in her absence. She hadn't shown up yet; I doubted she would.

*Jason was from Brooklyn.* I had a hard time letting go of it, for some reason that was unclear. It rolled around my brain for a while.

"How about you, Gail?" Susan asked. "You haven't told us. Who do you think murdered Dudley Crane?"

"I'll leave it to the police," she said.

"Not even a guess?" I asked.

No response. She turned from Susan and me a bit and made a show of emptying her large briefcase of materials onto the table. (Everyone else carried supplies in totes; Gail, who, besides studying for her new career in real estate, still worked part-time as a cosmetics sales rep, always looked ready for a day at the office.)

It bothered me that I was considering Gail's brother capable of the crime of murder. Unlike the police, who couldn't limit their world of possible suspects, I had limited mine to those I knew had motive to want Dudley Crane out of their lives. This meant suspecting my friends.

I looked around the table at some of my favorite people in the world, outside of my relatives.

Gail's summer wardrobe of trim sundresses seemed to have no end; Karen's inventory of youthspeak phrases was a delight to the rest of us; Susan, the most girly member of the group, sported a ruffle on some part of her outfit, no matter the season; Betty had a new set of photos of her grandchildren and great-grandchildren to start every meeting; and Mabel — we all hoped Mabel and her white, white curls would live forever, as we knew her beads would.

I couldn't know all their private and personal lives. I thought of a very old radio program that began with the words *Who knows what evil lurks . . .* Was it possible that one of my own circle was a killer, or related to one?

I hoped not.

Sometimes it was a blessing not to be a cop.

As always, great ideas flowed when crafters got together.

Karen, the only native Californian in the group, had already started on a series of posters for the mini-library, on California authors. She'd measured each frame to fit in the space between the bookshelves and the ceiling. She showed us miniature images of John Steinbeck, M. F. K. Fisher, Jack London, Gertrude Stein, Robert Frost, Anna Deavere Smith, and a half dozen others, including Dr. Seuss (who knew?) for the children's section.

We considered a Lincoln wall, to identify the library as belonging to Lincoln Point, but settled on having just one Lincoln poster, over the bookcases in the history section. Mabel was assigned the task of choosing it.

"And don't go beadin' his beard," Susan teased.

We made books and talked, as we did nearly every Wednesday of the year in the home of one or the other of us. We agreed to drop the subject of murder, but it came back over and over, like a bubble between two glued surfaces.

We'd start on an unrelated topic, but all roads led to Dudley Crane. Betty's granddaughter's beautiful engagement ring took us straight to Crane's Jewelers. Susan's evening in Tad Lincoln Park rolled into a discussion of the trees, which led to Dudley Crane's proposals to level them. Mabel's recent reread of a Louis L'Amour book turned into talk of Crane's classy Western wear, which he wore for campaign appearances. (The cynics among us thought he chose cowboy hats to remind everyone of the old West, not the new West he was trying to raise up in stucco houses and strip malls.)

Still, we made progress on our bookmaking, with no lack of supplies. Karen brought more women's magazines than I'd ever seen, including the stack on my hairdresser's table. Susan shared museum quarterlies and catalogs — she wanted to create an art and antiques book section. (I glanced at Gail, who had been singularly quiet all evening, tempted to ask if she knew any good books on gems.) Susan's designs were always ornate, like last year's Atlanta plantation home. She claimed she entered a Frank

Lloyd Wright dollhouse entry this year just to prove she could do minimalist.

Betty set herself to printing Jane Austen titles in gold. She had created a similar set for her recent Tudor (later declared *Tudorbethan,* a melding of Tudor and Elizabethan, by one of the judges, who pointed out its steepled roof and prominent cross gables).

Maddie joined us for refreshments, which we were not allowed to indulge in until we were close to our goals for the evening. Tonight was Susan's turn to feed us, and we were treated to a four-layer apple-and-peach stack cake.

"The official cake of the state of Tennessee," she announced.

Before I finished wondering if California had a state cake, Maddie was off to the computer and back with the answer.

"All I can find is Mexican hot chocolate for California," she said.

She won a round of laughter and great praise for her miniature rows of DVDs.

Her presence for the rest of the work session kept murder talk at bay. A very good thing.

Karen, who was the keeper of the library room in progress, took the books and Maddie's DVDs home with her — we managed to turn out about thirty books each, for a total of nearly two hundred volumes, big and small, classics and popular fiction, reference books and coffee-table books, for our miniature library.

I'd gotten what I wished for. A morning of tutoring, a relaxing afternoon, and an evening of crafts, albeit one with a grisly thread of conversation. A relatively normal Wednesday.

Unless you count the strange behavior of Gail Musgrave in the library and her reluctance to speculate about the murder of the man who was running a fierce campaign against her brother.

Technically, since the call from Linda came after midnight, it couldn't be counted as ruining Wednesday.

"Don't worry, Gerry, I'm not at a phone booth or anything, and I'm not going to come over."

Good, I thought. I wasn't proud of the unfriendly sentiment, but I'd been reading comfortably, about to turn out the light by my bed. "What is it, Linda?"

"I just want you to know I spent the whole evening at the police station. They let me go, but I think they think I did it, Gerry." Linda's voice was fractured, as if we had a bad cell connection, except that we were talking on landlines. "They think I killed Dudley."

That was a lot of "thinks." I set my Steinbeck anthology aside and breathed deeply. "I'm sorry, Linda," came out weakly.

I wondered what the police had to back it up, besides the broken desk. I was surprised Skip hadn't told me. Then again, it wasn't as if he shared his work with me as a general rule. In fact, he usually drew a hard line between work and family, even with his mother, though Beverly was a volunteer with the LPPD.

His giving me advance warning of Jason's possible arrest last Saturday had misled me. I was not a fellow police officer; I had no insight that would help him solve the case.

"I'm sure they'll find out who really did it, Linda." I hoped I sounded confident.

"I'm not so sure, Gerry. Maybe you could talk to Skip, and offer to help. He knows how smart you are."

"Linda, I have only one more day with Maddie, and —"

"For me, Gerry. Please. Just say you'll look into it. I need you to help me prove I'm innocent."

"Linda —"

"On Friday, after Maddie's gone."

251

I said the only thing that would get me some sleep. "I'll talk to Skip."

# CHAPTER 17

Over a breakfast of Maddie's favorite waffles and strawberries, we drew up an agenda on how to spend her last day in northern California — we'd work on the Bronx apartment in the morning; ride our bikes downtown for lunch and last-minute souvenir shopping for her parents and her best friend, Devyn (our previous attempt had turned up nothing, due to Maddie's short attention span for shopping); play board games in the afternoon; and, of course, have a special dinner with Beverly and Skip in the evening.

I hoped a good, fun day would erase the memory of two murders and her awful night cruising toward a rendezvous in a creepy neighborhood.

Maddie had saved a few of the DVDs she made to put into the living room of the miniature Bronx apartment, but I told her there were no such things when her grandfather and I lived there. "We had records," I said. "In this scale, about as big as a quarter."

She screwed up her densely freckled nose. "Was there an oven?"

I hoped she was teasing, and tickled her just in case.

We settled on making a couch for the living room, and a small item for each of the other rooms, so Maddie could say she worked on the whole apartment.

"Can we put a hockey stick in the hallway? Grandpa used to watch hockey on TV with me sometimes."

Not what I would have chosen, but I owed her a lot for the striking conversion that got her doing miniatures with me in the first place. I couldn't very well deny her a hockey stick, especially one that reminded her of her grandfather. "I think we can do that." I extracted a thin pine strip, about six inches long and three inches wide, from my wood stock. "Can you draw a stick on this piece of wood? Then we'll cut it out and paint it whatever color you want."

"Okay. I better do the one with the long hook since this apartment is supposed to be historic" — I didn't correct her usage — "and they use shorter hooks now."

I wasn't thrilled that she knew the history

of hockey sticks, but again . . .

The salad for the eventual kitchen counter was superb — green clay leaves (lettuce), red clay balls (tomatoes), and three tiny black beads (olives). We added a towel for the bathroom and pictures in frames for the bedroom.

At eleven o'clock we went to our respective rooms to change into what Maddie called capris and I called pedal pushers, for the bike-riding and shopping trip.

So far, so good. The few times I thought of Linda and her plight I was able to pull a Scarlett O'Hara on myself and assign it to tomorrow's agenda.

Lincoln Point was a bicycle-friendly town, with metal bike racks all along Springfield Boulevard. We chose a rack in front of the toy store, chained our bikes (both were presents from Richard and Mary Lou), and went in. The Toy Box was among the few shops still in existence along our main street — the fast-food and drinking establishments had fared better than the retail stores, as more and more people flocked to the large, upscale Stanford Shopping Center.

I couldn't help thinking that this was one of the problems the late Dudley Crane wanted to rectify. He went on record as wanting to make Lincoln Point a more business-friendly town, proposing an easier process for obtaining licenses and permits, and cutting back on some of the regulations that made it difficult for small businesses to survive.

The response from anti-growth candidate, Jack Wilson: "There's a reason for requiring landscaping whenever a new store moves into a strip mall. It's for the environment, for the beautification of our town, and for the edification of its citizens."

As usual, both sides claimed they wanted what was best for the citizens of Lincoln Point, but only one candidate would win in November. The closed sign on Crane's Jewelers reminded me that now one political party in the debate was handicapped by the death — the murder — of its leader. Tempting, but too simplistic, I knew, to blame the obvious benefactors.

The Toy Box was a favorite of Maddie's, as was the card shop in the middle of the block. We lingered a while, first in one, then the other, then back to the first. Unwilling to accept a supplement to the spending money her parents provided, Maddie chose her purchases wisely. A foot-tall stuffed giraffe from the toy shop for Devyn ("for when I tell her all about the Oakland Zoo"), and a box of art notepaper from the card shop, for Mary Lou. Nothing yet for Richard.

A lesson for life: boys were harder to buy gifts for than girls, at all ages.

"Maybe we should have lunch first?" I suggested.

We clicked knuckles. "Deal."

We considered the menu possibilities. I ruled out heavy-duty junk food; Maddie voted against the "really healthy" sandwiches and salads offered in the back of Sheridan's, our do-it-yourself ceramics shop. We walked past their window and looked at the array of unpainted vases, plates, bowls, baby shoes, and spoon rests. It was as crowded and varied as a miniatures store.

"Too bad we didn't think of this sooner. You could have painted something here for your dad," I said. "There's a mug with the kind of handle that he likes."

"I did that for him when I was a kid," Maddie said.

I checked out her expression to see if she was joking. (Partly.)

"Oh, look at the menu. They have a hummus-and-avocado combo salad," I said.

"No way." The reaction I expected. Maddie pointed across the street. The bagel shop. "How's that for a compromise?"

"Excellent idea."

Ten minutes later we were biting into hearty sandwiches (plain cream cheese on a plain bagel for Maddie, sun-dried tomato spread on a sesame bagel for me). Bagels by Willie was named after one of Lincoln's sons, who died at age eleven. Some biographies suggested he died of scarlet fever. I was thankful that Beverly's bout with it came a hundred years later.

Although Willie's chunky cookies were tempting, we decided to save dessert for later, at Sadie's, the ice cream shop two doors down.

It was good to relax and sit on a full-size seat after a long, hot bike ride and some serious retail shopping. I rotated my neck, horizontally and vertically, the way I learned in my on-again, off-again attendance at a senior workout class.

On the upward motion of the neck routine, I scanned the framed posters, all landmarks of New York City. I gazed at a team photo of the Yankees (even a non-sports fan like me recognized that uniform), the Empire State Building at night, the Rockefeller Center Christmas tree, the Brooklyn Bridge.

A mixed metaphor, I thought — a bagel

place named after Abraham Lincoln's son, with New York–style bagels and décor. Why weren't the photos of Illinois or Kentucky (though the town certainly had enough of those)? Or, why wasn't it called "East Coast Bagels"?

*Stop editing everything,* I told myself. Then the Brooklyn Bridge, in black, gray, and white splendor, caught my eye again. A little tickling in the back of my mind said I needed to pay attention to this.

Finally, I knew what had been bothering me.

I had to see Skip.

After what seemed like hours, Maddie ate the last potato chip and squashed the bag for the trash. I gave her a big smile and offered her another drink. She wasn't going to like what was coming.

"Sweetheart, I need to run an errand. I'm going to leave you across the street in the bookstore with Mrs. Norman. You remember her. She was my student —"

Maddie held up her hand. Her palm sparkled with potato chip residue. "Where are you going?"

She'd vetoed the idea the last time I wanted to leave her with Rosie Norman and go alone to the police station. I don't know what made me think I could get away with it this time.

"There's something I have to deal with —"

"With Uncle Skip?"

"It's not anything that would interest you, Maddie. And Mrs. Norman loves having you in her store, because you're so smart and you've read so many books —"

"I get it." Maddie frowned and jutted her lower lip out. The way her father did when he thought he'd be missing a fun time in the adult world.

"It'll take only a few minutes."

"Nuts," she said.

I bought a cookie for her — a grandma trick that at least drew a smile — and two for Skip.

As I hoped, Skip was at the station. The officer at the front desk (a balding Paul Hammerfield, who'd been my student) sent me back to the cubicles, where I caught my nephew with his feet up on the desk. He had a sandwich in one hand, a soft drink in the other, a file folder open on his lap. A fan on a shelf above him ruffled his wavy red hair.

I smelled pastrami, which went with the half-eaten pickle in a Styrofoam box.

"Tough life," I said.

Skip jerked down from his position, slamming his lunch onto the desk. He pulled an empty chair in place with his foot, and motioned for me to sit. "Hey, Aunt Gerry."

I sat on the rickety metal chair with a poor excuse for a cushion. "I brought dessert." I said this softly, since I hadn't thought to bring enough for the other five or six officers whose heads cruised by above the cubicle partitions.

Skip looked at the small brown bag. "From Willie's. None better. Except for your ginger cookies." He accepted the bag from me and bit into the first of Willie's four-inch-diameter chocolate-chip cookies. "But I'll bet you didn't come just to bring me treats."

"How did you know?"

"The adorable little redheaded squirt isn't with you."

"I guess there's a reason you're the detective."

"Almost detective."

I got right to it. "Tell me more about Tippi Wyatt. Exactly where was she from?"

"Brooklyn, remember? That's why no one around here cares that much, to be brutally frank. We've had no tips on Tippi, if you . know what I mean. Whereas, tips come in all the time for the Crane case. Cooney did it because Crane robbed his mother's estate. Wilson did it to win the election. Just Eddie did it because he's, Just Bad. Reed did it . . . that would be any one of three Reeds." He put his cookie down long enough to tick them off on his fingers. "Chuck, Linda, or Jason. Take your pick, with assorted motives."

"So is Jason Reed."

Skip gave me a funny look. "Huh?"

"Jason Reed is also from Brooklyn."

"So? Big deal. Aren't there, like, a million people from Brooklyn?"

Closer to two and a half million, but I didn't want to get off on demographics. "Where else did Tippi live? You said she moved to the Midwest."

"Yeah, some small town. I guess she was clean and sober in between, but the habit caught up with her and she was convicted on a minor drug charge."

"Where?"

Skip took a long breath, stuffed the remaining quarter of a cookie in his mouth, and turned to his computer. "I don't suppose you want to tell me what this is all about?"

"I will if I'm right."

While Skip worked the keyboard, I studied

the patterns made by the peeling paint and water stains on the walls of the large, divided room. It seemed easy to make a case for a new building, or at least an overhaul, for Lincoln Point's finest. I hoped it would be a logical decision on the part of the city council, and not just another excuse for a partisan battle.

"Tippi, Tippi, Tippi," Skip chanted as he hunted and pecked his way to a useful screen. "Here it is. Winona, Minnesota."

A small gasp escaped, not unnoticed by the almost-detective.

"What?" Skip asked.

"One more thing. Does that say whether Tippi had a child?"

A few more clicks, while my jaw became tighter and tighter.

"She had a kid in 1992. A boy, Edward Louis. Nothing recent on him."

The name didn't matter. The math was easy, even for me. Linda brought Jason to Lincoln Point from Winona in 1995; he was between three and four at the time.

"The boy's father?"

"None listed."

"The boy is now Jason Reed, Skip."

He took a deep breath and folded his hands across his chest. Not exactly open to my theory. "Let's have it."

"We have two individuals, Tippi and Jason, who traveled from Brooklyn, New York, to Winona, Minnesota, to Lincoln Point, California. Tippi Wyatt came here to look for her son, Skip. And that son is Jason."

Skip scratched his head. "That's a pretty big leap."

"Think about it. He's exactly the right age."

Skip fiddled with a couple of pens, rolling one over the other, as if they were ideas he was trying to smooth out. "If this is true, it's the connection we've been looking for." A low whistle came out. "Wow."

"Is that a good 'wow' or a bad 'wow'?" I asked.

"Good for us. Maybe bad for Linda and Chuck."

This was probably not what Linda meant when she'd asked me to talk to Skip. I had the odd feeling that I'd unintentionally sold out my friend. It occurred to me that Linda would have been better off this week if I hadn't kept trying to help her.

In spite of my brilliant sleuthing, Skip was adamant about keeping me out of the loop on all other matters. He wouldn't tell me what his next steps would be, nor what disposition had been made of the sapphire.

264

I did have one easy-to-fill request. "Can you come to the bookstore for five minutes and say hi to Maddie?" I asked him.

He opened his drawer and pulled out a blue-and-gold Lincoln Point Police Department patch. "I'll do better than that. I've been wanting to do this anyway."

A few minutes later, a crowd was assembled in Rosie's bookstore. Skip had recruited one of his fellow officers (actually, an attractive female policewoman to whom he gave the second cookie) to join us. Rosie gathered her customers, mostly mothers and children, for the ceremony.

Skip cleared his throat and assumed his best posture. "This Lincoln Point Police Department patch is awarded to Ms. Madison Porter, for cracking the case of the white truck."

The small but enthusiastic audience clapped, not knowing (I was fairly sure) a thing about a white truck case.

Maddie beamed (so did I), and I knew we'd been forgiven for excluding her.

I was so grateful, I added my own tribute.

"You're all invited to Sadie's," I said to more applause. "Free ice cream cones all around. Sprinkles included."

Maddie's farewell party back at the house

that evening was in full force. Although she visited several times a year, it was our tradition to make a big family fuss at the end of every trip. We did it up right, with BON VOYAGE balloons and matching plates and napkins.

"We don't need hats this year," Maddie had announced while we shopped in the party store. Fine with me — it meant fewer opportunities for Skip to catch his mother and aunt on film (or was it on bits? or bytes?) in a silly pose.

A cool evening breeze made it perfect for dining on the patio. At this time of the day, by the light of the setting sun, the Bay Area's dry, brown hills took on a golden color. (When she was six, Maddie informed me that the red streaks at sunset meant there was a lot of pollution in the air, but I refused to let science spoil my enjoyment.) Add to the scene the smell of hamburgers on the grill, expertly flipped by Skip, and the flutter of the hummingbirds drinking sugar water at my feeders, and every sense was satisfied.

As far as police talk went, Beverly was much more willing to share than Skip.

She'd put in a long day at her volunteer tagging job. I never would have guessed there would be that many abandoned vehicles on the streets of Lincoln Point.

"Another idiot today," she said. "This guy comes up to me while I'm tagging his beat-up old car and says I can't do that. 'Yes, I can,' I say, and he lashes out to hit me. Fortunately, the guy is way out of shape and I grab his arm on the way to my face. I was ready to call for backup, but I realized he was never going to connect. So I let him flail around and shout verbal abuse and went on my way."

"You should have called it in," Skip said. (Every family has a rule follower.)

His mother hardly gave him a glance, and went on to a story about a man who approached her with an open bottle of wine and asked if she could test it to see if he was being poisoned by his wife.

"I guess it's the uniform," Beverly said. "It attracts the oddballs among us."

Skip, on the other hand, kept his police business to himself (the nerve), using Maddie as a shield. He bestowed on Maddie her second award of the day, naming her Assistant Chef. This meant she got to do Skip's bidding, running back and forth from the grill to the kitchen to the outdoor table to the trash and, once, to retrieve Skip's cell phone from his car.

She loved it.

Maddie told more Los Angeles stories than usual, her way of easing back home, I guessed.

"You know what stinks?" she asked, a forkful of salad (a required course tonight) in her mouth. "In my school, the boys have the best locker room. We have to share ours with the janitor. And he puts these smelly mops in there just because he knows we don't like it, and because he just doesn't want to share."

Something about the juxtaposition of the words *janitor* and *just* stirred my brain. Just Eddie, the janitor, that was it. One of those strange neuron firings, or free-association trips I often went on.

"I'm surprised your mother isn't on a committee to correct the locker situation," Beverly said.

"She is," Maddie said. We all laughed, and from her reaction, I imagined Beverly, like me, was picturing petite Mary Lou Porter storming the PTA meetings with petitions for girls' rights. To be followed probably by leaflets on the nutritional value of the food in the cafeteria and a campaign for new girls' volleyball uniforms.

Between dinner and dessert, Maddie announced that she had presents for everyone. I didn't remember her ever doing this before, and took it as a sign of further maturity. I was amazed that, in spite of her snit at being left out, she'd spent part of her time in Rosie's store buying each of us a bookmark, the kind with a lovely photograph and a tassel at the end for ease of handling. I felt a surge of pride. I couldn't wait to tell Richard and Mary Lou what an outstanding job they were doing.

Skip's bookmark had a photo of a bright yellow sports car rounding a bend on a curvy road; the pattern on Beverly's was a Native American design that looked similar to a quilt that had been in the Porter family for years.

She'd also found a book of famous doctors for Richard.

"Mrs. Norman helped me with Dad's," she said.

And for me, a teary moment: THE WORLD'S GREATEST GRANDMA, printed in gold against a background of yellow roses.

For the second time that day, I offered ice cream all around.

Skip timed his leave-taking to coincide with Maddie's going to bed.

"Gotta run," he said, as soon as Maddie said her long good nights, with hugs that went on and on.

Coincidence? I thought not. He knew I had many questions about the murders of Tippi Wyatt and Dudley Crane. He knew I had a strong interest in finding the killer lest my friend be accused. He knew all this, and worked the evening perfectly, to avoid talk of the cases.

But tomorrow I would put Maddie on a plane, and then pay him a visit. Age and aunthood had its privileges.

And thanks to Maddie, and a slip of the tongue by Just Eddie, I had a new idea.

# CHAPTER 18

We arrived at the San Jose airport early to fill out the forms required for a child traveling alone. Maddie was past the age when she enjoyed getting little silver wings from a gushing flight attendant, but airline policy still called her an Unaccompanied Minor (UM, in airlines' literature).

"Only a few more times, Grandma."

That was Maddie trying to rush to adulthood. She'd be eleven next January; after that she'd no longer be a UM. How could she know how quickly life passes — how, a couple of decades from now, she'd want to slow it down?

"I promise to check out the rules for eleven-year-olds in plenty of time."

"Thanks, Grandma." She straightened her shoulders, bringing herself to her full height of four feet three inches, a little below average for her age (she had her mother's short genes, Richard said, not the tall Porter genes). "I love my bookmark," I told her. "That was so thoughtful of you."

Maddie smiled. "I'll miss you."

"I'll miss you more."

We laughed and hugged and continued our "more" game for several rounds.

"Don't finish the historic apartment without me, okay?"

Strangely, I found my granddaughter's grammatical errors charming. "Okay."

"I know you'll be busy anyway. Are you going home first after I board, or straight to the police station?"

Maddie slid one palm past the other, in a motion meant to emulate my path to the civic center, I was sure. Where did that come from? Did I have a little psychic on my hands?

"What are you talking about?"

"I know you're going to investigate all the stuff going on in town. You're just waiting so you won't have me to worry about anymore."

It sounded remarkably like a former president who said we wouldn't have him to kick around anymore, but Maddie was too young to know that.

On the other hand, she was quite advanced for her age.

The appearance of a flight attendant bearing gifts saved me from having to respond to Maddie. Dotty was on the dumpy side and a lot heavier and older than the "girls" in my college class who aspired to coveted careers as "stewardesses" and struggled to fit themselves into the weight and measurement requirements that ruled in the early days of air travel.

San Jose airport was bustling with a surprising number of children, their UM cards slipped into cases and hanging from navy blue lanyards with the airline logo.

"Hey, little girl," Dotty said to Maddie, who grimaced. "How would you like to wear the same wings our pilots wear? Huh?" Lucky for her, she didn't try to pinch Maddie's cheek.

Maddie looked at me and rolled her eyes. I made a note to give her non-pink luggage for Christmas, which might help upgrade her image. I gave her a "be nice" look.

"Thanks," Maddie said, taking the wings from Dotty with her thumb and index finger, as if they were from a dead insect. Come to think of it, she would have preferred to be holding the wings of a dead insect.

The airport PA system was at its best, with an unintelligible command that apparently Dotty understood. She gathered the families and led the children toward the gate for early boarding.

This was it. "Call me when you get home," I said, holding on to Maddie for one more second.

"I will. And if you need any help catching the bad guys" — she held her hand to her ear, thumb and pinkie extended, telephone style — "call me."

As I noted, my granddaughter was advanced for her age.

My excitement over the "just" and "janitor" juxtaposition that I picked up from Maddie seemed unwarranted in the light of day. Especially as I got closer to the civic center and the LPPD.

I had two things to back up my theory, both a little shaky. I couldn't barge into Skip's felt-walled cubby, shouting, "Just Eddie is Jason's father!" I needed to review my reasoning.

I pulled into a parking space in the police department lot. I rolled down the windows and took down the small notepad and pencil I kept clipped to my visor. Not that I would write anything comprehensible, but doodling would help me sort things out.

First, Tippi had named her son Edward. That was a matter of record. Yes, it was a leap from that to a father named Edward, who called himself Just Eddie. But it was possible. I couldn't let go of the scenario: Tippi Wyatt and Just Eddie have a son in Brooklyn, whom they name Edward Louis. Both parents are in and out of jail (I knew this about Tippi, and had no trouble believing it of Just Eddie), and eventually Tippi moves to the Midwest to get away from Just Eddie. When she has a relapse into drugs, she gives little Edward up for adoption (enter Linda and Chuck Reed). Just Eddie somehow (a miniature weakness in the theory here) finds out that his son is now Jason Reed, living in Lincoln Point, California, and comes out to be with him. Possibly he was waiting to make a move and kidnap Jason from the Reed home. (But I digress.)

My second clue, if it could be dignified as such, was Just Eddie's comment to me at the crafts fair (which seemed ages ago). When I asked him if he'd seen Jason, he'd said not to worry, and then something about a kid from Brooklyn's having lots of street smarts. At the time, I thought he was making a wild-card dig against my own New York roots. Now it seemed he was giving himself away. He knew where Jason was born because he was there.

What did these startling conclusions

amount to? I didn't know exactly. A possible motive for Just Eddie to want to be rid of Tippi? That would make sense if Tippi had custody and could keep Just Eddie from his son. Since Jason belonged to the Reeds, however, that was moot. Maybe Just Eddie just hated his former wife, or lover, from undreamed-of issues in their past.

For symmetry, I wanted to fit the murder of Dudley Crane into the picture, but there was no reason to think the two murders were connected.

Unless the same gun was used. I had to talk to Skip. By now he knew the answer to that, plus who was the rightful owner of the sapphire, plus all kinds of information that I was sorely missing. I had to find a way to get him to share, the way a family is supposed to.

I told myself I was here — about to enter the LPPD building and ask my cop nephew if I could be his partner — for Linda's sake, but if I was honest with myself, I'd have to admit that part of me needed to be involved in getting these cases solved, and quickly, for myself. I'd unwittingly driven my granddaughter within a few yards of a murder scene, which might account for the twinge I felt every time Skip mentioned that no one seemed to care about finding the killer of this stranger. And Dudley Crane — he wasn't a close friend, but he was an important part of my little community. A community I wanted to feel safe in again.

A familiar tune interrupted my thoughts. I couldn't quite place it, although it was coming from my own oversized purse. It took a couple of seconds for me to recognize the melody and figure out the mystery. Maddie had programmed my cell phone to ring with, "Take Me Out to the Ball Game." She knew I had no idea how to change it back to a simple bell sound. I smiled. She was probably planning to call me on this number as soon as she could.

I answered the frivolous ring.

"Is the UM in the air?" Beverly's voice.

"She is."

"Where are you now?"

Busted. "I'm sitting in my car, parked in the police department lot."

"Of course you are. How about an adults-only lunch at Sheridan's first? We can discuss the case."

This was standard for Beverly and me — not discussing murder cases, but getting together the day Maddie left for home. It was my sister-in-law's way of easing me into being alone again, a practice for which I was usually very grateful. This time the hole didn't seem so big. Maddie was right, that I did have the murders to distract me, but there was another reason that I couldn't express yet, even to myself.

Sheridan's restaurant was actually about six tables at the back of a ceramics shop where customers could paint their own designs on naked pottery. A few days later, they'd come back and their pieces would be fired and glazed, looking quite professional. Recently the two sisters who owned the studio had turned some extra space into a café. The fare was definitely adult, with salads, sprouts, avocados, fresh basil, and right-from-the-garden veggies — nothing that Maddie would like.

Today there were fewer people than usual at the high tables and stools available for painting. No big holiday was looming, like Mother's or Father's Day, when the studio was packed with children, dipping their hands in paint and preserving their pawlike designs on china.

I told Beverly about my call from Linda and briefed her on my current theory of Jason Reed's origin.

She blew out a low whistle. "And I thought I had a scoop. Just Eddie is Jason's father?"

I hoped Skip would be so accepting.

"Maybe. I wonder if Linda will allow DNA testing. I don't imagine they can take a swab, or whatever they do, from Jason without her permission. Tippi has no known relatives, so getting a sample from Tippi shouldn't be a problem."

Beverly, still wide-eyed, was definitely on board with my theory. "Then we'll need a sample from Just Eddie, too. It's anybody's guess if he'll submit to a paternity test. If he thinks about it, he might not, because it reveals a motive for killing Tippi Wyatt."

"Jason isn't theirs to fight over, though."

"Doesn't matter. They always look at spouses and significant others first." Beverly's voice had the ring of authority.

"Good point," was all I could add. We were at a standstill. Understandably, since our scenarios suffered from a distinct lack of facts.

A little late, I flashed back to Beverly's comment. "Wait. Did you say you had a scoop?"

"Nothing like yours. There is buzz around the station, however, about the sapphire." She shook her head. "Good thing I don't have to depend on my son for information."

"And?"

"It's the real thing, apparently. The gem's easily worth fifty or sixty thousand dollars, as Linda thought. It was faceted in India, which I guess makes it even more special." Like mine, Beverly's jewelry collection consisted mostly of costume pieces, and one or two items that were more expensive, like the pearls Ken had given me. Nothing on the order of that sapphire, however. "And you had it in your possession for a while, Gerry."

I smiled. "If only I'd known. So whose is it?"

"It belongs to" — Beverly mimicked a drumroll with slender arms — "Ta da . . . Jack Wilson."

The would-be councilman, Gail Musgrave's brother, running against the now-deceased Dudley Crane. My turn for a low whistle. I barely said, "Thank you," to Alysson, our waitress — who looked only a couple of years older than Maddie — when she brought our heaping salads.

"So it's Gail's sapphire also?"

"Not. Their father was in the foreign service. He brought it back from Ceylon for their mother."

"Who died about three months ago," I said.

"And who left it to Jack."

"Not to Gail?"

Beverly shook her head. "Gail didn't even

know about it. The father wanted the son to have it. Sound familiar? Good old boys, with old ladies following their wishes. Gail found out it existed when the will was read, and then, guess what? It was stolen about a month later."

"In the Crane robbery?" Now I was really confused. This was more complicated than I could handle over lunch.

"No, no, long before last week's robbery at Crane's."

"But between the time the mother died and the time Crane took over the estate handling. And before Gail and Jack relieved Crane of his estate duties."

Beverly finished chewing a healthy forkful of lettuce, cranberries, and nuts. She pointed her fork at me. "You got it."

"So someone stole the sapphire from Jack Wilson as long ago as three or four months?"

"Apparently."

"Jason?" I had a hard time picturing Jason climbing in a window of the Wilson home.

Beverly shrugged. "You can never get the 'whos' out of them, just the 'whats.' "

By "them," I assumed she meant the officers of the LPPD, including her son.

"Still, it's another piece of the puzzle."

And it made me a little better prepared to

talk to Skip, though I couldn't connect all the dots immediately. I mulled this over while Beverly did the math for the check.

"Don't look now," Beverly said.

But of course, I did, and gazed straight into Chuck Reed's belt buckle. Quite a surprise. This didn't seem like his kind of establishment. For one thing, Sheridan's did not serve alcohol; plus, the idea of Chuck's biting into a cucumber-and-hummus sandwich was laughable. Skinny as he was, I pictured him eating from a Styrofoam box at any of the fast-food places along the boulevard.

"Afternoon, ladies," he said.

I gave him a slight, unsmiling nod. The last time I'd seen Chuck was at the fair, after his fight with Linda, when he bellowed some threat at me, about my keeping out of his family business. As if he were even close to being a family man.

Beverly was more friendly. "Hi, Chuck. What brings you into a pottery shop?"

Chuck pointed to the counter where one could sit on a diner-style stool and have a cup of coffee and a slice of Debbie Sheridan's rhubarb pie, in season. Today, there were no bar customers. Debbie (one of the few Lincoln Point citizens too old to have been my student) was behind the counter, straightening napkins, sugar packets, and condiments. She gave Chuck a big wave.

"Her," Chuck said. He marched over to the counter, leaned his long frame over, and planted a kiss on Debbie.

I turned away as quickly as possible, but I could have sworn I heard a wet smack.

Silly as it was, I wondered if I'd ever be able to eat there again.

Beverly walked me to my car, where I planned to stash the leftovers from lunch before knocking on Skip's door, so to speak.

As we approached my Ion, I saw something on the windshield. A parking ticket in the police department lot? How embarrassing. But the lot was open to the public, and the spaces weren't metered. I checked the area for something obvious, like a sign that read RESERVED FOR CHIEF OF POLICE, but saw no such restriction on the spot I'd chosen.

I clicked open the trunk for Beverly so she could claim her picnic cooler, borrowed for my days at the crafts fair. I went around to the front of the car and plucked the piece of paper from under my windshield wiper.

I unfolded lined, white paper, the size of the pages in a black-and-white marble-cover composition book. BACK OFF, I read. OR

SOMETHING BAD WILL HAPPEN TO YOU, TOO.

What? The lettering was like that of a child's, in ballpoint pen, but more suited to crayons. A joke? Maybe, but my knees didn't know the difference, and I had to support myself by leaning on the hood of the car.

I looked around the lot. Other than Beverly, who had placed her red-and-white cooler on the ground while she closed the trunk, I saw only a woman with a child in a stroller. A balloon tied to the handle whipped around the woman's face, and both mother and child laughed over it. The day was sunny, with a pleasant breeze. The note in my hand seemed out of place, meant for the darkness of an urban alley, not the cheery suburban setting of downtown Lincoln Point.

I thought how lucky that Maddie wasn't around. It hit home to me again how much I worried about her safety when she was with me.

"What is it?" Beverly asked. "Don't tell me you got a ticket? Too bad we don't know anyone who can fix it."

Nothing to worry Beverly about. A joke. Kids out of school with nothing better to do.

"It's an ad for that new Chinese restaurant. You probably have one, too," I said.

I hoped not.

I asked myself: Why is it that lately every time I'm with my nephew, I'm hiding something? Before this week's episodes with Linda, Tippi Wyatt, and Dudley Crane, I led a normal life. Some would have called it boring, in fact. Now I was party to borderline obstruction of justice, and the object of a threatening note.

I'd immediately tucked the note into a zipper pocket on the outside of my purse, with no intention of showing it to Skip. It would only serve to give him ammunition, I reasoned. He'd probably say, "Ditto, Auntie. Back off." If I remembered correctly, he had recently used the same phrase on me.

I nearly changed my mind about going into the station. I was afraid deception would show on my face, that somehow Skip's cop training would tell him I had something in my purse that should be reported to the police.

When he greeted me in the foyer, a few seconds after I stepped through the sliding front doors of the building, I jumped.

"You look surprised to see me," Skip said. "When I'm the one who should be shocked." He had that teasing look in his eyes that I'm sure he used successfully in his dating life. And maybe also in his cop life.

"I, uh, have an idea I wanted to share with you."

"I'll bet you do. Maddie's gone home, and now what? Might as well play detective."

My nephew was fast becoming just another annoying young man, like my son. "Skip, I have enough to do. That's not why I'm here."

"Come on back," he said, leading the way to his cubicle. "It's a good thing you're my favorite aunt."

"I'm your only aunt."

"Exactly."

Smart guy. I wasn't sure he deserved my help, with that attitude. On the other hand, I was the one who needed information.

After only slight jostling among officers coming and going in the narrow passageways of the cubicle maze, we settled in front of Skip's desk. The agreeable breeze that wafted outdoors was singularly missing back here. I imagined it took a few days for the old building to cool down after an extended heat wave.

"I think I know who Jason Reed's biological father is," I said, positioning myself to capture a bit of action from the fan.

While I ran down my logic, Skip swiveled back and forth in his chair, expressionless. I wished I'd brought him one of Willie's cookies again, to soften him up.

"Interesting," he said, when I'd finished.

"Interesting how? As in, you'll look into it? Get DNA and all that? Are you at least testing to see if Tippi is Jason's mother?"

"I can't talk about the details, Aunt Gerry. You know better than that." Skip leaned closer, and lowered his voice. Cubicle protocol, I figured. "I know I've given you a heads-up a couple of times this week, about the Reeds, and maybe that was a bad precedent. I'm sorry if I misled you. I have to treat your ideas the way I would handle any tip that came in over the hotline."

"Tips? Is that what I'm giving you? Maybe I should call in on the hotline, then. I'll bet I'd get more satisfaction." I couldn't remember being so upset with my nephew since he was a teenager and kept Richard out past his curfew.

Skip tapped a pencil on his desk. "I'm sure it's frustrating for you. I know you feel a certain connection to Tippi Wyatt, having been at the crime scene, for all practical purposes. And with Maddie, at that. And I know Dudley Crane was a friend. And that you want to protect Linda. But you wouldn't want me to do something against policy, would you?"

He was right. I was learning something new about my nephew. This was the first time I'd tried to interact with him on a professional level, and he was being just that. Professional. I had no right to be upset.

But that didn't mean I'd have to give up completely, either. He was a public servant, and I was the public.

"How about a couple of 'concerned citizen' questions, then?" I asked.

A deep sigh from Skip, followed by a gesture that said, "Be my guest."

"Has Tippi's body been buried already? Or sent somewhere?"

Skip hesitated, as if he were consulting some rulebook about what to tell a concerned citizen. "We're waiting on information about possible relatives."

"Meanwhile you can get a DNA sample, right? Oops, sorry, that was outside tip-givers' boundaries."

Skip laughed.

"And the gun issue? Whether the same gun was used for both murders?"

Skip gave me a look that said, "not a chance," which immediately turned to surprise when "Take Me Out to the Ball

Game" rang through the room. It was good to hear his hearty laugh.

"Maddie," I said.

"Sweet."

We took turns telling Maddie we missed her already and promised we'd call often.

I left soon after, quitting before I was too far behind.

# CHAPTER 19

As soon as the automatic doors opened to let me out of the police building, I peered in the direction of my car. The feeling of panic I had when I read the note came back. From a distance my windshield seemed bare, however, and after several friendly "good afternoon" exchanges with non-threatening types crossing the civic-center plaza, my nervous system settled down.

I did a number of errands that I'd let slide in the last couple of weeks. I stopped at the library to pick up flyers for the Friends' book sale and bought a book on California history for Angela at Rosie Norman's book-store. I drove by the theater to see what was playing for when Beverly and I resumed our movie nights, though I knew they'd be showing the same Maddie-level movie all summer. I browsed the card shop and chose a sympathy note for an old friend in San Francisco whose husband died, and a birthday greeting for a woman who helped out with the library's literacy program. I made a run to buy boring paper products, toothpaste, vitamins, and other staples for the house.

The tasks took a chunk out of the afternoon. I told myself this spurt of running around town had nothing to do with not wanting to go home to an empty house.

I thought I'd exhausted the options offered by Lincoln Point — I had no dry cleaning in the summer, and all my shoes were in good repair — until I spotted red-white-and-blue banners hanging from a small building, a block off Springfield Boulevard. The campaign headquarters of Jack Wilson. As a concerned citizen, I felt an immediate need to get myself informed before Election Day.

I parked around the back of the building, scanning the area as I left my car, and beeped the alarm to on. Nothing like a little note to make one paranoid.

The door to the Wilson headquarters was wide open, which meant no air-conditioning, but it couldn't be worse than the LPPD, I figured. Right I was. The building, a converted cottage, had a nice cross breeze. The ambience was also helped by the fact that there was no peeling paint, nor stains left by felons past, on the walls. They were freshly painted, a stark white, the better to show off posters of the candidate, in his navy blue suit and red power tie, in full smiling splendor.

Gail Musgrave, the sister who was passed over for the family jewel, as I now thought of her, sat close to the front door at a desk piled high with brochures, all with the same smiling photo of Jack Wilson. A large, boxy briefcase that I recognized as Gail's cosmetics samples bag was by her feet. Double duty today, I guessed, doing both of her part-time jobs.

The room was quiet. The phones and faxes sat silent, as if they'd been turned off. Not what I expected to find, until I remembered — it was late Friday afternoon in the summer. Everyone was on the road already, for Tahoe to the north or Santa Cruz to the south, for a weekend away.

Gail looked crisp, as usual, in a sleeveless, pastel flower-print dress. "Hi, Gerry. What brings you here?"

The same question Beverly had asked of Chuck Reed in Sheridan's. Was I that out of place? Considering that I'd never been here, nor to anyone else's campaign headquarters since I was in college (Mary Lou would be ashamed of her mother-in-law), the answer was, yes.

"I thought I'd get caught up on the issues," I said, sounding hollow even to myself. I picked up a brochure.

Gail laughed. "Sure you did."

"Lots of people have just happened to find themselves in the neighborhood today." This from Karen Striker, entering from a doorway to the right, carrying a large carton that partially hid her tanned thighs.

For once I was glad not to have the Porter red hair and corresponding quick-to-blush skin. "I guess there's not much going on in this town, and the appearance of a fifty-thousand-dollar gem is big news."

Karen smiled and brushed her denim shorts clear of dust from the box she'd set down. "I'm trying to convince Jack to bring in the gem and charge people to have a look. Or, excuse me, make a campaign contribution to have a look."

Karen seemed to be a good customer of Gail's, as well as a campaign worker — in spite of very casual dress, her makeup was extensive and perfect. Her fingernails were done in a summery salmon color, and her toenails, prominent against her yellow flip-flops, matched.

"We have our sapphire back, and all is well," Gail said. "I'm not sure I want to parade it around town." She was making an attempt to be light, but I detected a serious undertone. I didn't miss the "we," either.

I had so many questions. Too bad this was not the time to ask her to speculate on where the gem had been, or why her father had chosen to keep it a secret from her. And what she thought of her parents' decision to will it solely to Jack.

"As long as you're here, help yourself to some iced tea and cookies," Karen said, pointing to a small kitchenette off the main room. "I don't recommend the coffee, which has been sitting there all day."

Iced tea sounded good. Plus, a little refreshment break would extend my stay naturally. "I think I will. Thanks," I said, and headed toward the doorway Karen indicated. My plan was to come up with a growth/no-growth question to give my visit some credibility.

The room, probably the kitchen in the original bungalow, had been divided clumsily into a storage area and a small nook encompassing the sink, stove, and refrigerator. Rolled-up posters, boxes of bumper stickers, and bags of campaign buttons overflowed into the snack area. No chairs or tables would fit.

I squeezed between unopened cartons and

made it to the counter, where a tray held a pitcher of tea, condiments, and a plate of store-bought filled cookies.

A coatrack, out of place only inches from the counter, held a navy jacket on a hanger. A red tie was looped around the hook of the hanger, producing the effect of a store-window mannequin. Jack Wilson's costume, as seen in the posters in the main room.

I smiled as a memory came to mind, of my husband, who also used to keep a nice jacket and tie at his office, in case he was called to an impromptu meeting with a client. Otherwise, he worked in his favorite blue cotton shirts, sleeves rolled up.

Thoughts of Ken, combined with the cramped quarters, threw me off balance. As I reached for a cup, my oversize purse swung around and knocked Wilson's jacket from the hanger. Luckily no tea was spilled in the incident.

Other things spilled, however, from the jacket. Two bronze-color pens, with JACK WILSON FOR COUNCIL in bold letters, and a small notepad. I looked over my shoulder, hoping to be alone with my misdeed and make things right before anyone noticed. I heard Karen and Gail talking in the outer room and knew I was clear.

I put the pens back in the outside pocket,

and picked up the small notepad. In bright blue letters, I read (not that I was actually reading, but the letters passed before my eyes, unbidden), CRANE'S JEWELERS, INC.

Odd that Jack would have a pad from Dudley Crane's store. I would have expected Jack to go as far as he needed to — the Milpitas mall, for example — for jewelry purchases, rather than patronize the business of his staunch rival.

The first two pages of the pad had intriguing doodles. I guessed it was Dudley's hand that had drawn the excellent representations of various pieces of jewelry. A pendant, a ring, a bracelet, a choker — all featuring the same stone.

A stone I recognized, even in a sketched version. One that had been at the bottom of my tote. The Wilsons' Ceylon sapphire.

In printed letters, along the vertical edge of the top page, I read, J — PICK ONE!

I heard the phone ring in the main room. Bad timing. Either Karen or Gail would have to answer, leaving the other one free to come back here. The pages of the notepad were furled, and I didn't think I could get them straightened out quickly enough to insert the pad neatly into the jacket pocket.

Only one thing to do. I stuffed the pad

into my purse.

When Karen appeared moments later, I was stirring unneeded sugar into my iced tea. I never did that, but I wanted to look busy enough to have stayed in the kitchen longer than it would take to pour a cup of tea and return to the outer room.

"Everything okay back here?" Karen asked.

"Oh, yes. I was trying to decide whether to take a cookie." I was sure my hand was shaking, but Karen didn't seem to notice anything off about my outward appearance.

"Please do. First, you're skinny, and second, we need to finish these up. The weekend kids are great about bringing homemade goodies." Karen covered her mouth, a gesture I remembered from when she spilled the beans the other night about Jason's birthplace. "Sorry. I didn't mean you should eat the inferior stuff. No offense."

I laughed and took a cookie. I bit off a piece. "None taken."

Karen needed to work on her brain-to-mouth timing, as I would often tell my high-school students, but I was glad she had her own gaffe to cover up and wasn't aware of mine.

I needed to get out of the building. Between the threatening note from my windshield and Jack's (Dudley's) notepad, I felt my purse was the most interesting thing in Lincoln Point at the moment and I wanted to go home and study its contents.

We walked into the outer room, where Gail was finishing a phone conversation.

I looked at my watch. "Is it that late already? I'd better be going."

"We're about to lock up anyway," Karen said. "We're just waiting for Jack to pick us up. We're going to dinner and then there's a meeting this evening to discuss what to do in light of the empty spot on the ballot." She lowered her voice appropriately at "empty spot" as if to honor the deceased.

"Is it an open meeting?" I asked.

"Oh, definitely," Karen said. "It's at eight in city hall. You should —"

Gail put her hand out, nearly blocking Karen's mouth. "Well, technically, yes, it's open. But it will be very boring, I promise you."

*On the contrary,* I thought, *it might be even more interesting than my tote.*

"Thanks for the warning," I said, and moved toward the door to the outside. At which point, I'd be officially walking off with property not my own.

Moving in a straight line, but turned

sideways to wave good-bye to Karen and Gail, I bumped into a solid mass. About my height, and muscular.

"Gerry?" Among the hundreds of faces of Jack Wilson that surrounded me on the walls, the real Jack emerged in front of me, obstructing my path. "What a surprise," he said.

I really had to work on my community involvement.

"Gerry's curious about the sapphire," Karen said.

Gail gave her a silencing look. I suspected there would be some discussion later over Karen's naïvete and openness, quite unbefitting a political campaigner. I tried to remember when Gail had become so serious and uncommunicative. Perhaps she was simply tired, schlepping cosmetics by day, taking classes at night, and working for her brother's campaign.

"Well, of course, I'm curious," I said. "Isn't everyone? But I'm especially interested in how it came to be in Dudley Crane's possession."

Now who was not thinking before speaking? I had no evidence that the sapphire had been anywhere but with Jack Wilson, and then with Jason Reed (and then me). It was my guess, and only a guess — once I ruled out Jason's sneaking into a private home to steal a piece of jewelry — that Jason and/or Just Eddie had stolen it in the Crane robbery.

The effect of my guess rippled through the room. Gail dropped a stack of brochures on the floor. Karen looked puzzled and began to cough. Jack stretched his thick neck nervously.

"I'm sure I have no idea what you're talking about," Jack said. At nearly six o'clock on Friday afternoon, while most voters were in shorts and tank tops, Jack Wilson was in a three-piece suit. Maybe that wasn't the only reason he was sweating. "I doubt that poor Dudley was the one who stole the gem."

"Of course not," I said.

Jack turned to Karen and Gail. Before my eyes, he snapped his fingers. "Can I get a cold drink here?"

I thought that behavior went out when love beads came in. I decided to leave before witnessing the women's response.

"I'll see you all at the meeting tonight," I said. I pulled a brochure from my tote and waved it. "Meanwhile I'll just go home and read up on the issues."

I stuffed the brochure back into my tote, where it would eventually fall to the bottom and join expired coupons for soft drinks and paper towels, plus receipts for parking garages, the ice cream shop, and photographs developed in years past.

I seemed to be doing a lot of thinking in my car lately.

As I'd gone about my errands earlier, I'd thought about the timeline Beverly had given me on the gemstone. The whole story seemed more and more suspicious. The gem was present and accounted for, apparently, in Gail and Jack's mother's possession, until it was bequeathed to Jack only.

Now I wondered if, by any chance, Gail had contested the will and then, conveniently, Jack reported the gem stolen, making her challenge moot.

A wild leap, many of which I'd been making lately. There was nothing to suggest that Gail was anything but loving and loyal to her brother. Or that Jack would go to such lengths as to fake its theft, to keep it from his sister.

I turned off Springfield, onto Gettysburg, working out a reasonable scenario. The gem had been in my tote; I needed to know its route, from the beginning.

I thought I remembered correctly that if a will is contested, it has to be filed with the court, and becomes a matter of public record. I made a note to check that out. It wasn't pleasant to be hoping for dissent in a family, but my newest theory depended on it.

I needed someone to talk to, but I knew Beverly was at a meeting of police volunteers. Nothing to do but work it out on my own. I spoke my thoughts half out loud, as if Ken were present to bounce things off. I'd done that less and less lately, which I wondered about. I wasn't sure I wanted him to slip away like that.

For now, I addressed my visor, which had a photo of Ken clipped to it.

Suppose Jack gave the stone secretly to Dudley Crane to fence, to avoid dealing with Gail's challenge. Dudley came up with some designs, which he doodled on a pad for Jack. The whole show of bad blood between the men was just that, a show. They might even be on the same side of the growth issue, but that wasn't what mattered to them anyway. Probably neither candidate cared what happened to Lincoln Point. The voters were being misled and riled up (how aggravating, Ken) while Jack and Dudley were coconspirators in a fifty-thousand-dollar fraud. Twice that amount, if Jack's insurance paid for the allegedly stolen gem.

The stone, then, would have an interesting history. It would have been reported stolen (by Jack) when it wasn't, and not reported stolen (by Dudley) when it was.

I sensed another tip on its way to my nephew.

But first, I had to talk to Jason, who might have been the one to (truly) steal the stone from Crane's Jewelers, where it shouldn't have been.

# CHAPTER 20

I turned down my street at about six thirty. The meeting at city hall was at eight, giving me plenty of time to prepare dinner for one. Most of the time I didn't mind being alone. I was free to cook what and when I wanted; there was no one to challenge my choices, whether of leisure activities, spending habits, or décor, no one to explain myself to. "Sweet," Skip called it, referring to his own single life.

But right after sharing my space with someone as wonderful to be with as my granddaughter, I missed the company. I was tempted to call LA, but I knew I should leave my son and his family to reconnect after nearly a month.

Since I'd be leaving soon again for city hall, I parked on the street in front of my driveway. It had been a long day, beginning with leaving Maddie off at the airport. I had acquired what seemed a massive amount of

304

information, which sent several murder scenarios running through my head. I looked forward to a break, with fresh iced tea, leftover mac and cheese in Maddie's honor, and maybe a short session with my Bronx apartment.

I wanted to look through my fabric scraps for something that would be reminiscent of the white piqué curtains I'd put up over the sink in the life-size apartment. One of my favorite memories was of the window that wasn't there. Ken had painted (poorly) a beach scene on the wall over the sink, and I'd hung the curtains, creating the illusion of a window that overlooked the ocean. The perspective was perfect, but Ken was not as good an artist as he was an architect, and the pea-soup color waves brought a smile every time I thought of them.

My smile dissipated quickly as I exited my car and walked toward my door. Not another trauma — so soon after my windshield incident? There, on my lovely, newly re-painted blue front door was a note.

I approached slowly, as if the note might leap out at me at any moment, and knock my body down, the way it had already knocked my head around. I could tell before I detached it that the note was on different paper from the earlier one, and not folded.

That was it — it was innocuous, from a neighbor ("borrowed your lawn mower," it might say, as June had written once) or from a delivery person. Whatever my intellect devised, the pounding of my heart said my nervous system thought otherwise.

I snatched the note from the door, summoning a spirit of annoyance, pretending to myself that I cared more about a smudge the masking tape might leave on the paint than about the contents of the page.

BACK OFF, I read. The same message, seemingly printed by a different hand, as if someone wanted me to know that *everyone* wanted me to back off.

I'd come straight home from Jack Wilson's campaign headquarters, so I ruled out that group. I thought of them only because I'd so recently upset Gail and Jack with my curiosity and intrusive comments.

I had my key ready, then thought about calling the police before entering my house. Too paranoid? Before I could make up my mind, a dark-clothed figure came into view from the side bushes. The figure brushed past me, missing me by only a few inches, and ran down the driveway to a bicycle that had been lying on June's lawn.

I was stunned, but not so much that I couldn't study the retreating figure. A short, chunky person, wearing a hooded sweat-shirt. In this heat? He had clearly dressed for the occasion.

I caught a glimpse also of a backpack, limiting the number of possibilities to every single kid in Lincoln Point between the ages of six and eighteen. This backpack had a distinct design — different shades of green and black patches. A camouflage pattern. Most likely a fairly common design, but the one I was most familiar with belonged to Jason Reed. And Jason was short, and had a bike like the one I'd just seen.

I felt better knowing (at least, in my mind) who had been threatening me. I saw it for the childish attempt it was, to keep me out of his business. Strangely, instead of being angry, I felt more and more sorry for Jason.

Still, when I entered the house, I made the room search that had become too regular a procedure for my taste. I carried my portable phone as I checked nooks and crannies, and punched in Linda's number when I saw that all was well inside.

"Is Jason there?" I asked. No "hello, Linda." Sympathy and compassion notwith-standing, I was out of patience with the Reeds.

"Did you talk to Skip? Did you find out who killed Dudley?" she asked. No "hello" from her, either.

"I talked to Skip. Now, can you please just tell me if Jason is there?"

"He's not. He's out on his bike."

I didn't know whether to be glad or not, or even whether I should care. "I'd like you both to come by when he gets home."

"I don't know when to expect him."

"He's on his way," I said.

The mac-and-cheese casserole was way past its time; I could tell by how far back in the refrigerator it had landed. Peanut butter and black currant jelly on the last of my homemade bread would have to do. I held my gourmet sandwich in one hand and sorted through odd scraps of fabric with the other. A calming and productive activity. I found a patch of oilcloth that would go nicely in my next picnic scene, and a fun animal print I could offer to Betty for the room box she'd created for her newest grandchild.

By the time the doorbell rang, I'd almost forgotten the stress of the day. I looked through the peephole to see Linda, with Jason, who hadn't bothered to change his sweatshirt. Dumb? Cocky? Or both?

We settled in the atrium with cold drinks. I'd sent Maddie off with every remaining cookie, so my cupboard was bare of sweets.

"Sorry I don't have much to offer," I said, mostly to Jason. Ken would have chuckled as I apologized to the kid who was badgering me, trying to ruin my peace of mind.

Linda waved her hand. "We're fine."

Jason kept his chin on his chest, his usual posture.

I was conscious of the time — I wanted to get to the ballot meeting by eight — but I didn't want to rush headlong into all my theories and accusations. I started with a question.

"How did your desk get into Dudley Crane's hand?" I asked Linda.

"You don't beat around the bush, do you?"

*You don't know the half of it,* I thought.

"Well? I don't have a lot of time, Linda. And we have a lot to talk about."

"I know. I told the police all this already on Wednesday. And you said you didn't want to talk to me until Maddie left, so —"

This was Linda, assigning blame. "The Governor Winthrop desk, Linda?" I paused after each word, for clarity, and to make a point, I hoped.

"I took the desk home with me. I wanted to show it to Jason, to let him know I found it."

"Why not show him the gem itself, instead of planting the gem in my bag?"

Linda shrugged. Her eyes darted toward her son. Jason had plunked himself on a chair under the jade tree, making him seem all the more shadowy and brooding. He sipped from a soft-drink can.

"She thought I'd take it back from her," Jason said. "She doesn't trust me." His voice was still high, as a child's.

"No, no, it wasn't that," his mother said.

But we all knew it was exactly that. I also understood that Linda had lost many men in her life, one way or another, and she couldn't risk alienating Jason. At fifteen, he was of the age when many kids left home — homes a lot more stable than the Reeds'.

"When was the last time you saw your desk?"

"Monday, after the fair. It was on my workbench in the garage," Linda said, looking at Jason.

"She thinks I did something with it."

"Did you?" I asked.

"No, it wasn't me."

"Jason, isn't about time you told us the truth? Nothing can be worse for you than getting into all these lies, to your mother, to the police." I thought of using the "oh, what a tangled web" quote, but figured it would be lost on Jason and Linda both.

Finally, Jason poured it out. "It was Just

Eddie," he said. "He started, like, following me around at school. Told me he had some things lined up that I could help him with, and make some money on the side. I said no at first, but he kept at me, and he was all friendly and made it sound like he really cared about me."

Linda sipped her tea, calmer than I would be if my son were telling a story like this. Not the first time she was hearing it, I guessed.

"So, it was Just Eddie who took your mom's desk from the garage?"

"I guess so."

Not too convincing, but I pressed forward.

"And this was after you and Just Eddie robbed Crane's Jewelers a week ago Tuesday?"

Jason shook his head and opened his mouth, as if to correct me, then pressed his lips together, the way his adoptive mother did when she was stressed (a case for nurture, not nature?) and nodded. "Yeah."

"And one of the things you took in that robbery was that sapphire?"

"Yeah."

So far, so good. If true, this fit with my idea that Jack Wilson had given it in secret to Crane, to fence, but it was stolen for real before he could do anything with it.

"How did you end up with the gem instead of Just Eddie?" I asked.

"I . . . uh . . . it's complicated."

"And you're sure Just Eddie took the desk from the garage, after your mom removed the sapphire?"

"Yeah, Just Eddie," Jason said.

Why did I feel Jason had slipped from the truth again? I wished I could accept what he said at face value — it would be so handy to think that Just Eddie killed Tippi over some issue with Jason, and then murdered Crane, framing Linda. I had a clear picture of Just Eddie wanting Jason back, and therefore getting rid of both mothers, in a way. I was sure that, given more time, I could smooth out the details, such as, what about Chuck? Maybe Just Eddie figured (as I did) that Chuck wouldn't care one way or the other where Jason ended up.

I wanted to press Jason, still feeling he was holding back something important, but Linda could wait no longer for her own agenda.

"Did you talk to Skip?" Linda asked. "What do the police know? Do they have any other evidence against me? Besides the desk?"

"Should they?"

"No, but people plant things."

Like you planted the sapphire on me, I wanted to say.

"Here's the bad news, Linda. My nephew is not about to tell me privileged information. But I have some ideas that I've come up with on my own."

"Such as?"

I looked at Jason. As aggravated as I was with the family, I had no desire to traumatize a young boy, delinquent or not.

"He knows," Linda said.

I raised my eyebrows. "He knows . . . ?"

"He knows Tippi Wyatt is his mother." Linda's head fell to her chest. Now the two of them looked as much like natural mother and son as I'd ever seen.

"Have you agreed to DNA testing?"

"There's no need to. I knew as soon as I heard the woman came from Brooklyn by way of Winona."

"But you weren't going to say anything?" Until I butted in, I meant.

I wondered how hard the police had come down on her. This gave Linda an excellent motive to kill Tippi. Jason's birth mother might have wanted him back. But she was being framed for Crane's murder, not Tippi's, and I was once again traveling in dizzying circles.

One thing at a time. "The adoption wasn't

exactly above-board, was it?" I asked Linda.

Linda shook her head, her eyes sad and watery. "I was old, Gerry. In my forties. And Chuck wasn't that enthusiastic, as you know. He —"

"Don't say that about my father," Jason said, in an angry voice. "My father loves me."

"Of course he does, Jason, now that he knows you." Linda turned to me to explain, as if Jason could take only so much reasoning. "He just wasn't willing to go through a big ordeal to get a child through the regular channels, so I did the best I could to make a family."

"I know you did, Linda," I said, and meant it.

I looked at Jason, who was sobbing quietly. I had never seen him look so vulnerable, not even as a toddler. He seemed to have been born with a chip on his shoulder that grew to mammoth proportions in the dozen years that I'd known him.

"I'm sorry I almost knocked you over, Mrs. Porter." I could barely understand him, but I knew his apology was genuine. "I was afraid you'd find out I wasn't legal, and I didn't want to be taken away from my parents."

My heart went out to him. In the last

analysis, Jason was not a hardened criminal. He was a kid who couldn't catch a break, one I'd known since he was a toddler. I thought again how lucky Maddie was, to have two birth parents who loved each other and who doted on her on a daily basis. To say nothing of her northern California fans.

"You didn't hurt me, Jason. And I would never want to hurt you or take you away from your parents."

"I just wanted to, like, scare you off."

"And you thought that sending me two notes would do it?"

"Not two," Jason said, seeming surprised. "I just put that one on your door."

"You didn't put one under my windshield wiper earlier today?"

Jason's eyes widened, his face scrunched in confusion. "No, I swear. Just the one."

Unfortunately, I believed him. I was glad Linda was so wrapped up in her own problems that she didn't think to ask me about the second note.

I hoped I'd have as easy a time forgetting about it.

"Thanks for not lecturing me, Gerry," Linda said, as she left my house. Jason was ahead of her, already in her car. "I've learned a lot this past couple of weeks. I know what Jason and I have to do . . . about the robbery, and we're ready to do it. I was just hoping you might smooth the way a little? With Skip? Jason is only a kid, and Just Eddie dragged him into it, making stealing things look glamorous, you know."

I was happy that I didn't know, that my son hadn't been seduced by adventures outside the law. "I'll do my best."

I didn't have the heart to tell Linda how low my stock was with my nephew at this time.

# CHAPTER 21

Seven thirty in the evening, and I was exhausted. Did I really want to leave my comfortable home and drive across town for a boring meeting at city hall? I'd forgotten why I wanted to go in the first place.

I felt so bad for Linda, having to go to the police with her only son and listen to him confess to committing a crime. I toyed with the idea of calling Skip, but in the end opted to keep out of it. What would I say to him? "Go easy on them, they're our friends?" Skip knew that already. I ran the risk of insulting him and, worse, hurting Jason's chances for leniency.

I wanted to ask Skip if he'd done anything about my idea that Just Eddie was Jason's father. The fact that Just Eddie had been courting Jason gave a modicum of credibility to my theory. (Isn't it every father's dream that his son will be his partner in crime?) I hadn't had the heart to bring the matter up with Linda and Jason. They had enough to think about.

There was also the matter of insurance fraud. I considered calling in an anonymous tip about Jack Wilson's sapphire. I tried to see it from the point of view of the LPPD. In May, Wilson reported that his sapphire had been stolen. Last week it turned up in my tote bag, thanks to Jason and Linda Reed. It would seem to the police that Jason stole the gem from Wilson a couple of months ago.

I could only hope that Jason would tell the whole story, not only about Just Eddie's involvement in the robbery, but that the gem had been in Crane's vault. The police would have to wonder how the gem ended up there. Surely they wouldn't think that Dudley had stolen the gem. They could figure out the fraud, the conspiracy between Dudley Crane and Jack Wilson, themselves.

I took the Crane's Jewelers notepad from my purse and studied the intricate pencil drawings. Dudley had been quite an artist. The pieces came to life under his hand. He'd used different pencil strokes to depict the tips and the facets and added some "rays" to show how the gem would reflect light. The ring setting looked worthy of a gift to Elizabeth Taylor; the bracelet version included smaller stones on either side. I had to remind myself that I wasn't the one being asked to make a selection for my jewelry collection.

The question was whether to turn the pad over to the police. I saw the "J — PICK ONE!" notation as sufficiently incriminating. Dudley Crane asking Jack Wilson to choose a setting for the piece to be fenced.

I could hear my nephew now. After a grueling interview about how I came to have the pad in my possession in the first place, he'd give me five other explanations for its existence. The half-used Crane pad had been thrown in the trash, and any one of Lincoln Point's citizens had picked it up and used it for doodling. Crane was drawing a few options for some other stone. For some other customer. At some other time, perhaps years ago. It could have been a homework assignment in jeweler's school. And so on.

What was it doing in Jack Wilson's jacket pocket? He picked it up as litter and was planning to toss it in the trash but hadn't gotten around to it yet. Or someone else put it there. It could have been Gail, or Karen, or Louie at the dry cleaners. It could have been Skip's nosy, detective-wannabe Aunt Gerry, wanting to make trouble.

Besides the pad, all I had was my gut feeling, which, I had to admit, wouldn't add much to the case for sending a man to prison.

The ramifications of Jack Wilson's being arrested for fraud finally came to me. Later than they should have, and I could only blame the constant twists and turns my mind had to take over the past few days. Even if Wilson was eventually cleared of a crime, the fact of his indictment would most likely ruin his political career.

More was at stake than this year's seat on the city council.

Too much to keep straight. It was almost more than I could handle.

One thing keeping me from throwing up my hands and abandoning my pseudoinvestigation was the note on my windshield. Its message had the opposite effect from the words. I couldn't back off until I found out who put the note there. What was my alternative? Put an ad in the *Lincolnite* that "GP has officially backed off"?

My musings energized me. I splashed water on my face, changed out of my shorts into a long sleeveless dress, and headed out the door.

I was curious to see how Jack Wilson handled himself. I realized I'd ruled out

Wilson as Crane's killer once I figured out they were coconspirators, but that was not a good reason. It wouldn't be the first falling-out among thieves that resulted in murder. One or the other of them could have gotten greedy. Maybe one of their fights, their last one, wasn't just for show.

Lincoln Point's government was based on a city manager/council system. Seven council members were elected for staggered four-year terms. Each year in January, the council elected one of its members mayor and another city manager. It was never clear to me what the difference was, except that it was the mayor, currently Larry Roberts, older than me by a decade, who was the public face of the city.

Meanwhile, the public building of the city, city hall, was in no better shape than the police department facility or the library. The meeting was held in a large, non-air-conditioned assembly room, with a stage at one end, and battered folding chairs in long rows throughout the hall. Tall, narrow windows, open only at the top, provided minimal ventilation. At the back of the room, by the entrance, were uncovered picnic tables with coffee, tea, and cookies-by-the-tub. I wondered where those homemade goodies were that Karen talked about. Going directly to Wilson campaign headquarters, I assumed.

Three spots on the council were open this year, but only one seat had been contested. The two incumbents were shoo-ins. Now, with Dudley Crane dead, unless another candidate stepped forward at this late date, Jack Wilson was also a shoo-in.

I skipped the refreshment tables and walked toward the center of the hall, overflowing with people. No wonder I'd had to park two blocks down from the civic center. Who knew that council meetings drew this many citizens? It seemed everyone — or at least as many adults as I'd ever seen at a Fourth of July parade — had gathered in this old building on a hot summer night.

If Jack and Gail had intended to keep the meeting attendance down by discouraging people as they'd tried to dissuade me, they failed.

When I finally tuned in to the conversations around me, I learned that it wasn't the discussion of the city-council seat that was the main attraction for the assembled masses. The talk was of murder, and how to make Lincoln Point safe again.

As I passed Mabel and Jim Quinlan, I overheard snippets of Jim's story. He was recounting the tale we'd heard at the crafts fair, of his and Mabel's being in the vicinity of Tippi Wyatt's body the very night she was murdered. That made three of us who seemed to care about Tippi, the stranger who was the first murder victim in the city in more than a year. I couldn't help be sad that, if I understood correctly, Tippi Wyatt's search for her child had led to her death.

"Thinking of running for council, Geraldine?" Because it was Postmaster Brian Cooney, creeping up behind me, who asked this question, the tone was not light and friendly, but belligerent, as if the speaker was presenting a dare or a threat.

"Oh, are you, too?" I asked him. Why not let him think I had a position on Lincoln Point development that he might care about? He gave me a pouty frown and moved on. This was the man who called himself Mr. Puppeteer at our fairs and holiday parties. I made a mental note to check out his show sometime to be sure it was suitable for children and not a reenacted horror story.

I looked around for a seat, greeting friends as I walked through the crowd. There was Susan Giles in a white off-the-shoulder blouse. I waved to Gene and Judy, who ran the dry-cleaning establishment; Sadie, who'd been scooping ice cream on Springfield Boulevard since I was a child; Carol and George from the coffee shop; Debbie Sheridan (Chuck Reed's new girlfriend, apparently) from the ceramics shop and restaurant.

Jack Wilson, his sister, and best friend, Karen (maybe now an official assistant?), sat in the first row in front of the stage, surrounded by a phalanx of adoring young people who looked like they'd torn off their I LOVE JACK WILSON buttons just before they entered the hall, in order to seem nonpartisan.

If anyone asked, it would be easier to list the people who were not here. Beverly was home resting, I hoped. Maddie's visit had put an extra strain on her, as much as they loved being together. Linda was understandably among the missing, as were her two ex-husbands, probably for different reasons.

In a far corner by the stage, I saw Just Eddie, leaning against the wall. I wondered if he'd been hired to work tonight. I also wondered how soon he'd be in jail.

"Gerry, Gerry, over here." Betty Fine beckoned me to an empty seat next to her and her granddaughter, Lucy (now in her thirties, and not the best student I'd encountered in my career at Abraham Lincoln High).

"Do you usually come to these meetings?" I asked Betty, settling beside her.

Betty had availed herself of the free coffee, which attacked my nostrils. I was sorry I'd offered to hold it for her while she struggled to get a tissue from her purse.

"Oh, no, and I doubt this is typical. This is my first, and I see lots of my neighbors who've never been, either. We're all worried about our safety."

The council members, six men and one woman, sat in a row on the stage behind a podium. *They had a lot to deal with tonight,* I thought, *including the discomfort of their obligatory suits and ties.*

At a few minutes past eight, Mayor Roberts (in an older gentleman's formal Western wear) strode to the podium, adjusted the mike, and called the meeting to order with the sound of wood on wood, the bang of a gavel.

"My, my," he said, stroking his bolo tie. "How nice to see so many people at this special meeting. I hope you'll all consider coming back to our regular meetings, which are held every second and fourth Tuesdays."

I detected a ring of insincerity. I would have bet that the council would never get any work done with this many people present on a regular basis, and preferred to work uninterrupted. Minutes of meetings were available in the library and archived on the city's website. In the last couple of years, meetings were broadcast on our local cable channel. I doubted many citizens even knew what number that channel was (I knew only because I'd watched my own appearance last spring, for a feature about the library's literacy program).

Sad to say, unless something affected us or our pocketbooks directly, most of us paid no attention to the work involved in the day-to-day operations for even a small city like Lincoln Point. Not many became passionate about library policy, public art, bicycle and pedestrian lane markings, transportation issues, or the upkeep of our parks. Something told me the politicians preferred it this way.

Roberts addressed the crowd in a somber voice. "Ladies and gentlemen, at this time, I'd like to call for a moment of silence for one of our fine citizens, a well-known and respected Lincoln Point businessman, and a worthy candidate for public office, Dudley Crane. Let us pray that he may rest in peace."

The hall fell silent. I used part of my time

to pray for peace for Tippi Wyatt also.

"Thank you, everyone. We extend our sympathies to the Crane family. They tell me that that they will let us know as soon as possible when memorial services will be held." (When the police released his body, I guessed.) Roberts had resumed his official tone, and the moment was over.

"Crane was a cheat," I heard behind me. Not so loud as to be disruptive, but rather timed to coincide with the rustle of clothing and throat clearing that immediately followed the period of silence. Cooney, again. I remembered hearing that he was unhappy with how Crane dealt with his mother's estate. Cooney claimed Dudley skimmed off the top a good deal more than the percentage due him under their contract. I hoped none of Dudley's relatives (only a daughter who lived in Seattle with her family), if they were present, were within earshot.

Roberts banged his gavel. "As you know, this is a special meeting to discuss the single, previously contested seat on the city council. We're not in regular session, so we can dispense with the formality of time limits, and so on. And you won't need to fill out the little blue cards before you can speak." Here, Roberts, the six council members behind him, and a smattering of the audience laughed. An in-joke for the more civic-minded among us, who'd attended meetings before and knew the protocol.

"I wonder what that means," Betty whispered to me. I shrugged my shoulders, not wanting to distract anyone who would mind missing a word of Roberts's speech.

"This is a critical time for our fair city" — I couldn't believe a twenty-first-century politician still used that phrase — "a turning point as far as our growth and development as a community."

We all knew at least that much. The city council appointed the planning commission, who formulated and recommended plans for the city, especially its physical development. They also selected a downtown committee, which oversaw outreach to the business community. The council had great power, through its appointees, to regulate growth and economic opportunities in Lincoln Point.

Among Crane's supporters, there was no clear second-in-command who might step up. If Jack Wilson ran unopposed, Crane's proposals would never see the light of day.

It was common knowledge, even among the most casual voters, that the open seat would be a tie-breaking seat. Six council members — four who were not up for reelection, and two incumbents — were split down the middle. I was ashamed to admit that I couldn't name which member stood for which position.

A man I recognized from a real estate office stood up, still dressed in a business suit. "It seems to me we ought to do everything we can to offer a pro-growth candidate, to balance the ticket. Otherwise, why have an election at all?"

"That's why we're here," Roberts said. For the life of me, I couldn't remember which side Roberts came down on. "We want to give you a chance to present a candidate. There's a certain amount of city funds available to assist if someone wants to run." This last announcement met with a round of applause.

A man I didn't know stood up, cap in hand, respectfully. "Why do we need an election to tell us that we should have more cops on the street? Does anyone in this town feel safe right now?"

A murmur of no's rippled through the assembly. From there it took off. A free-for-all, that Roberts's gavel and microphone were no match for. The orderly meeting became a rerun of the rally on the street earlier in the week.

"More development means more money for services."

"What are they doing with the money we already have?"

"Do you want them to raise our taxes?" (I didn't follow the thread of this person's argument, but she may not have meant it to be logical.)

"What good are low taxes if we're not safe on the street?"

"I'm afraid to leave my house at night."

"What about our kids? Who's next?"

Roberts banged his gavel over and over. I guessed he wished he had those little blue cards, after all. He shouted through the mike. "Please, please, we'll never get anywhere if we don't have order." The uproar ran its course, and the hall settled down. "If you raise your hands, we'll be happy to answer your questions."

A young man raised his hand. "Has there been any progress on the murder case?"

Not what Roberts expected when he invited questions. Before he could answer, Mike Rafferty, the chief of police (Skip's boss, whose son had been my student in AP English) stood up. When I turned to see him, I recognized at least one row of policemen, including my nephew, sitting in the back of the hall. I wondered if I could get through the crowd quickly enough to corner Skip when the meeting was over.

"We are using all our resources to investigate the crimes of the past week," the chief said. I was glad he made it plural, though he might have meant the jewelry-store robbery and Crane's murder. Rafferty was not in uniform, but his large physique and booming voice gave him the look and sound of authority.

The next few questions had the same "who killed Crane?" bent to them, and the chief's answer was a verbal anagram of his first statement.

*Was this time well spent?* I asked myself. I thought not. I could have stayed home and made an entire restaurant out of the little white plastic "tables" that held up the covers of pizza boxes. (I had an abundance of them from dinners with Maddie.)

Maybe I could salvage the evening. Before I could reconsider, my hand was in the air. "Mrs. Porter," Chief Rafferty said. I hoped he had only the fondest memories of me at PTA meetings.

I stood up. I thought I'd conquered my fear of public speaking during my first week of teaching, but this was an altogether different situation. I cleared my throat. I reminded myself that probably a third of the attendees had been my students during my thirty-year career. "Chief Rafferty, do you have any reason to believe that the murders of Tippi Wyatt and Dudley Crane are related?"

The buzz went through the hall. I picked out snatches of commentary, "good question" being the most prominent. I relaxed my hold on the chair in front of me and sat down.

"Good question," the chief echoed. "I'm sure you know that we can't divulge any information that would compromise our investigation."

I wondered if the "we" included my nephew.

I was happy with the follow-up questions — Was the same gun used? Were there fingerprints anywhere? Any more information on the woman? Did the woman have any relatives in Lincoln Point? The answer, however, was the same for all, a variation of "We can't comment on an open case."

With not much accomplished, to my mind, Roberts declared the meeting over. "We'll review tonight's discussion and submit a report, which will be available to you in the usual formats. Thank you all for coming." He pounded the gavel one last time.

I heard everything from "boo" to less polite ejaculations, over the din of hundreds of chairs scraping against the floor. Was this typical of council sessions? No issues were resolved, and people were more upset now than before the meeting started. We never even got back to the original agenda: Who would fill the ballot slot left vacant by Dudley's murder?

I probably should have stayed home and played with my furniture.

But then I wouldn't have (literally) run into Skip.

Of course, he did it deliberately. I could tell by the smirk and the twinkle and the . . . well . . . the Skip look. "I kept waiting for you to ask a question," he said to me. "I knew if you were in the room, you would, and" — he threw up his hands in mock glee — "you did."

"So, will you answer it for me?"

"You weren't happy with the chief's answer?"

"No, and neither were you, or you wouldn't be looking over your shoulder right now as you're asking me."

"Nice catch."

We walked out to the sidewalk and toward Springfield Boulevard, where my car was parked, eventually breaking away from the crowd. I secretly (stupidly) hoped there would be a note on my car while Skip was with me. "Imagine that!" I'd say, and submit the note for handwriting analysis.

"Do you want to grab a coffee?" Skip asked. We both looked up and down the street. The only beacon was the light from Sadie's ice cream shop.

"Ice cream it is," I said.

Being the only show in town, Sadie's was crowded, but with an escort like Skip, we got a table pretty quickly. Two high-school girls (I could spot them a mile away) vied for the privilege of giving Skip a menu. The other girl handed one to me and led us to a booth by the large window that looked onto Springfield Boulevard.

Sadie's was brightly lit, with everything — floor, walls, chairs, tables, servers' uniforms, signage — in pink and white. In our window seat, we were practically on display on the otherwise dimly lit boulevard.

I'd thought about what might have provoked someone (besides Jason) to warn me to back off. I'd concluded that the only reason anyone would have to think I was "investigating" was that they saw me at the police station. I seldom visited Skip there, and anyone who knew me would be aware of that. Now here I was slurping a mocha shake, across from a cop (eating a caramel cashew sundae) in Sadie's window for all the world to see.

I couldn't worry about it; for the moment anyway, I couldn't be safer. And there was a slight chance that Jason had lied about the second note.

"Linda and Jason will be showing up at the station in the morning," I said.

Skip nodded. "I caught the call right before I left for the meeting. I'm glad. And, really, if you had anything to do with their coming forward on their own — almost on their own — thanks."

"Meanwhile, there's another crime you may not be aware of yet."

I told Skip the history of the sapphire. He was relaxed, spooning ice cream into his mouth, but listening attentively. I could tell he hadn't already thought of the conspiracy theory. Maybe, before going on, I could take advantage of the moment.

"Was the same gun used in both murders?" I asked him. I could see my car, parked across the street. I strained to determine if there was anything under the windshield wiper. I hoped there was no stalker in the shadows, reading my lips.

Skip gave a hearty laugh. "Nice shot. You don't let me rest a minute, do you?"

"It was worth a try. It doesn't seem that long ago that I could fool you into thinking a fairy left money under your pillow."

"Nah, I never believed that crap."

"Your mother's heart will be broken." I drew a long, refreshing mouthful of chocolate shake through my straw. "Back to the sapphire. I, uh, may be able to help you when it comes to making a case for insurance fraud."

I dug in my purse and pulled out a business-size envelope that I'd used to protect the Crane notepad. I pulled out the pad and handed it to Skip. "What do you think? Doesn't it look like Dudley Crane and Jack Wilson had something going on the side?"

Skip whistled as he flipped back and forth between the pages that were written on. A good sign. He turned the book sideways to read the "PICK ONE" message.

Before he could ask, I said, "In case you're wondering, it fell out of a jacket."

# CHAPTER 22

Saturday morning, I felt I'd done all I could, with my limited information, to set things right in Lincoln Point. I'd been of some help with the Crane's Jewelers robbery by working with Linda and Jason. And I felt sure the Crane-Wilson insurance fraud wouldn't have come to light as quickly if I hadn't found the drawing and presented it to Skip.

Two out of three wasn't bad. It wasn't my job to find a killer.

There was no way Skip was going to include me in the murder investigation, and I had no good reason for wanting to be part of it, other than wanting to clear Linda and Jason. And "capture" whoever had threatened me.

I wanted to contact Mr. Windshield Note, tell him to be advised that *I am, indeed, backing off.* I hoped he would get the message and assume all my future police depart-

337

ment visits would have to do only with an aunt visiting her nephew.

My phone rang as I was covering the tops of my collection of "pizza tables" with contact paper in a red-and-white-checked design. I envisioned an Italian restaurant with wine bottles on each table. I'd seen the perfect tall, thin wood bottle shapes in packages at the crafts store. I'd paint them a dark green like Chianti bottles.

I picked up the phone in the laundry room, which had one of my many crafts tables. How appropriate — the call was from fellow crafter Karen Striker.

Before she could tell me why she was calling, I roped her into brainstorming an idea for the bottom of the Chianti bottles.

"Hmm. I'd use some netting, like, from a thin, close-weave strainer. Then, you know, you can spray paint it a basket color and glue to the bottles."

Excellent. I could see it take shape in my mind, how I'd also roll some of the netting together and form a handle. "Thanks, Karen," I said. I almost said, "Like, thanks."

"Don't forget to put candles in a few of the bottles," she said.

"Good idea. But I'll bet that's not why you called."

"You're right. This really is a solicitation

for help with our campaign."

I couldn't believe Jack Wilson was still campaigning. Thanks to the do-nothing meeting of the evening before, Jack was de facto on the city council. Unless the police were ready to bring the case to the DA and he was indicted for fraud. Either way, he didn't need to campaign.

Karen was still talking. ". . . ask for your support. Look, Gerry, I don't know where you come down on the growth/no-growth thing, but I think you'll be happy with Gail's platform."

"Gail's platform?"

"Yes, didn't you hear the first part of this? Sorry, I tend to babble. Gail is running for the council seat. I'm her campaign manager. Sort of. I mean I'm just learning."

"And Jack . . . ?"

"At this time, Jack has some legal issues to deal with." Karen clicked her tongue. "Oh, what am I saying? You know it's about the sapphire, Gerry. You practically told us yourself yesterday."

I was amazed at the quick work of the LPPD. No doubt the chief of police had something to do with giving Jack a heads-up so he could turn himself in. No perp-walk, as Skip would say, for a prominent citizen like Jack Wilson.

I was still processing the news. Gail Musgrave was running for city council.

Karen kept up her end of the conversation. "You know that Gail has been a Lincoln Point businesswoman for many years. She's now studying to be a broker right here in town, and she has her finger on the needs of the community. Her platform is one of responsible development." I heard no "likes" or "you knows" and pictured Karen reading from a cue card. "Gail feels that only with . . . well, I guess I don't really need to pitch to you, do I? The fact is, we could use some volunteers, Gerry. And I thought, since you're retired . . ."

Karen was too young to know that life in retirement was often busier than ever. "Isn't Gail guaranteed the seat if she runs unopposed? As Jack would be?"

"Not exactly. She needs thirty-three percent of the vote in any case. Some old clause in the election rules says that if a candidate doesn't hit that minimum, the city can keep the seat vacant for six months and then start all over again."

"And Gail's afraid she might not make it, since she doesn't have the name recognition her brother does."

"Right. She's kind of an unknown quantity, and we're trying to change that."

340

I looked through the glass sliding doors of my laundry room, at my Eichler neighborhood and beyond. Maybe it was time for me to get involved in the workings of my city. It was very comfortable to work with literacy students as a way of contributing, but, truthfully, I had the time and the resources to do more.

Didn't I grow up with John F. Kennedy's, "Ask not what your country can do for you . . ."? Wasn't I in college during the bumper-sticker revolution: "If you're not part of the solution, you're part of the problem." So what if I was a late bloomer? I could still get out there and do my bit.

I felt so patriotic, I nearly pledged allegiance to the little flag decal Maddie had stuck to my washing machine when she was about four years old.

"What do you need?" I asked Karen.

Excited about my new "job" — I'd signed up to answer phones and do routine clerical work at the formerly-known-as Wilson, now Musgrave, campaign headquarters — I decided to start spreading the word immediately.

I began with Beverly. Today was one of her seat-belt checking days, so I punched in her cell-phone number.

341

"Go, Gail," Beverly said, when I gave her the news. "And go, Geraldine. I'm so glad you're doing this."

I heard the swoosh of traffic in the background. I knew Beverly was a good multitasker and her job wouldn't suffer for this call. "Me, too. And I know Gail would be an excellent council member."

"I guess she has the last laugh, or whatever you want to call it. She'll have the sapphire *and* the office."

"Life is strange."

"Speaking of strange, I saw the oddest thing a few minutes ago. Oops, just a second, I need to check off one in the offender column." Beverly faded away for a short time, to mark on her clipboard, I assumed, then came back. "I saw Just Eddie heading out of town in his old truck, with a pile of furniture in the back."

My throat caught. "What? Beverly, how long ago was this?"

"Maybe five or ten minutes. Why the excitement? Don't tell me you'll miss him?"

Just Eddie must have gotten wind of the fact that Jason was about to turn himself in and tell all. "I'll explain later."

I hung up quickly and punched in Skip's number.

"Lincoln Point Police."

342

"Skip Gowen, please. It's urgent."

"I'll put you through."

After three rings, I knew it was going to the answering machine, so I hung up and called the desk again.

"I need you to put out an APB on . . . on a white truck with furniture in the back."

How dumb was that? No surprise that I didn't immediately hear the sounds of sirens in the distance.

"And who's calling, please?"

"Geraldine Porter. I . . . thank you, anyway."

I hung up and dialed Skip's cell.

I heard a very sleepy, "Hello?"

Of course. Saturday morning. Skip was sleeping in, either alone or . . . Embarrassing as it was to wake him, I had a mission.

"Skip, I just hung up with your mom. She saw Just Eddie trying to skip town. His truck was full of —"

"Just Eddie is already in custody. The last call that woke me up" — he cleared his throat meaningfully — "was to tell me he's on his way in, in a cruiser. I figured I had a few minutes to get to the station."

"What about Linda and Jason?"

"I was on a code five, a stakeout, from midnight until four this morning, so Paul took their statements. Anyway, you'll be interested to know that Just Eddie is actually Edward Doucette. He has a record in New York. Jumped bail. And he's probably linked to a few other robberies in this county."

A fugitive from justice hanging around our youth? "How did he get a job with the school district?"

"He used his stepfather's name. School records had him as Edward Duchin. Sad to say, police departments are not great on reciprocity. A really complete national database is a dream waiting to happen."

"And Eddie's cheap and flexible," I added, knowing school budgets.

"Yeah, and he's been supplementing his income with robberies. Somewhere there's a pile of loot."

"Okay. Sorry to wake you, Skip. And did I thank you for the ice cream last night?"

Skip laughed. "I'd be happier if you were a twenty-five-year-old, single girl saying, 'Thanks for last night.' "

"I'm blushing."

I hung up, confused. Either someone else was driving Just Eddie's truck, or Beverly was mistaken. I called her back.

During the first three rings, I dismissed the thought of Beverly's making an error. She'd been dealing with the Lincoln Point car population for years. On seat-belt checks, on the abandoned-vehicle watch, and on duty occasionally at the impound lot. She knew cars.

So, who else could have been driving Just Eddie's truck?

On the fourth ring, it came to me. Jason had been holding something back during our three-way chat after his semi-stalking me. He'd been quick to give up Just Eddie, but I'd had the feeling there was someone else. It came to me — whom would Jason protect? The man he thought of as his father.

Chuck Reed.

Beverly answered before the fifth ring. "Sorry, Gerry, I had a run of offenders to tick off."

"Did you see the driver?"

"I see lots of drivers."

"In Just Eddie's truck. Are you sure he was the driver?"

"Well, he was going kind of fast. And to tell you the truth, I look at the seat belt, not the face. But, now that you mention it, the driver was too tall and skinny for Just Eddie."

"Could it have been Chuck Reed?"

"Definitely could have been. What is all this about, Gerry?"

"Later, I promise. Thanks."

345

I punched in Skip's number again.

It was all starting to make sense. Chuck was in on the robberies. It was Chuck whom Maddie saw on the videotape the night Linda was stranded, the night Tippi Wyatt was murdered. He was driving Just Eddie's truck. Making a delivery of stolen goods, maybe, and he caught Tippi snooping around — perhaps looking for Just Eddie — and killed her. Or he may have killed her somewhere else and dumped her body there in the middle of the night.

And Dudley Crane's murder? He was not the most honest man, it was turning out, and may have tried to fence the sapphire through Chuck. It wasn't a stretch to imagine Chuck's getting greedy. I figured I was on to about 80 percent of the truth, the rest conjecture; but one thing I was sure of was that Chuck Reed would have to make one stop before he fled town.

He was on his way to Bird's Storage, with the "cheep rates" sign that had annoyed Maddie. Why else would he need Just Eddie's truck again, unless he had to get the pile of loot Skip mentioned, that wouldn't fit in his own small sports car?

Skip's machine picked up. A fine time for him to be between cell towers, or in the shower.

I left a convoluted message, not quite as foolish as my earlier request for an APB. I hoped Skip would get the message in time. By now I was convinced that Chuck Reed was guilty of a double homicide.

So what on earth possessed me to grab my keys and go after him? Where was the mild-mannered, retired English teacher who wouldn't even ride the Ferris wheel on the Lincoln Point Fairgrounds?

I can only say that my newfound desire for community service propelled me out the door before I could think things through. A Lincoln quote came to me, one that I'd had lettered on the blackboard in my classroom: "Let us have faith that right makes might, and in that faith, let us, to the end, dare to do our duty as we understand it."

I got in my car and drove the route I'd taken a week ago, toward Bird's Storage, very grateful that my granddaughter was safe with her parents in LA.

# CHAPTER 23

More than once on the familiar Highway 101, I moved to an exit lane, ready to turn around and go home. I tried Skip several times, with no luck.

I figured Chuck had about a twenty-minute head start. Maybe that was enough time for him to empty out the storage locker and he'd be gone by the time I got there. I could only hope.

When I turned off the Guadalupe Parkway exit — the same one I'd taken on my Rescue Linda mission — all I could see was the big X in the *Lincolnite,* marking the spot where Tippi's body had been found. I shook away the image. It was broad daylight, I reminded myself. Nothing bad could happen.

I slowed down and drove to the front of the out-of-service gas station. In daylight I could see the CLOSED FOR REPAIRS sign clearly. Traffic whizzed by on the freeway behind me, but this neighborhood was deserted. I guessed there might be more action during the workweek in some of the surrounding buildings, many of which looked like small factories or distribution centers.

I drove around to the back and entered the parking lot between the gas station and the lockers. I rounded the corner, then braked and surveyed the large area. I knew from the videotape exactly where the surveillance camera was located, high on the building, up and to my right. I got my bearings and determined I was parked on the X. I gulped and moved forward, still out of camera range.

Just Eddie's truck was parked in front of an open metal door. If Chuck Reed exited the garagelike space at that moment and looked straight ahead, he'd see me, clear as day. I backed up, conscious of the noise my tires were making on the gravel. I was afraid I'd get a flat, driving over what looked like a thick layer of nails and broken glass.

I was afraid of more than that. My jaw seemed to have a charley horse, and my knees were locked so that I could barely operate the pedals on my car.

I couldn't believe that cops — my own sweet nephew among them — did this all the time. Sure, they were armed and had training, but human beings were not predictable, especially ones crazy enough to rob and kill, and no amount of training could be foolproof. I made a note to give Skip and all his friends at the LPPD hugs and thank-you's the next time I saw them. I hoped there would be a next time.

I headed around the building and drove into the lot from the opposite corner from the X. Now Just Eddie's truck was between me and the open door, at a distance of about twenty-five yards. I convinced myself that this made a big difference.

I'd tried Skip again when I was behind the wall, probably right under the back of the camera.

I had been in the vicinity of the storage locker for about five minutes. Chuck must have realized that Just Eddie was in custody and that he didn't have much time, I reasoned. But maybe he thinks the police will be looking for his own red sports car. No matter, I had to do something to stall him. Otherwise it was useless for me to have conquered (almost) my fears and driven out to this place of bad vibes.

My best shot was to do something to the truck so he couldn't drive it away. At least not until the police could get there. *What police?* I asked myself. The cop at the desk where I left a crazy woman's message? Or my nephew, who had little reason to trust his interfering aunt?

I thought about my options for disabling the truck. It was so old and decrepit, it shouldn't be hard. I was sure there was no alarm system in it, and no remote door opener.

Slashing the tires came to mind, but I didn't think my Exacto knife would do the job.

What other tools did I have in the crafters tool kit I kept in the car? Wire cutters, I answered. I peered at the truck. The windows were open, which meant no locked doors (apparently, Chuck thought this was a safe neighborhood, in spite of its being a crime scene recently), but even if I did get inside to cut the wires, Chuck would no doubt be able to hotwire it in a flash.

I reached down to the floor on the passenger side, where my tool kit was. I opened it and rummaged around. Nail file, useless. Scissors, useless.

I'd seen a child sabotage a bad guy's RV once by pouring sugar in the gas tank. I didn't have any sugar. I wished I'd paid more attention in science class; I might have been able to come up with a mixture that was deadly for pickups.

I searched my purse. Nail-polish remover? Dry-skin cream? I was ill-equipped.

Back to the tool kit. I had pliers. Maybe I could disable the battery? Not likely. My pliers and wire cutters were meant to make neat turns in thin beading wire, or clip off stray ends — not cut through heavy-duty battery cables.

I shrank beneath my steering wheel when I heard a loud noise. Chuck, wearing a large cowboy hat and tight jeans that would have looked better on a younger, more fit man, had exited the storage with a dark green military-style duffel bag. I hoped it wasn't his last trip. I lifted my head slowly and looked over the door of my too-red Ion. All clear.

I felt around the tool kit one more time, with my right hand, keeping my head just high enough to see the truck. Something in the top tray of the box caught on my hand and wouldn't let go. A blob of glue, from my roll of sticky dots. The clear adhesive circles were impossible to remove once applied. Good for crafters (as long as you were sure of where to apply them), but bad for keyholes.

A single quarter-inch dot, pushed into the keyhole of the door of the truck would keep

Chuck busy for hours.

I got out of my car — reluctantly — and slid along the wall, moving as quickly as I could in a squat, without making noise. Halfway down the wall, between two other metal doors, was a large, battered black Dumpster. I took a two-second rest to stretch out my legs. Then, onward.

First, I'd have to close the windows and lock the doors of the vehicle. Then I'd have to apply the glue and get back to my car, which I'd kept running. I was carrying only a strip of dots and a thin tongue depressor, to push in the key slot and tuck in the dots.

I could hear Chuck moving around in the storage area. I managed to close both windows, the old-fashioned roll-up kind. I hoped Chuck was old enough to have compromised hearing, or perhaps drunk enough not to be aware of his surroundings. The truck was parked front-end out, for easy loading, giving me some protection as I rounded the cab from one side to the other. I locked both doors, leaning against them until I heard the clicks.

It took longer than I expected to get the dots into the keyhole. The glue kept sticking to the tongue depressor and coming back out with the wood. It didn't help that the early afternoon sun beat down on me, adding to the fear-generated perspiration on my hands. More than once I wiped my forehead on the short sleeve of my T-shirt. Finally, I broke off a piece of wood, making a sharper point, and successfully stuffed a dot of glue into the keyhole.

Now to get back to my car.

I made a dash for the Dumpster. Just in time. Chuck left the storage area carrying a small box in one hand. He lowered the door to the unit with the other. He went around to the front of his truck, first to the passenger side (my side) to deposit the box, I assumed. I couldn't see his face, but I imagined a quizzical look when he noticed the windows rolled up and the door locked. He carried the box to the driver's side, walking more quickly, looking over his shoulder. I shrank back behind the Dumpster, my heart pounding so loud I felt I was broadcasting my presence over a PA system.

Now the old truck was between Chuck and me, so I didn't get a chance to enjoy his attempts to put his key in the lock. What I did see was Chuck throwing the box to the ground. He shouted a word not in my everyday vocabulary. Then he shouted it several more times. He took off his hat and slammed it on the hood. I saw the truck rock back and forth and figured he was trying to pull the locked door open.

I congratulated myself on a wonderfully executed plan. All it needed was an exit strategy, which I did not have. What I did have was Chuck, finally noticing the one other car in the lot (flashing red, it seemed to me, but partially hidden by the Dumpster) and walking toward me.

I wished I'd climbed into the Dumpster, but it was too late for that. My only hope was to outrun him to my car. I got up, ignoring the stiffness in my knees, and ran. I didn't stop, not even when the pocket of my shorts played, "Take Me Out to the Ball Game."

My one smart move had been to leave my car running. I dashed in and made it out the driveway as the shot rang out, hitting my trunk. I knew I was safe, because Chuck had no way to drive after me. And also because a fleet of Lincoln Point police vehicles rounded the corner in front of me and headed into the lot.

I pulled over. My phone had stopped ringing. I checked the message.

"We're on our way," Skip's voice said.

I leaned my head on my steering wheel and didn't lift it until a few minutes later, when Skip opened my door and put his arms around me.

# CHAPTER 24

"You blacked out," Beverly told me, by way of explaining why I woke up in the hospital on Sunday morning.

I suspected it was because the ambulance had been dispatched to the crime scene and, since Chuck didn't need it, I was the designated patient. Then, while I was here, they did some tests and gave me something to bring on a twelve-hour sleep.

Now I was being wheeled out the front door to the curb where Skip was waiting for us with my car.

"Detective Gowen at your service," he said, and Beverly cheered.

"When did that happen?" she asked.

"Technically next Friday, but the chief called me in and told me last night."

On the drive to my house (with me on pillows in the backseat, unnecessarily), Skip and Beverly briefed me.

Jason was on probation. I was confident

that his chances of having a real family life had improved. Linda already turned over a new leaf by putting a thank-you note and a lovely basket of flowers in my hospital room.

"You should know that Linda would not leave your bedside until she was called into work," Beverly told me. "This is the good side of Linda, back in full force."

"Nice to know," I said.

"And she can't wait to tell you how grateful she is to you." She turned to her son, in the driver's seat. "And to you, too, of course, sweetie."

"Right," said the detective.

"I wonder if she had a clue what her second ex-husband was capable of," I mused.

Beverly had an answer. "I believe her when she says she had no idea about Chuck and his involvement in the little ring of thieves. Evidently Just Eddie enlisted Chuck — birds of a feather find each other, I guess — without telling him they shared a son, in a manner of speaking.

It remained to be seen which state had first dibs on Just Eddie — New York, California, or perhaps one in between. According to Skip, he'd copped to a kidnapping charge (in the matter of Linda Reed) but was giving out details on a string of robberies in tiny dribbles, hoping for a good deal.

Of course, Chuck's gun matched the one used in both murders. "You could have told me the same gun was used," I chided Skip. "I might have figured the whole thing out sooner."

"I'm fully aware that you deserve half my shield," he said.

"I'm just glad you understood my message."

"Two messages," he said. "Paul Hammerfield recognized your voice on that first call and did his best to rally everyone to find the truck."

"He was an A student," I said.

Beverly had some new bumper stickers to show me: MUSGRAVE FOR COUNCIL. "Everyone I know is behind her one hundred percent," she said.

"Even Cooney?"

"Okay, every thinking person is behind her."

"Services for Dudley Crane are set, now that they have his killer. I guess he got greedy with that sapphire. For a while all the crooks were threatening each other with exposure."

"With Jason Reed caught in the middle," Beverly said. She'd brought a tin of brownies and began distributing them to us.

There was still one loose end. "Tippi Wyatt?" I asked.

"We located an aunt in Brooklyn and sent her remains. Chuck laid it out for us. Tippi had found her way to Lincoln Point, using the same ex-con network that Eddie used. She was snooping around town for a couple of days, trying to find something on Eddie so she could get Jason back. She knew the adoption was borderline and thought she would shake things up. She followed Eddie's truck to the storage facility that night."

"But Chuck was driving."

"Right. And she saw things she shouldn't have seen, probably put two and two together, and became a liability."

All Tippi had wanted was her family. Like Linda. And Jason. I sighed deeply at the irony: Jason tried to protect Chuck Reed, the man who wasn't his father, but gave up to the police Just Eddie, who was his real father.

I thought I'd start the week right. On Monday morning, I picked up the phone and punched in speed-dial number three, my son's home in Los Angeles.

I brushed off Richard's comments about my bravery (Beverly and Skip had phoned during my brief and unnecessary hospital stay). He hadn't seen my sweaty palms, nor my shaky knees, nor my alleged blackout.

"What would be a good time for me to visit?" I asked.

"You're not kidding?"

Richard had every right to be surprised. I hadn't been on a plane since Ken died. In fact, except for one trip to Monterey for a dollhouse show, I hadn't traveled outside a thirty-mile radius of Lincoln Point in two years.

Ken and I had traveled a lot. Back to the Bronx and Jersey to see his cousins and catch an exhibit or a show. To Florida to see relatives who left New York for warmer climes. To Yosemite, to Hawaii, wherever there were mountains or an ocean. It didn't seem right to go on journeys for pleasure without him.

Whether it was the events of the week, or some internal timer that went off inside me, I knew I was ready. I realized also why it hadn't bothered me as much as usual on Friday when Maddie left — at some level I knew I'd be seeing her soon in her own home.

"I'm not kidding," I told Richard. "It's time I got out there, don't you think?"

"You miss your granddaughter, huh?" Mary Lou said.

"I miss you all."

"Hi, Grandma," Maddie said, seizing control of one of the lines. "I missed all the excitement."

How glad I was. "I'll tell you all about it when I see you."

"Promise? Everything?"

"I promise."

"Wait till you see my room. I have two new things. Do you want to know what they are?"

"I certainly do."

"A locker for my sports stuff."

"How nice."

"And a dollhouse!" she shrieked.

I shrieked back, as only a grandmother can.

"Are you really coming to see us soon?" she asked.

"I have to come, Maddie, I need you to reprogram my cell phone."

# GERRY'S MINIATURE TIPS

## Miniature Tips for Found Objects

Your junk drawers, sewing baskets, and button jars are a treasure trove for dollhouses and miniature scenes.

- Look through your button jar for ones that can be furniture "feet," bowls, lamp shades, a piece of sculpture, or artwork for a wall or curio cabinet.
- Rounded buttons can be used for drawer pulls on furniture or cabinets.
- Belt buckles or watchband buckles can be picture frames.
- Drinking straws can be cut for use as lamp bases, long or short. (Add a filigree for a fancy look.)
- Lose an earring or two? The other one in the pair can be used to trim miniature hats, purses, or other accessories.
- For that tiny scrap of fabric: Cut in a small circle and put over a cylindrical piece of

wood, painted a food color. Add a string around the top and you have a jar of homemade preserves. Make several and line them up on a kitchen shelf.

- The small metal cap from a carbonated water or beer bottle is a perfect pie pan. Fill it with liquid fabric paint of a natural color and dot it with "blueberry" or a fruit color of choice. You can also leave a section empty, as if a slice has been removed, and paint "spilled" filling.
- Clear plastic caps that come with bottles of cold medicine, or on tops of sports drinks, are excellent wastebaskets. Paint them or use as is, and fill with scraps of paper. Vary the scraps: some can be wadded up, some flat; others newsprint or colored paper. Mark a few scraps to look like letters and envelopes.

### MINIATURE TIPS FOR FOOD

- For spaghetti: Cut many pieces of heavy thread or thin string into various sizes. Arrange on a plate (any circular piece of heavy paper, cut to size, will do). Use paint or hairspray to hold pieces in place. Add pools of red fabric paint mixed with clear glue for tomato sauce. Meatballs are dabs of brown paint.
- Use the pits of "real" fruit for miniature

fruit. A cherry pit painted the appropriate color can be an orange, a peach, or a plum.

- Use strong scissors to cut a red-and-white-striped paper clip, and you have a candy cane!

- That annoying Styrofoam packing can be crumbled to look like popcorn. Pile crumbs into a bowl made from a domed metal or plastic button. You can remove the button backing or simply cover it over with the "popcorn."

### MINIATURE TIPS FOR SHOWER CURTAINS

- For the curtain: Use thin plastic from a shower cap, a food storage bag, or a plastic bowl cover. Cut to size, and run through a glue bath (equal parts white craft glue and water). Manipulate the wet plastic to form appropriate draping (not sharp pleats). Allow to dry, then punch holes at the top of the piece, for inserting rings.

- Rings: For the rings that hold the curtain, start with old-fashioned pencil-tip erasers, which now come in a variety of colors. Snip a ring from the bottom (the part that fits over the pencil). You should be able to get three or four eighth-inch rings from one eraser. (Save the triangle-shaped tips to use as trees in an outdoor scene!) Cut a slit in the ring for inserting into the holes in the curtain. Glue the ends of the ring back together once they're in the holes of the plastic curtain.

- You can also use small metal jewelry findings, but they're harder to open and difficult to thread through the plastic holes.
- If the bowl cover or shower cap has no design, apply one with dabs of paint or tiny stickers.
- For a rod, use any dowel of the right diameter, or cut a drinking straw to fit.

### Miniature Tips for Window Scenes

Location, location, location!

Move your dollhouse or room box to any location by adding a scene outside an already cutout window or by adding a "fake" window.

- If there is a cutout window, tape a postcard, a scene from a magazine, or your own drawing or photo to set your house or box wherever you choose. If the back is to be displayed, cover the entire section with a piece of felt.
- If there's no cutout window, glue the scene over the kitchen sink, for example, or behind a sofa, and add curtains or drapes, giving the effect of a window where there is only solid wall.

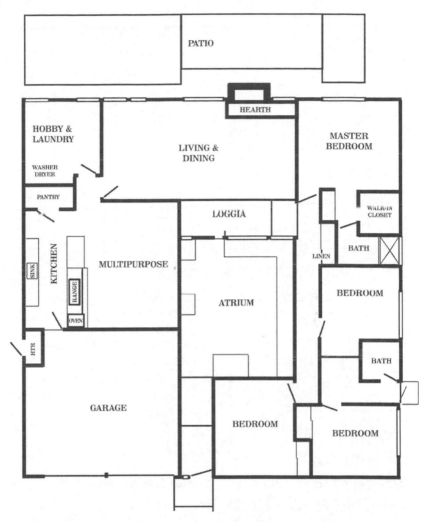

*GERALDINE'S EICHLER HOME*

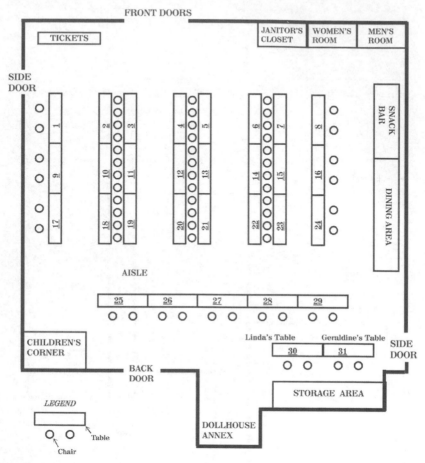

*ABRAHAM LINCOLN HIGH SCHOOL MULTI-PURPOSE ROOM CRAFTS FAIR LAYOUT*

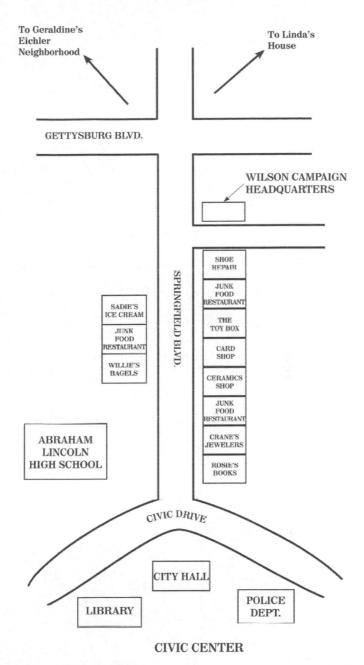

**LINCOLN POINT, CA**

# ABOUT THE AUTHOR

**Margaret Grace** is the pen name of Camille Minichino. She is a life-long miniaturist and is currently at work on the next Miniature Mystery.

As Camille Minichino, she is the author of eight other mystery novels as well as short stories and articles. She lives in northern California and can be reached at www.mini chino.com and www.dollhousemysteries .com.

We hope you have enjoyed this Large Print book. Other Thorndike, Wheeler, and Chivers Press Large Print books are available at your library or directly from the publishers.

For information about current and upcoming titles, please call or write, without obligation, to:

Publisher
Thorndike Press
295 Kennedy Memorial Drive
Waterville, ME 04901
Tel. (800) 223-1244

or visit our Web site at:

http://gale.cengage.com/thorndike

OR

Chivers Large Print
published by BBC Audiobooks Ltd
St James House, The Square
Lower Bristol Road
Bath BA2 3SB
England
Tel. +44(0) 800 136919
email: bbcaudiobooks@bbc.co.uk
www.bbcaudiobooks.co.uk

All our Large Print titles are designed for easy reading, and all our books are made to last.